LETHBRIDGE-STEWART

IT CAME FROM THE ISLE OF MAN

John Peel

CANDY JAR BOOKS · CARDIFF
2024

ISBN: 978-1-915439-78-9

Range Editor: Andy Frankham-Allen
Editor: Shaun Russell
Editorial: Keren Williams
Licensed by Hannah Haisman
Cover by Paul Cooke & Will Brooks

Printed and bound in the UK by
4edge, 22 Eldon Way, Hockley, Essex, SS5 4AD

Published by
Candy Jar Books
Mackintosh House
136 Newport Road, Cardiff, CF24 1DJ
www.candyjarbooks.co.uk

For Ken Deep

PROLOGUE

'**ALISTAIR LETHBRIDGE-STEWART** – why are you brewing your own tea?'

Lethbridge-Stewart found himself looking guiltily at his wife, teapot in hand. 'Ah, yes, well...' he stammered, wondering how she could make him feel so terrible for doing something so innocent. 'I didn't want to bother you,' was all he could come up with. He realised how lame it sounded.

'I am your wife,' she said, primly. 'We'd be in a very bad marriage indeed if my making you a cup of tea was a problem.' Despite her cold tone, there was a flicker of amusement in her eyes. 'Or have you been reading Agatha Christie again and suspect me of slipping cyanide into your Tetley's?'

'What a preposterous idea!'

'Oh, I don't know,' she said. 'I love you dearly, Alistair, but there are times I could get really mad at you. And this is one of them. I *enjoy* seeing you off with a good breakfast inside you – and that includes a nice cup of tea. At least I make it better than that swill you drink in the NAAFI. Let me indulge myself.' Her eyes narrowed. 'And I can assure you that in all of the medical literature in the history of the human race, there is not one single account of a miscarriage being induced by brewing tea!' She snatched the pot from his hand and started warming it.

He'd been caught out, of course; Fiona had always been able to penetrate his motivations. 'It's not that. It's just...'

'I *know* what it is,' she snapped. 'I know that you have to protect this country – and sometimes the world – but you *don't* have to protect me, Alistair. Women have been getting pregnant since the dawn of time. There are countries in this world where expectant mothers work in the fields right up until they drop their babies. And then they pick it up and carry on working. If they can manage that, I can make my husband a cup of bloody tea!'

'I know that,' he admitted weakly. 'It's just that...' His voice trailed off again.

'I know what it is,' she said, this time tenderly. She stroked his cheek. 'And, honestly, I do sometimes enjoy being treated as if I'm Dresden China. But, for the most part, I prefer to be my scruffy hard-working self.' She smiled, a little sadly. 'Yes, I *did* have that ectopic pregnancy last time – and it's not something I'd want to undergo again. But *this* pregnancy is fine, honestly. The doctor says I'd make a good brood mare. I'm not sure that's exactly flattering, of course, but if *he* isn't worried, and *I'm* not worried – well, then, *you* should stop brooding over it. It's not ectopian and I don't need mothering.' She smiled. 'Save that for *after* the baby is born – then I promise I'll allow you to smother me all you like. I shall have deserved it.' She poured him his tea. 'Now drink this and then get going. Today may end up being another day when you have to save the world again. And stop worrying about me.'

She might as well have asked him to stop breathing. He sipped his tea.

And worried.

CHAPTER ONE
This Island Earth

IT WAS possibly the kindest, most humane invasion ever. Nobody was killed – nobody was even bruised by it. At least, not at first. Not while it went according to plan.

But it was an invasion, nevertheless…

Albert Rudley strode on up the gentle hillside, simply enjoying the fresh air and sunshine, while Queenie snuffled and pranced about at his feet.

The compact little spaniel lived for these walks, busying herself with whatever little doggie pleasures filled her mind – chasing butterflies she could never catch, uncovering bugs she really wouldn't want to catch, and following scent trails undoubtedly laid down by other dogs. She left a few scents of her own for those that would come after. All was right with her world.

Albert, too, was quite content. He'd been born here on the Isle of Man, and lived his entire life within a stone's throw of Peel Castle, save for the three years in the Tank Corps helping to liberate France and the rest of Europe from the bloody Nazis. But as soon as he was able, he came back to be a Manxman again. Five years ago, he'd taken over running *The Fox and Grapes* on Waterloo Street after his dad had suffered his stroke. He had married Elsie Nugent a couple of years before that. There had been some sort of a medical issue with Elsie, leaving her unable to have any kids, but that was fine with Albert. It wasn't that he disliked kids, exactly – just that he'd never had the urge to raise any of his own. He wasn't entirely sure how Elsie felt about it – it wasn't the sort of thing Albert was comfortable talking about; women's issues were for women, after all.

So, five years back, the pair of them had moved into the pub. Elsie looked after Dad – who was crippled, but still alert and cranky – while Albert learned the ropes of running *The Fox and Grapes*. To his surprise, he discovered that he enjoyed it. It was pleasant chatting with the customers, and it was lovely to have the odd half bought by one or another of them. He never touched the stronger stuff; it had never really appealed to him, except maybe a touch of whisky when he had a cold or something. The only aspect of the pub he didn't like was all the smoke from endless cigarettes.

He loved the early morning walks he took with Queenie into the hills and woods, in the crisp spring air, with nobody else around for miles. It fair set him up for the day.

Glancing back over his shoulder, he could see the pinkish sandstone buildings that made up most of the town, and the railway tracks leading to Douglas, and now left to rust thanks to Dr Beeching. Beyond that was the causeway that led to the castle itself, quietly rotting away on St Patrick's Isle. It warmed his heart to see so much familiarity. It made him comfortable clear down to his soul.

Life was grand, and it was quietly predictable – which might describe himself pretty accurately, too, he reflected. He strode on, whistling tunelessly. He'd never been able to carry a tune, but that didn't bother him when he was alone like this, and it bothered Queenie even less. She was having the time of her life; she *always* had the time of her life.

Then he heard her growl.

She was staring into the bushes, and her hackles were actually raised. Clearly she could sense something he couldn't. Probably a stray dog, or maybe a fox or even a badger.

'Down, lass,' he cautioned her. She was a feisty little thing, but she'd certainly stand no chance against a badger or a larger dog. A fox would most likely run away. It could even just be a hedgehog – Queenie had an irrational dislike of the little beasties. If it was, she'd end up getting a few needles in her nose, which would teach her a lesson; but he'd rather it was a lesson she didn't learn. As much as he loved any human being, he loved his good girl.

'Gentle, lass, gentle,' he cautioned her. He never had her

on a leash, but she did wear a collar, which he slipped his fingers into. She fought against the restraint slightly, but she was too used to obeying him to fight much. Still, she was clearly bothered badly by whatever it was that she sensed.

He could see nothing. Well, nothing out of the ordinary, at least. There were a few gorse bushes, some broken undergrowth and a couple of trees. There was nothing stirring, and nothing out of place. There didn't appear to be anything at all to upset his girl. But she was still growling unpleasantly and staring at the nothing she'd detected. And she pulled forward, despite his grip.

'Steady, girl,' he told her, but she clearly wasn't listening. He decided that the safest thing to do was to scoop her up into his arms. She struggled against this, but then licked his hand before returning to her low growling. She strained to go forward.

Albert shrugged mentally. He was curious himself as to what had got her so worked up. There was nothing really dangerous on the island – the worst it might have been was a dog of some kind, and dogs didn't scare him. On the other hand, just to be on the safe side, he picked up a short, broken branch. No point in going off half-cocked, after all.

He moved forward, and Queenie started to shake and snarl more loudly. Clearly, he was getting closer to whatever it was that was setting her off. He still could see nothing at all out of the ordinary.

And then he could.

It made no sense to him, but the trees and bushes ahead were broken and crushed, pushed down into the earth as if some immensely heavy weight had slammed down upon them. But there was no visible cause for this – just an area of broken wood some six feet wide, running off in both directions. It looked for all the world as if something huge and heavy had smashed down on this part of the hill. But there was nothing there now.

He set Queenie down, and the dog immediately set to barking at nothing again, dancing around his feet and darting at the odd area and retreating again. Albert had no idea what this was all about, but he reached forward to pick up one of the broken branches.

He couldn't.

He could reach to the edge of the flattened area, and then his hand stopped. He wasn't touching anything, but the *nothing* wouldn't allow him to reach any further. He pushed, and *nothing* pushed back. He pulled his hand back and tried again a couple of feet away. Once again, he was able to reach out until he was directly above the edge of the flattened patch – and then he simply couldn't press forward. He couldn't feel anything at all, but there had to be something there, because it was stopping him.

He was starting to understand why Queenie was in such a nervous state. This was definitely creeping him out. He'd known fear before, of course – three years of warfare had taught him to face it and go on even when he'd rather have pissed in his pants and run away – but that had been fear of *something*. You'd have to be insane not to be scared of the Germans and the likelihood of death or dismemberment. But here there was *nothing*, and that *nothing* scared him as much as a bloody Kraut with a machine pistol.

He stepped back a few paces, and the fear died down. Forward again, and he was sweating and shaking.

It was this *nothing* that was somehow making him afraid! The invisible barrier ahead of him, stretching in both directions, was somehow also causing him to fear advancing. It was trying to push him away from it. That had to be what Queenie was feeling, why the girl was so unusually skittish. And the longer he stood there, the worse the fear was becoming. The more he defied it, the stronger it got.

Finally, he could stand it no longer.

'Heel, girl,' he ordered. The spaniel looked at him with what appeared to be relief. She was growling and snarling to try and protect him, of course. She didn't know what was threatening her master, but – good gal that she was – she was willing to defy it even at the possible cost of her life.

As Albert retreated, though, she dashed after him, clearly happy to be leaving that place.

What was he to do? Albert didn't know. Should he report this? Oh, he could just imagine how it would be if he tried telling anybody that he'd run into an invisible *nothing* that had made his knees shake… They'd just laugh at him, and he wouldn't really blame them. But those three years in the Tank Corps still sat within him. Back then, in the War, it was your duty to report, even if it made you look foolish, and that code of behaviour was still strong in him. He'd better tell the police. That was *his* duty.

What they did – or didn't do – with his information… Well, that wasn't his business, was it? He'd do his duty, personal embarrassment be damned. After that, it was up to the coppers what they did, wasn't it?

Maxim Dayanna steered his GAZ-67 jeep north, keeping the banks of the Irtysh River in sight to his right.

He'd grown up in Khanty-Mansiysk, now some thirty kilometres to the south, and the spectacular Siberian landscape was ingrained in his blood. Even as he tried to focus on his mission, he couldn't help noticing and loving the tree-laden hillsides. The short months of summer were fading now, and the temperature was starting its plunge to sub-zero figures. It was around freezing now, and there wasn't much time before his co-workers would be brought in to await the spring thaws. There was snow in the peaks – but there was *always* snow in the peaks. Siberia, after all, was still pretty much a byword for *suffering.* The gulags were further to the north, with their fill of dissidents, but Maxim had a firm rule never to get involved in politics. As long as he kept his head down and his mouth shut, he had a job, a wife and a small apartment back in town. He wasn't stupid enough to bother having political opinions. And if he ever *did* have opinions… well, he kept them to himself. It would be unwise to share them with anyone, even his wife. You never knew who to trust.

Not even to do their jobs properly. Maxim – like many people in the area – worked for a metals firm that extracted nickel from the mineral-laden earth. The Soviet Union produced a large portion of the world's nickel – and he knew for a fact that (for once) this was not propaganda but simple truth – and Khanty-Mansiysk produced a large proportion of the Soviet Union's nickel. He felt a certain amount of pride in this fact, and in the knowledge that his job was contributing to the public good.

He was basically a roving trouble-shooter for the area,

keeping an eye on the various mines and work gangs. It was an interesting job for the most part; he never knew from day to day what he'd be called on to do. He was grateful for this, because so many jobs were simply routine – men and women went to factories and did the same thing, over and over, every day of their miserable lives. He, on the other hand, could be running a work-gang one day and trouble-shooting machinery the next.

And, right now, he was looking for a couple of lost workers. They had gone out the previous evening to check on a potential new mining site and hadn't returned. At first it had been assumed that they had simply decided to camp out overnight, but then it was discovered that they had taken no supplies with them. One of them, Gorski, was a nephew of one of the directors of the company. Maxim had met him a few times – as few as possible. He was lazy and irresponsible, but unconcerned about his job performance because of his uncle. Maxim's attitude was that if Gorski was lost in the mountains somewhere, then the bears were welcome to him. Understandably, though, this was not his uncle's point of view, and so Maxim was in search of someone he'd rather not find.

The young idiot had probably acquired some of the foul cigarettes he enjoyed, and a few bottles of the potent locally-produced vodka and got drunk. It wouldn't be the first time, and it was unlikely to be the last. He'd probably slept in the cab of his truck when he realised he was too drunk to drive back. This was most likely a complete waste of Maxim's own time and abilities, but when the supervisor ordered, you did as you were told.

At least the drive was pleasant, and this was the road Gorski would have taken to and from the mine area. If the young idiot had tried driving back while he was still drunk, he'd be in a crumpled wreck somewhere on – or slightly off – it.

Maxim wondered if he was a bad person for hoping he'd find the truck wrapped around a tree and Gorski's dead body impaled on a branch. Then he decided that he didn't care if he was a bad person, and went right on hoping.

This was more like a track than a road, really. It wouldn't be graded or surfaced unless the local Soviet decided that the mine site was worth operating. Thankfully the GAZ was four-wheel drive, and designed for this kind of situation. It had been a workhorse in the war years, and still operational and optimal these days. He was rather fond of the sturdy, slightly battered vehicle. It took on whatever landscape it found itself facing and always triumphed – a good analogy for the Soviets, really. The rest of the world might sneer at them – or fear them – but the Russian people simply buckled down and went on.

The woods were growing thicker as the road ascended. He estimated that he couldn't be more than a dozen kilometres from the mine site now. He thought for a moment, and then stopped the jeep to allow it to rest. He knew that the vehicle wasn't alive, but he tried to treat it as if it was. That way it would last longer. Besides, he wanted a smoke.

He lit up and surveyed the area. He was still far below the snow line, but the temperature had dropped a degree or two, and he was glad he had bundled up before leaving town. He watched the smoke from his rough cigarette curl upwards in the gentle breeze. Below him to the east he could see the glitter of the Irtysh between the trees. Far off were the mountains. It was still and peaceful, save for the sounds of the birds.

He carefully crushed the end of his spent cigarette – he didn't want to start a forest fire – and tossed it aside. He drove on again, enjoying the loneliness and peace.

Then he saw movement in the trees. Just flashes of something heading down the hillside towards the road. He instinctively reached for the rifle on the passenger seat. Larger animals didn't come down this low in general, but there were black bears and a few tigers in the area, so he always kept a weapon handy. Not that it mattered, as he had no intention of stopping, and his GAZ could outpace any bear or tiger.

Then he saw that the figure was waving, and he realised it was no beast, but a man. He slammed on the brakes and then gripped the rifle more firmly. There had been no report of bandits in the area, but, again – why take unnecessary chances?

The man was staggering, and waving, stumbling as he ran, clearly exhausted. After a moment, Maxim recognized him – it was Gorski, of course. What had the idiot done now? Where was the truck and his companion? Maxim experienced just a moment of temptation to shoot the fool and then claim he hadn't recognised him… But, no, that wouldn't be right. And shooting the boss' nephew – even by accident – would probably get him sent to the Gulag. Or, if he was very lucky, shot in his turn. He replaced the rifle and waited for the idiot to stagger up.

He looked terrible but, oddly, not hung-over as Maxim had expected. His eyes were bloodshot, though, and filled with panic.

'Thank God!' he croaked, collapsing against the side of the jeep.

'There is no God, comrade,' Maxim corrected him. 'If you wish to thank something, then thank Soviet efficiency.'

'Stop talking nonsense. Water?' Maxim produced his canteen, and Gorski took a long swallow before reluctantly handing it back. 'Food?' Maxim had bread and a large chunk of sausage. Reluctantly, he cut slices of both and handed them across, watching impassively as Gorski ate as if he had been lost weeks instead of hours.

'Where is your companion?' Maxim asked. 'And your truck?'

'Gone.'

'Could you be a little more specific? I will have to file a report on this, and you know the Commissars won't accept *gone* as an answer. Gone *where?*'

Gorski stared at him, as if he'd somehow forgotten the language. He was looking a little better, though, after eating and drinking. He made a visible effort to pull himself together. 'The truck is destroyed, comrade, and Alexi…' He shrugged. 'I haven't seen him since I ran from the bear. Maybe it got him – it didn't catch me.' While he was clearly disturbed, it didn't seem to be about his companion.

'How did the truck get destroyed?' Maxim demanded. 'Did you run it into a tree while drunk?'

'I wasn't drunk,' Gorski growled. 'I wish to God I was, but I wasn't. I wasn't even in it when it was destroyed.'

Maxim didn't bother to rebuke him a second time for his decadent reference to a deity. 'Are you saying that somebody else destroyed it? An imperialist saboteur, maybe?' He didn't bother to hide his scorn.

'I don't know *what* destroyed it.' Gorski didn't appear to have noticed the dripping sarcasm. 'One moment it was fine – the next…'

'You're making no sense, comrade,' Maxim complained.

'How can I make any sense over something that makes no sense to me?' Gorski asked, plaintively.

The man was an utter fool.

'Take me to where the truck was damaged. If I am to report it, I must see it.'

'That may not be a wise idea.'

'Why not?'

'Because whatever destroyed the truck may still be lurking about. I wouldn't want the jeep to be destroyed also.'

Maxim scowled. 'You think there's somebody there who is making a career out of destroying transportation?'

'How should I know?' Gorski yelled. 'I wasn't stupid enough to see if it would add *me* to its list of victims!' He shook his head. 'I don't want to go back there and give it another go at me.'

'Coward!'

'Yes, okay – if you like. I'm a coward. But I'm alive. If I go back there, I may end up a dead coward; how is that any better?'

'Do you want to go back to the Commissar with this tale of yours?' Maxim asked. 'You may end up a dead coward there as well.'

That penetrated the other man's fears. Even his uncle's influence wouldn't protect him that far. 'How about I take you most of the way?' he suggested. 'And you go the rest of the way on foot?' The compromise clearly didn't make him feel much better.

'Whatever will get you to do your duty,' Maxim agreed.

They both clambered into the GAZ and continued upward toward the mine site. The air was crisp and cold, but there was no sign of any early snow yet. Conditions weren't right for it just yet, but Maxim knew it was on its way. A week, maybe less. It would be good to get back to town and get warm again. He glanced at Gorski, who seemed to have somehow shrunk in on himself.

He really is scared, he realised. He knew that the youth was reckless and arrogant, but he'd never heard it said before that he was a coward. It was hard to reconcile the two different versions of the man.

'We're getting close,' Gorski finally announced. 'Stop here.' Maxim obliged the man, who was now starting to sweat with fear. 'Leave me and the jeep here. You'll find the truck up the road about half a kilometre.'

'Fine.' Maxim switched off the ignition and pocketed the keys.

Gorski looked alarmed. 'You can't take the keys! What if it destroys you, too?'

'Perhaps you'd better pray to your non-existent God that it doesn't?' Maxim suggested. He wasn't foolish enough to leave Gorski in a working jeep and expect to find it here when he returned. For a moment, it looked as if Gorski would pluck up the courage to attack him and steal the keys. Then he collapsed in on himself again, shaking his head. That was smart of him.

Maxim picked up his rifle and checked it. Without another word, he set off along the road. He didn't look back.

The slope was gentle, so he didn't have to exert himself too much. There was only the sounds of the wind and the rustling of the branches.

Maxim could see no signs of any animals, and there were no discernible tracks of predators. It was just a regular, pleasant day in the countryside as far as he could tell. There was no sign of whatever had so terrified the young man shaking in the GAZ.

Then he saw the vodka bottle just off the road. He knelt to check it out. The cap was missing, and the bottle was empty, but there was still the whiff of alcohol to be detected.

So, Gorski *had* been drinking… Or, perhaps, the still-missing Alexei? It was looking like Gorski was trying to excuse his own poor behaviour, as Maxim had suspected all along. He considered taking the bottle with him as proof, but realised that if he needed it, it would be here on the way back, so he left it and carried on.

Ahead of him, the road curved slightly. He knew he was only about a kilometre or so from the mine site, and that he would soon see it. But as he rounded the bend, he could see through the gap in the trees something very puzzling.

It was snowing.

There was nothing so surprising about that, really, even if it wasn't the weather for it. It snowed a lot in Siberia, after all. But this was not any kind of normal snow. It was snowing about forty metres ahead of him…

In a straight line.

It was as if there were some sort of magic line across the road, and on one side of the invisible line it snowed. And on the other it did not.

Snow did *not* behave in this manner – not even in Siberia…

He realised he was gripping the rifle defensively. He chuckled at this instinctive reaction. What was he going to shoot at? Snow? But he realised that he was scared, deep inside, at some sort of an instinctive level. He almost wished that he could believe in a god, because prayer might feel good right about now…

As he drew closer to the cut-off point for the snowfall, he saw the wreckage of Gorski's truck. It looked as if it had entered part-way into the snow and then *something* had completely smashed in the engine and cab. The rest of the truck looked perfectly fine – like some immense guillotine had slammed down onto the truck and severed it, crushing the front and leaving the rear intact.

Nothing on Earth that he knew about could do such a thing. Well, perhaps a stamping mill – but there was nothing even remotely like that here.

He stared at the snow, which was piling up just beyond the truck. In a straight line. No, wait – he glanced in both directions and realised that the line was in fact gently curving in a circle. It was large enough that a small section appeared to be straight. This odd line had to be kilometres long.

It made absolutely no sense whatsoever to him.

He reached the truck and tried to examine the shattered and crushed front end. But *something* stopped him. It was as if there was a smooth, invisible wall which had sprung up from nowhere. He pushed, and the nothingness gently pushed back.

He finally felt a tinge of sympathy for Gorski. Whatever was happening here was way beyond his experience. He could feel panic rising inside him. There was clearly only one sensible thing for him to do.

Report all of this, and make it somebody else's problem.

Colonel Maggie Hickenlooper glared sourly out of her office window at the shimmering haze on the Nevada rocks and sands.

She'd taken this posting to Groom Lake and The Ranch[1] because it had been pretty much the only promotion she was ever likely to be offered. Even at this date, the US Air Force was mainly monolithically male. Students might be demonstrating, women might be burning their bras and getting voted into office – but the Air Force managed to survive on its traditional institutional blindness. It wasn't necessarily that they were *against* women – more that they simply didn't know how to deal with them. So, when the time had come that she had earned a promotion, the Powers-That-Be decided she could have one – and *only* one – stuck out here at Homey Airport on Groom Lake.

A testing ground. The jocks, the flyboys – *they* got to play with captured Russian fighters, running them against their Air Force equivalents. Colonel Hickenlooper, though, being a woman, wasn't allowed to fly anything but her desk. Even the brains trust got to play with their drones – the D-21 at the moment, as long as *that* lasted. *She* got to file papers, sign reports and stare out of her window over the vast desert, knowing that Vegas was a hundred miles or so away.

Hardly what anyone could call job satisfaction – were it not for one thing.

The Ranch was also where they stored the Artefacts.

Maggie had heard rumours about this at her previous postings, but that was all they had been: tall tales about alien technology that had been scooped up and squirreled away under the aegis of Project Blue Book.

In her early days in the Air Force, she'd been the designated officer to submit UFO reports to Blue Book (every field had one such officer, usually somebody currently out of favour with the top brass, or, as in her case, a woman). There had been any number of reports that had bothered her. She knew the pilots involved, and knew that they weren't prone

---

1 Better known to us now as Area 51.

to seeing things that weren't there, or reporting sightings of Venus as 'unidentified'. But it hadn't been her job to pass judgment, merely to pass the reports along. Those in charge of Blue Book were the ones who had to explain everything away. Ostensibly, they were 'investigating', but that was a euphemism for 'brush it under the rug'.

When she had arrived here, she'd finally been introduced to the Artefacts.

Stored in three large, guarded hangers, it was a collection of a lot of things – mostly junk. Chunks of metal, some circuitry boards that were inevitably charred and useless. There were even a couple of what might be bodies – or, at least, body parts.

And one fairly intact craft that had been studied for almost two decades. It was – or, at least, appeared to be – dead. Nothing worked, not even the interior lighting. You had to wear a miner's helmet in order to walk around it. Scientists and technicians over the years had taken a few bits of it apart, and learned pretty much next to nothing from any of it. Now it was considered to be mostly pointless junk. Even scientists got bored when there was nothing that they could do to get anything working.

Still, Maggie always got a kick out of looking at the ship. Just knowing it existed was astounding to her. It was clearly built by non-human hands, by minds that didn't think in human ways, and for bodies that didn't resemble human beings one bit. It was absolute proof that there were alien beings out there, among the stars – and that at least a few of them had managed to make it all the way here to Earth.

Why? She had no clue. It could be simply the lure of exploration – God knew that there were plenty of humans driven by that urge. Or it could be pretty much any of the explanations offered by cheesy sci-fi flicks – from invasion to stealing women for Mars (or wherever). It just seemed odd to her that the craft had been sitting here for twenty-odd years and a second had never even turned up. Was it because the crew of the craft had over-extended themselves and gone further than their technology really allowed? Or were the – well, call them *people* – the people who built it too busy elsewhere to wonder what had happened to this ship? There was no way to know.

She sometimes had flashes of humour that suggested maybe it was a getaway ship for alien bank robbers, the alien equivalents of Bonnie and Clyde.

The phone on her desk abruptly rang, and she snatched it up. 'What is it?'

'Colonel, you'd better get up here.' It was a voice she didn't recognise. 'We've got a bogey.'

A bogey?

'Where the hell is *up here* and who the hell are you, flyboy?'

'Uh, oh, yeah – sorry, ma'am. Lieutenant Mendez, sir, in the radar room.' He sounded very flustered.

'I'll be right up.'

At last – something to actually *do*, instead of filing reports. It took her a second or two to recall where the radar facility was, and then she hurried from her office.

A bogey… Something real – maybe – instead of just reading reports about them from pilots. She found herself getting excited as she hurried to the monitoring station.

There were five people in the room when she arrived.

One – with insignia indicating his rank – was presumably Mendez. Two were clearly the operatives, bent over the screens in the darkened room. She had no idea who the other two were; probably just soldiers drawn in by the potential drama.

'Mendez,' she snapped. 'What do we have?'

The one she'd decided was him replied. He definitely looked shaken and unsure of himself. 'Um… Bogey at sixty thousand… Travelling at Mach six point four.'

'Meteor?'

'No, ma'am,' one of the two operators replied. 'It's changed course twice.'

Crap.

'Is it something of ours?'

The operator gave her a *at Mach six?* look, and then shook his head. 'We have nothing in that area, and definitely not at that height.'

No, well, they wouldn't – but she had to run through the possibilities. 'Russkies?' That was just as dumb a question –

there was no way the Russians could have something with that sort of capability.

'No, ma'am.'

'Nothing wrong with your screen?'

The other operator spoke up. 'I have confirmation of the sighting, ma'am.' He blinked. 'It's slowing down.' He looked shocked. 'It's dropped to Mach one point five.'

'Jesus…' she muttered. How could *anything* drop almost four thousand miles an hour instantaneously? It should have broken into millions of tiny pieces raining down over the Nevada desert. 'What's its heading?'

'Changing,' the first operator answered.

She turned to one of the two airmen still hanging around. 'Get on the phone to the commander and inform him,' she snapped. 'He'll probably want to scramble and intercept.'

'At Mach one point five? Uh, I mean, yes, ma'am.' He saluted and hurried off.

Maggie turned back to the radar. 'Have you got a course yet?'

'Uh… it's heading in this direction,' the operator replied. 'Still slowing.'

'Jesus H Christ,' the other onlooker grunted in a wide Texan accent. 'You think they want their artefacts back?'

It was as good a theory as anything at the moment. 'Find me some binoculars,' she ordered. He saluted and scooted away. 'How long 'til it reaches us?'

'Ninety seconds at that speed, ma'am.'

Well, an intercept was out – and probably needless. Whatever that thing was, it would be on them way before they could scramble anything. Even an egg…

She looked around. The radar room was windowless, of course, but there would be *somewhere* close with a window. She was torn between staying where she was and attempting to see what the heck this thing was.

'What's its altitude?'

'Ten thousand and dropping fast.' The operator shook his head. 'You think it's aiming for a landing, ma'am?'

'God knows, and He hasn't bothered to inform me.' The youngster she'd sent after binoculars was back, waving a pair. She snatched them from him. 'Stay here,' she ordered. 'And let me know if anything changes.'

She hurried from the room to the closest door and stepped outside – into the blazing desert heat. She didn't even notice it. She raised the binoculars to her eyes and scanned the skies. There were far-off wisps of clouds, but nothing moving in the air.

No – *there!*

It was a light, intensely bright – presumably glowing from friction and attempting to radiate out the heat it must have built up. She could tell nothing at all about it because of the glow. There was no shape to be seen, neither could she judge its height. It appeared to be slowing still, but that could just be her imagination. It was heading towards the Ranch, but it was impossible to judge whether it was aiming to land or not.

But one thing was very, very clear. Whatever this was, there was some sort of intelligence behind it. Given the speeds it had been travelling at and the way it had slowed so abruptly; it was possible that it was some kind of unmanned – or maybe *unaliened* – vessel. A drone of some sort, but vastly more sophisticated than the D-21s they had been testing.

It was almost overhead now, and still glowing wildly. There was no indication that it intended to land here, as it was still hundreds of feet in the air, and maybe higher. She heard the howl of an alert sounding, but paid it no real attention. The commander had no doubt ordered the pointless scramble anyway. It wouldn't look good on anyone's record if he did nothing.

And then it passed overhead, and zipped off into the desert beyond. She followed it with the binoculars, even though it hurt her eyes to watch.

Then it stopped. Dead. In the air.

Because of the glow, she couldn't accurately estimate distances, but it seemed to be maybe ten miles off. Then it dropped out of sight behind a bunch of hills.

She dashed back into the radar room again. There were half a dozen officers in there now, but she didn't wait to see if she outranked them.

'What the hell just happened?' she growled at the first operator.

'It appears to have landed, ma'am. Twenty-two miles

north-northeast.'

Another voice: 'The commander's ordered a fly-by.'

And then everyone was talking at once.

What the hell had they just witnessed? Could it possibly be the landing of a craft from another world?

Things were about to get… interesting.

CHAPTER TWO
It Came from Outer Space

BRIGADIER LETHBRIDGE-STEWART was not in the best of moods.

He was lost in his own concerns as he strode through Dolerite Base towards his office. He acknowledged salutes as he did so, and promptly forgot who he had just seen. Thoughts of Fiona were occupying his mind right now. Well, *thoughts* was too mild a word – *fears* might be more accurate. He'd done some reading up on the subject, of course, but ever since the failure of her first pregnancy, he had been afraid that this second one might end up just as badly.

He *knew*, of course, that most pregnancies went off without a hitch, but that wasn't overly comforting. Somehow it was all of the possible complications that stuck in the mind – those resulting in the death of mother or baby… or both. Umbilical cords wrapped around necks, breech births, biological infections… He shook his head, but the thoughts refused to flee his brain. What if the baby was born dead? What if Fiona should have complications?

What if… well, almost *anything*?

This was worse than fighting ICU's, Egyptian gods… even vampires in the night. At least with threats like those there was something physical to grapple with and defeat. But how could you thrash your own mind into compliance?

He reached his office and shut himself in with his thoughts. He hung up his overcoat and laid his briefcase on the desk. Then he glanced at the telephone. Should he give Fiona a call and check that she was still okay? But he knew what she'd say (it was what she always said): 'I'm fine, Alistair. I'm not the first woman in the world to have a baby, you know.'

Maybe not, but she was the first woman in the world to have *his* baby. And he wanted it to be perfect, and for Fiona to sail through the process with a healthy glow and a smile on her face – not screaming and cursing him for getting her pregnant in the first place.

Would she need painkillers? Epidurals? A C-section?

Dear God… He buried his head in his hands. Were all impending fathers wrecks like this? They were on bad TV comedies, of course, but in real life…?

There was a rap on his door, and he immediately straightened up, pushing his fears aside. Wouldn't do for the men to see him in a state like this.

'Enter!'

It wasn't technically a man. Sergeant Jean Maddox strode in and stood to attention. She was the head of communications for the Fifth, solid and highly efficient.

'Morning, sir. Message from the Department of Defence. Peter Grant is on his way to hold a briefing at oh-nine-hundred hours.'

He glanced at his wall clock – ten minutes from now. 'Any idea what this is about, Sergeant?'

She hesitated. 'Officially, no.'

'Unofficially?'

Maddox dealt in all sorts of scuttlebutt also, considering that to be a part of her duties, whether in her job description or not. 'Something to do with the Isle of Man, sir. There's been some kind of police activity there. Anne has also been doing some research that's related.'

'I appear to have missed a hive of activity,' he said drily.

'Yes, sir.'

He nodded. 'Have you informed the staff?'

'I'm on my way to do so, sir. I thought you should know first.'

'Quite right, of course.' He smiled tightly. 'Don't let me keep you.'

'Sir.' She hurried off in her calmly efficient way.

A very fine officer, and about due for her annual evaluation, and, frankly, a promotion.

He considered what she had said: the Isle of Man? Did anything ever happen there? He realised with some surprise that he'd never actually been to the place. Well, there was no saying he'd be going there now. It could be simply something that the Fifth wanted to keep an eye on. Plenty of reports turned out to be nothing, but it was always better to be safe than sorry – especially in this line of work. Well, he supposed he would find out very shortly.

Lethbridge-Stewart strode down the corridor to the Briefing Room.

Several people were already there, and jumped to attention as he arrived. 'At ease,' he responded, and then glanced about. There were Maddox, Captain Bill Bishop, Colonel Douglas… and Anne Bishop, who was scowling slightly.

'Mr Grant and Mr Bryden are on their way down, sir,' Maddox reported.

Dolerite Base was secreted under Edinburgh Castle, and the lifts were the main access routes. Lethbridge-Stewart winced slightly. Grant was a decent enough chappie in his own off-hand way, but Bryden always managed to irritate him. Grant was DoD, but Bryden was the industrialist who helped to fund the Fifth and, as a result, felt it was his right to poke his nose into everything going. But because of his funding, they couldn't keep the man out, much as they might wish they could.

Lethbridge-Stewart looked at Anne. 'I understand you know what this is about?'

'Don't jump the gun, Brigadier,' she replied with a slight smile. 'I wouldn't want to steal Mr Grant's thunder.'

'Naturally,' he said.

The door opened again, and Corporal Wright escorted the two officials into the room. Grant was a smiling, amiable man with a mess of red hair and an air of slight foolishness that masked a sharp mind. Bryden was a tall, hawk-like man with a piercing gaze and a secretive nature. If he'd ever learned how to smile, those muscles had atrophied with disuse.

'Brigadier,' Grant called cheerily. 'Gentlemen.' A bigger smile. 'Ladies.' He shook his head. 'Still can't get used to that lift of yours. I suppose my stomach will catch up with me by the time I have to leave.'

'Let's get on with it,' Bryden suggested firmly.

'Can't we have tea with the meeting?' Grant asked, slightly plaintively.

Lethbridge-Stewart nodded at Wright. 'See what you can rustle up, Corporal.'

'Sir.' He left the room as Grant and Bryden took their usual seats.

The MoD man slapped his briefcase on the table, opened it and started to haul papers and files out of it, creating a tide of mess all about him. 'It's in here somewhere…' he muttered. 'Aha!' He pulled out a file marked 'SECRET', and slid it across to Lethbridge-Stewart. 'There's an ongoing incident on the Isle of Man that seems to be right up your street.'

'What is it?' He broke the seal on the file and opened it.

'Not a clue,' Grant said cheerfully. 'That's your department, not mine. Some sort of force field sprung up overnight. A man walking his dog found it and reported it.'

There was a detailed Ordinance Survey map of the island in the file, and Lethbridge-Stewart spread it on the table. Everyone craned their necks to look at it. A red line had been drawn in, stretching from just outside of Peel into the ocean, a vast rather deflated sphere. The majority of it was at sea, but there appeared to be several square miles of land enclosed.

'Nobody has any idea what's causing it?' Douglas asked.

'None. Nothing seems to be able to get through.' Grant looked expectantly at them all. 'It extends vertically, too. No idea how far, but, luckily, there's not much air traffic in that area. Wouldn't want to fly into an invisible brick wall, would we?'

Lethbridge-Stewart frowned slightly. 'It certainly sounds as if it may be our type of event,' he agreed. 'I'll get a team assembled and ready to go within the hour.'

Anne spoke up. 'It's not quite that simple, Brigadier.'

He raised an eyebrow. 'Why am I not surprised that you already know something about this?' Anne exchanged a glance with Maddox, making her source of the extra information obvious. 'So, what is the complication?'

'That's not the only one.' She tapped the edge of the map. 'There are two others.'

Bryden leaned forward, attentively. 'And you know that how?'

'I piggybacked a signal on ATS-2 when I first heard about the Peel incident,' Anne explained. 'The satellite was passing over the area, and I thought I might detect something.' She gestured at the map. 'A force field of that size would need substantial power to generate it, and I theorised I'd be able to detect an energy signature.'

'I'm assuming you did?' Lethbridge-Stewart asked, glad to have Anne back in the fold.

'Indeed. A strong, positive one. Much higher in the energy spectrum than anyone on this planet could generate.'

Lethbridge-Stewart sighed. 'Aliens? Again?'

Anne nodded. 'It does look like that,' she agreed. 'Anyway, as I was plotting the size and scope of the… barrier, I got a second ping. My signal was still tucked into the satellite, and it came across the second field, and, later, a third.'

'That's all there are, though?' Bishop asked.

'Yes, three in all. This one on the Isle of Man. A second in Siberia and a third in the Nevada desert.'

Lethbridge-Stewart glanced at Grant. 'You haven't heard of those two?'

'News to me,' the man from the Ministry replied. 'Well, you know how proprietary the Yanks are, and how tight-lipped the Reds can be. Wouldn't really expect them to keep us informed.'

Lethbridge-Stewart said nothing, but glanced at Anne, thinking of a report she'd submitted a few months back.

'Both other readings are identical to the one on Man?' Bryden demanded.

'Aside from the fact that the areas enclosed are larger, yes.' Anne looked around the room. 'The problem, then, is bigger than it looks.'

Lethbridge-Stewart sighed. 'Well, Siberia and Nevada are outside our province,' he stated. 'But it might be an idea to get onto the Americans and Russians and see what they know – and if they'll cooperate. But in the meantime, we need to get started on our own investigations.'

The door opened, and Wright half-stumbled in, carrying a large tray filled with cups, a large teapot, milk and sugar. Bishop hastily cleared space on the table, onto which the corporal gratefully dumped the rattling tray.

'Just in time, Ev… erm, Wright,' Lethbridge-Stewart said. 'I need a team readied for the Isle of Man. Six men should be enough, plus you. Get the ball rolling.'

Wright gave him a quick *why me?* look, but saluted. 'Righto, sir.' He left the room.

Lethbridge-Stewart turned to Anne. 'You'd better go along with them and do your thing. See if there's a way to penetrate that… field. It's presumably there to prevent us entering the area, so entering it is our top priority.'

'Of course, Alistair.' She rose. 'I'll start getting my equipment ready.' She grinned. 'Save me a cuppa.' She hurried from the room.

'Maddox,' Lethbridge-Stewart ordered. 'You'd better get busy.' He thought for a moment. 'Put in calls to Admiral Hennessey and Air Marshall MacMillan first.' He looked to Grant. 'I'm assuming they know about the barrier?' He'd worked with both men in the past, and he knew that they were both capable and responsive.

Grant glanced at his watch. 'They will by about now.'

'Good. I'm sure they'll send people out to take a look, so we had better co-ordinate on that. Then I'll need a call to Captain Kramer in New York, and patch it through to me as soon as it's answered.' Maddox nodded, and Lethbridge-Stewart continued. 'Finally, I'll need to speak to Major Bugayev once that's finished.'

Maddox dashed from the room.

'Goodness me,' Grant said. 'Such a flurry of activity.' He picked up the pot of tea. 'Shall I be mother?'

'Any thoughts on this, Brigadier?' Bryden asked sharply, ignoring his companion.

'I'm thinking that we need more data,' Lethbridge-Stewart responded, accepting the cup of tea that Grant extended to him, and adding milk and sugar. He tapped the thin file. 'There isn't very much in here. But it doesn't appear to be earth-shaking – yet. Whatever that barrier is for, it's been there a day now and nothing appears to be happening.' He sipped the tea and managed to avoid grimacing. Fiona had been correct – this stuff was muck.

'Whatever's inside it may be getting ready to emerge,' Bishop said, worriedly. 'It may be a sort of a cocoon – peaceful till it bursts. Do you think a small force is enough?'

'Until we have further information, we won't know if even a *large* force will be enough. And the situation seems to be calm at the moment – sending a large force into Peel might alarm the locals and create panic. I'll trust Anne to call for help if she feels it's necessary.'

'Sir.'

'Don't look so impatient, Captain – I'll be needing field teams to head out in case we get co-operation from our counterparts in the US and Siberia. I'll want you to start prepping a team to potentially go to the Nevada site. Keep it as small as possible.' He glanced at Grant. 'I'm sure the ministry will be happier the less people we transport out.'

That brought a smile to Bishop's face. 'Sir.' He finished his tea, saluted and dashed.

Lethbridge-Stewart turned to Douglas. 'Dougie, that leaves you with the same mission to Siberia, I'm afraid.'

He grinned back. 'I'll go pack my thermal underwear.'

The room seemed suddenly empty. Lethbridge-Stewart was left with only the civilians now.

'Well, I think that's all we can do for the moment. We'll know more if I get responses to my calls, and if the Americans and Russians are willing to exchange information.' He started to stand. 'Thank you, gentlemen.'

Bryden made a slashing motion with his hand. 'Just a moment, Brigadier,' he said sharply. 'I still have something to say.'

Lethbridge-Stewart fell back into his seat. 'By all means, Mr Bryden,' he said, not really meaning it. He was quite certain he knew what was about to be said because the industrialist *always* brought it up.

'Isn't it time you released some of that alien technology you've been hiding away in your closet? There must be *something* in there that would be very useful in this situation.'

Lethbridge-Stewart sighed mentally. 'First of all, Mr Bryden,' he said, as calmly as possible, 'we don't yet know what *this situation* even is, so there's absolutely no telling what might or might not be useful. It could be anything ranging from an alien invasion to the equivalent of a short weekend in Bognor. Those barriers *might* be a cocoon, growing some sort of monsters, but they might just as likely be an alien version of a tent for backpackers.' He saw Bryden getting ready to speak, but pressed on. 'Secondly, we still don't have any idea what kind of side-effects the technology might have. Most of the aliens we've faced would think nothing of deploying equipment that might… oh, consume all of the oxygen in our atmosphere and choke us to death. Until we can be certain that this won't happen, it stays under lock and key, so to speak.' Again, Bryden made to speak, and again Lethbridge-Stewart cut him off. 'And, thirdly, I know that you and your brother are hoping to discover some sort of device that will give your company a marketing edge in your field, but even if I were to release some sort of alien thingamajig, there's no way you could mass produce it in time to help out in this situation.'

'It might help out *next* time,' Bryden snapped, finally getting in a word or six.

'There's no way to be sure of that. And, in any case, nothing will be released until Dr Travers signs off on it. And she's heading to the Isle of Man right now.'

'She has not signed off on *anything* yet,' Bryden pointed out.

'Which is why you haven't received anything yet,' Lethbridge-Stewart agreed.

'Can't you light a fire under her?'

'Even if I could, I wouldn't. She has the expertise in this matter that I lack, and I will not over-rule her decisions.'

'The Ministry could,' Bryden said, darkly.

'Indeed, they could. But the fact that they *haven't* shows that they back my judgement in the matter.' This time Lethbridge-Stewart did stand up. 'I understand your concerns, Mr Bryden, and I am sure that some of them are out of regard for this country and its safety. But the situation has not changed since the last time you raised this concern, and it is unlikely to change in the near future. Now, if you'll excuse me, I *really* must get busy on sorting this matter out.'

Bryden started to speak again, but Peter Grant plucked at his sleeve. 'I rather think you'd better let it go, old chap. The brigadier has enough on his plate already, don't you think? Better let him – ah – soldier on, as it were.' Urging him towards the door, Grant gave Lethbridge-Stewart a sly wink.

He gave him a small smile of appreciation, and then put both men out of his mind as he hurried back to his office.

Lethbridge-Stewart heard his phone ringing as he reached it. Closing the door behind him, he reached over and scooped up the handset. 'Yes?'

'Admiral Hennessey on the line, sir,' Maddox reported.

'Thank you, Sergeant.' There was a click, and he said: 'Admiral.'

'Stewart? Just out of probably the same briefing you've no doubt just had. What are you planning to do about this... thing?'

'I have a team preparing, sir. I'm calling to ask you exactly the same question.'

'Yes, right.' Hennessey thought for a moment. 'This... barrier or whatever it is, extends into the Irish Sea, so we'll have to issue some sort of warning to shipping to stay away from it. God knows what excuse we can cook up this time. I envy you land-based chaps – you can always claim it's an unexploded German bomb, or some such. Anyway, I have a light cruiser – the *Agamemnon*, I think – in the general vicinity. I'll send it in, and tell the captain to cooperate if needed.'

'Thank you, sir,' Lethbridge-Stewart said warmly. 'I really do appreciate that.'

'Keep me posted.' The line went dead.

Lethbridge-Stewart replaced the receiver and started to think about who he had better send where – assuming he received co-operation. The phone rang again, and this time it was MacMillan. The bluff air marshal came straight to the point.

'I've just heard about the Isle of Man. I've ordered a Canberra to make a pass over Peel and take surveillance photos. As soon as they're developed, I'll have copies sent over. I'm assuming you'll have a team on the ground by then?'

'It's preparing to leave right now, sir.'

'Thought as much. Let my office know when they're in place, will you?' He hung up.

Lethbridge-Stewart stared at the phone thoughtfully before putting it back in its cradle.

Things were progressing well. He was pleased that he hadn't needed to fight for co-operation from either man. It looked as if the Fifth was becoming acceptable to the entrenched powers, and that was encouraging. It was often hard enough fighting the enemy without having to fight those who were supposed to be friends as well.

If only he could believe it would be as simple to gain the same assistance from the Yanks and the Reds… Ah, well, negotiating was one of the… joys of command.

He pulled out the thin sheath of papers from the file he'd been given and started to skim quickly through them.

There was a rap on the door, and Anne popped in.

'Well, we're ready to depart, Alistair,' she informed him. 'Evans really has turned over a new leaf, and he's got the men ready.'

Lethbridge-Stewart wasn't surprised to hear this, as he'd been keeping a close eye on Evans (or, Gwynfor Wright as the Welshman was now officially called) since the man had been stationed in Scotland, but Anne had been *away* for some time, it was only in the last month that she'd agreed to become more involved with the Fifth again. Which was just as well, since Jeff Erickson really hadn't been up to the task. The net result of which meant Anne had missed much of Wright's development.

'It's *Wright* now,' Lethbridge-Stewart reminded her.

'Of course.' She smiled. 'It's a nice touch, changing his name to honour his sister.'

'Quite. I was surprised, I must admit, when the paperwork arrived. Even more so, considering that they weren't that close when Sally was alive…'

'Guilt does funny things to a person. Anyway,' she added, returning to business, 'we've a plane standing by,' Anne continued, 'and it should be ready for us by the time we reach the airport.'

'Good.' He tapped the papers he'd been reading. 'The first report of this… whatever-it-is came from a publican, one Albert Rudley. It might be an idea for you to take rooms at his pub.'

'Good thinking, Alistair. I love a little brandy of an evening.'

She was teasing, of course, but he pretended to take her seriously. 'I meant that this way you could ensure the story doesn't get spread *too* far. We *are* still trying to keep these kind of incidents under wraps.'

'Of course. Wright would just *love* to keep an eye and ear open in a public house.'

'You'd better be off, then, before I start taking you seriously, Dr Travers.'

'Righto, Brigadier. I promise I shall drop you a postcard or two…' With a cheeky grin, she waved and left, no doubt to say her goodbyes to her husband.

A moment later, the phone rang again. Lethbridge-Stewart didn't know how she managed it, but Jean Maddox seemed to know precisely when he was free. Perhaps it was better if he didn't enquire.

'Captain Kramer for you, sir.'

'Brigadier…?' There was a low-level hiss on the transatlantic call, but he could understand her, at least.

'Captain. Good of you to call.'

'Are you contacting me to wish me a happy birthday?'

Lethbridge-Stewart gave a start. 'It's your birthday?'

'Of course it's not – don't you recognise sarcasm when you run into it? I'm merely complaining that you only call when you're knee-deep in crap. So, what stinks right now?'

She was in a mood today…

'We've had an incident. And so have you. I thought you might want to pool resources on this one.'

There was a slight pause. 'I don't have a clue what you're talking about. Can you can the military jargon and speak plainly for once?'

She hadn't mellowed a bit.

'It appears that there was some kind of alien landing on the Isle of Man sometime overnight.'

'Isle of Man? Isn't that one of those piddly little rocks off your coast somewhere?'

'Halfway between the mainland and Ireland, yes.'

There was real confusion in her voice. 'Why the hell would even aliens want to invade a spot like that?'

'We don't know that it's an invasion – there's some sort of force barrier been thrown up, and aliens are behind it. I have a team on the way to investigate. I assume you're doing the same.'

'Why in Hades would we care about whatever happens on that place? Unless it *is* an invasion?'

'Because you have a similar incident that's on US soil.'

'We do?' She sounded shocked. 'Are you— No, scrub that, of course you're sure or you wouldn't have mentioned it. Trust me, Brigadier, this is the first I've heard about any such incident. They're really into need-to-know over here, and they usually think I don't need to know anything. What can you tell me?'

'It's at Groom Lake.'

'Ah, crap – that explains it. They don't even tell themselves what's going on there.'

He took a deep breath. 'Captain, can you get us clearance to send a small team in there? We might do better if we cooperate on this.'

'I can't even get *me* into Groom Lake. How the hell do you expect me to get you in?'

'I wasn't *expecting*, I was *hoping*. The more information we have, the sooner we may be able to clear this matter up.' He considered informing her of the Siberian incident, but decided that one case of telling her she was out of the loop was enough for one day.

'I do have a contact there,' Kramer admitted reluctantly. 'But she's hardly cooperative. Hickenlooper is a bitch on wheels.'

Lethbridge-Stewart felt a surge of excitement. 'Hickenlooper?' he echoed. '*Maggie* Hickenlooper?'

'Yeah, I've heard rumours that her parents did christen her something, but I've never been convinced she ever *had* parents.' Lethbridge-Stewart could almost hear her scowling. 'How come you know her name?'

'We dated a couple of times when we were both in Korea.'

'You dated *Hickenlooper*? Do you have pictures, or something? 'Cause nobody would believe me if I told 'em.'

'She's not that bad,' Lethbridge-Stewart said, defensively.

'Public opinion wouldn't agree. But I'll tell you what – I'll give you her number, and you can try and talk to her yourself. Ah – she *does* have fond memories of you, I hope? You didn't get fresh and have her haul off and knock your head off?'

'A gentleman doesn't kiss and tell.'

'A gentleman doesn't; how about *you*?'

'Captain, please, this is important.'

She chuckled. 'The United States Armed Forces have me in a thankless job, Brigadier; allow me the opportunity to milk it for all it's worth, will ya? Okay, got a pen?' She reeled off a number, which he jotted down. 'Just remember – you didn't get that from me, okay? In fact, don't mention my name at all. I don't want to get on her bad side. And she doesn't have a good side.'

Mischievously, he couldn't stop himself saying: 'I thought her left side was… rather interesting.'

'Okay, once the world's been saved again, you owe me a drink and far more details.'

His moustache twitched. 'It's a promise. Thank you.'

Maddox had been busy.

The large map table in the middle of the room was now a world map. Peel, Groom Lake and Khanty-Mansiysk were all marked. He crossed to where she was organizing markers for the various teams, ready to place them as required. He noted that *HMS Agamemnon* was already in place.

'Another call to place,' he informed her, handing across the number for Groom Lake. 'Colonel Hickenlooper.'

'On it, sir,' she said. 'Ah – the call to Captain Bugayev may take a while. I'm having trouble tracking him down.'

'Yes, well, he does like to stay off the radar,' Lethbridge-Stewart admitted. 'Just do your best, Sergeant.'

'Of course, sir.' She moved off to start on the next call.

She was a damned efficient officer, and he couldn't imagine Dolerite Base working as well without her. And, speaking of working…

Anne was busy packing a case with various devices. Lethbridge-Stewart didn't have a clue what any of them were for, but clearly she felt that they were essential. She glanced up as he entered.

'I'm off in five minutes,' she informed him. 'Wright has the team assembled.' Her voice softened slightly. 'He's doing well;

I've not seen a man change in quite the way he has for a long time. I do believe you're a good influence on him.'

Lethbridge-Stewart was never comfortable with praise. 'Ah, yes, well – he does seem to be motivated. Entirely his own doing.'

The phone rang. Anne glared at it, and then answered it. She held out the handset. 'Jean, for you.'

'How the devil did she know I was in here?'

Anne grinned. 'How does Jean ever know *anything*? But she does.'

Lethbridge-Stewart took the phone. 'Yes?'

'Colonel Hickenlooper for you, sir. Switching you now.'

'Alistair?' He felt a shiver of recognition for that accented voice, even though he hadn't heard it for more than a decade. Maggie Hickenlooper had always been an... interesting woman. 'What do you want? I'm kind of busy right now, but your gal said it was urgent.' He'd never heard Maddox referred to as a *gal* before.

'It is, rather,' he replied. 'It's good to hear you, Maggie.'

'Get to the goddam point, will you? There's a... situation here.'

'There's one here, too. And one in Siberia. And they're connected.'

Anne had finished her packing, and started to head for the door. He waved her to stay, and she did so, remaining silent and attentive.

'The devil you say. You *know* about our... incident?'

'Yes – impenetrable barrier in the desert just outside your base. It's the reason I'm calling. We have one also on the Isle of Man.'

'And the Russkies?' Her voice was interested.

'In Siberia. I'm trying to get in touch. I'd like to suggest a joint investigation, since we appear to have a common problem.'

Anne's eyebrow perked up at that. As well they should.

'Did the Reds agree?' Maggie asked.

'I'm still trying to contact them. But when I heard that you were in charge there, I thought—'

'Well, *stop* thinking. I'm just junior grade here, Alistair. I don't have the authority to agree to anything like this.'

That was a disappointment. 'Come on, Maggie,' he urged. 'I'm sure you could *get* authority if you asked in the right places. You were always good at getting your own way.'

'It's one thing to get my own way on a date,' she growled. 'And quite another in this benighted place.' She sighed. 'Okay, I'll see what I can do. What can you offer us? Or, rather, *who?*'

'I was thinking of my scientific advisor. She's top notch, and very experienced with alien incursions.'

'*Very* experienced?' Hickenlooper chuckled. 'Not sure I want details. I *am* aware that you've been having some problems lately, though, and if she's been dealing with them, she sounds like somebody I could use.' He could almost hear the gears working in her brain. 'Okay, Alistair – send her over, and I'll work something out.'

'One of my men also?' He might as well push his luck while she was in a cooperative mood.

'As long as it's only one. We don't want another Limey invasion, you know. We still remember 1812.'

'Thank you.'

'How's your wife?' she asked, abruptly. 'Do you have a son yet?'

How the devil does she know about that? 'Ah – no, not yet.'

'Good luck.' The line went dead, and he hung the phone up.

'Change of plans,' he informed Anne.

'So I gathered,' she said drily. 'I'm now going to Nevada?'

'Yes, and you'd better take Bill with you. I'm sure he won't want you on the loose alone so close to Las Vegas.'

She grinned. 'Beats the heck out of the Isle of Man.' Then she frowned. 'Who are you going to get to go there now?'

'I imagine it had better be me. Probably a good idea to keep an eye on Wright, anyway. And I can make it back here if I have to in double-quick time.' He glanced at his watch – it wasn't even 10am yet. 'Now all I need is for Maddox to track down the Russians…'

CHAPTER THREE

The Beast from 20,000 Fathoms

LETHBRIDGE-STEWART, WRIGHT and six men flew into what had once been RAF Jurby on the north of the Isle of Man.

The old training station had closed down just a few years earlier, and the Territorial Army was in the process of converting it for their own use. This meant that Lethbridge-Stewart had been able to commandeer a truck and a jeep to make the trip down to Peel. The drive – down the A4 and then the A10 – wasn't much more than a dozen miles, most of it in view of the coast. Lethbridge-Stewart had never been to the island before, but barely took in the view beyond noting that the Irish Sea looked choppy and rough. Peel – the island's main fishing port – looked as if it had been carved out of the rocky landscape.

The Fox and Grapes wasn't difficult to find, and Albert Rudley was professionally warm and cheerful. His dog, Queenie, barked excitedly at the strangers. Rudley was in late middle age, running to fat and losing much of his thin hair. His wife, Elsie, was a solid, down-to-earth woman who quietly managed her husband as he managed the hotel. When Lethbridge-Stewart enquired about the odd barrier, she sighed theatrically and told her husband to take 'the military gentlemen' up to it. As the lunchtime crowd was thinning out, Rudley felt he could be spared. Naturally, excited by the prospect of a second walk that day, Queenie demanded to come along.

The journey – on foot – took barely ten minutes; straight up the hill, in fact. Even Wright wasn't winded when they reached it.

'Queerest thing I ever did see,' Rudley remarked. Then he grinned. 'Not that I actually *did* see it,' he added. 'Felt it, really.' He demonstrated by leaning against – nothing.

Lethbridge-Stewart noticed that Queenie's hackles were slightly raised; obviously the dog could sense something that puzzled – though not alarmed – her. He tapped at thin air with his swagger stick, and struck something he couldn't see. He felt the unease that was bordering on low-level fear that Rudley had reported, but he was able to push it to the back of his mind.

'How far does this extend, Mr Rudley?' he asked, his moustache twitching.

'Don't know,' the publican admitted. 'I've not checked it out.'

Lethbridge-Stewart turned to Wright. 'Have the men follow it in both directions for about five minutes.'

Wright dutifully organised the men and they split into two parties to investigate. Lethbridge-Stewart gazed down the hill and out to sea. Everything looked perfectly normal, and there was no sign at all that the barrier existed. He considered the matter carefully.

If this were some sort of an invasion, it was the oddest one he'd ever experienced. It seemed like a crisp but pleasant autumn day, with nothing at all out of the ordinary.

Except the invisible force field.

'I hope you're keeping quiet about… this,' he said to the barman. He waved his hand vaguely. 'Wouldn't want to cause a panic.'

Rudley snorted. 'Not much chance of that. Anybody I've told thinks I've been drinking up my profits – even the wife.' He sounded a bit disappointed. He seemed a bit aggrieved that nobody seemed to be interested in his tale – probably the only exciting thing that had ever happened to him in his life. Then he perked up a bit. 'Nice to see that you take it seriously, though.'

'It's my job to investigate this sort of thing, Mr Rudley.'

'You get a lot of this, then?' Rudley waved his hand. 'Invisible barriers and the like?'

'No,' Lethbridge-Stewart said, hastily. Wouldn't do for the man to start spreading stories. 'Most of the time it's simply… something misinterpreted. Might be in this case, too. I'm sure that there's a perfectly natural explanation for whatever is going on.'

'Aye?' The man wasn't convinced. 'See-through walls crop up a lot, then, do they?'

Wright's return saved Lethbridge-Stewart from having to answer that.

'The thing appears to extend clear in both directions, sir,' he reported. 'It's easy to follow the crushed vegetation. I used binoculars, but I can't see anything at all beyond it except – well, what's supposed to be there. No sign of movement.' He frowned. 'The only odd thing is that the birds seem to be unhappy. There's a lot of them sitting on branches on the far side of the barrier. Just sitting there.'

Lethbridge-Stewart studied the trees beyond this section, and he saw that Wright was right. There were dozens of crows in the trees – all of them sitting there, barely moving.

'The barrier must have cut across their normal flight paths,' he mused. 'They're disturbed that they can't get through.' But it gave him one piece of information; apparently the barrier was impassable from either direction. So, was it there to keep people out... or to keep whatever was on the other side in?

He rather wished he'd brought Anne with him. He was certain she'd have cooked up a half-dozen experiments to conduct by now, but he couldn't think of anything to do that might actually be useful. He considered leaving a guard, but what would be the point? The barrier apparently ran for miles, and he didn't have enough men to patrol it. Still, he ought to leave a man on watch, in case *something* happened.

'Detail a man to stay here and keep an eye on this... thing,' he instructed Wright. 'Give him a walkie-talkie and instruct him to report in every fifteen minutes. Or immediately, of course, if anything happens. Have him relieved every three hours.'

'Sir.' Wright moved off to assign his men. Lethbridge-Stewart liked the way he was finally shaping up.

Lethbridge-Stewart turned back to Rudley. 'Well, we might as well go back to your establishment. I have a few messages I'm waiting for.'

'Don't worry, the missus will keep them safe for you.'

'I don't doubt it,' Lethbridge-Stewart said drily. 'But they're likely to be Top Secret, so I really had better take charge of them as soon as possible.'

'Top Secret?' the publican scoffed. 'You can't make a public thoroughfare *top secret*, mate. People come up here all the time.'

Considering the fact that they had seen absolutely nobody since leaving the town, Lethbridge-Stewart found this claim unlikely. 'It's not my decision.'

'No, it's them bloody politicians, ain't it?' Rudley complained. 'You know what's likely causing this? All them rockets they keep firing off, that's what. Making holes in the ruddy sky – who knows what will fall through when you do that, eh? You tell me that.'

'I really couldn't,' Lethbridge-Stewart replied, mustering all the patience he could. Really, sometimes people amazed him with their ignorance. Still, there was absolutely no point in trying to set the man straight. In fact, it was probably better that he didn't even try to correct Rudley – this way, if he tried to tell anyone about this mystery, he'd simply sound like a crank. It would make whatever cover-up story Lethbridge-Stewart had to cook up a lot easier.

Thankfully, as they made their way back to the pub, Rudley seemed more interested in playing with his dog than in speculating about the barrier.

That suited Lethbridge-Stewart, who spent his own time trying to guess what might be going on. If only Anne was here, maybe she'd have a few ideas. She always did! But she'd be on her way to Nevada by now, which might eventually be more fruitful. After all, it would be hard to hide whatever was happening in a flat desert where you could see for miles…

Maggie Hickenlooper stared out across the sun-baked landscape, frustrated and annoyed.

Finally, something interesting had happened in this benighted area, and she could see practically nothing. Even the binoculars were useless.

The object – whatever the hell it was – had landed gently in the desert. When a patrol went to investigate, they were stopped by an impenetrable, invisible barrier. It seemed to stretch roughly in a circle approximately twelve miles across. The object has sat there for a couple of hours, and then, quite suddenly, a huge cloud of sand had been thrown up near it. Since then, they had been able to see nothing but sand.

In those clear hours, though, a few thousand pictures had been taken, and these had been blown up to the limits of visibility and were being studied inside the Ranch by the top brass. She had been pointedly excluded. Good old sexism at its finest. Still, she doubted that the photos were revealing very much more than she could see here on the spot.

'What the hell is going on in there?' she growled to herself. 'What do those... things want?' Naturally, she couldn't reply.

Back at *The Fox and Grapes*, Lethbridge-Stewart found a motorcycle parked outside and a young airman waiting for him inside. He jumped stiffly to attention, saluted and handed over a large manila envelope.

As Lethbridge-Stewart had suspected, it was marked TOP SECRET in large, bright red letters. Lethbridge-Stewart signed the receipt and the airman dashed off.

The pub was empty now, and Elsie had cleaned up, so he went to one of the tables, opened the envelope and spread the enclosed photos out.

They were from the Canberra's cameras, as he had expected, and told him very little. They'd been taken from at least ten thousand feet, and mostly showed the town and surrounding areas. There was no way to tell where the barrier was positioned, of course, since it was invisible, but he knew it stretched south-west from the town. He examined the pictures, but it was almost impossible to see anything except the obvious – lots of trees, fields, water and the edge of the town.

'Mr Rudley,' he called out. 'Would you come and have a look at these with me?' Maybe a local eye could spot something he couldn't.

The landlord came over, wiping his hands dry on a towel. 'I won't get in trouble looking at top secret pictures, will I?' he asked, anxiously.

'No, not at all,' Lethbridge-Stewart assured him. 'I'm clearing these for your examination.' *Especially since they don't seem to show anything,* he thought. 'I can't tell if there's anything here that shouldn't be, and I thought you might be able to help.'

The innkeeper nodded and bent to examine the photos. In less than a minute, he tapped one. 'Right here, mate,' he said. 'This is just south of where I took you earlier.'

Lethbridge-Stewart bent to study the picture, but didn't know what he was looking at. It appeared to show a small field on the edge of the woods with some sort of a building at the edge of the trees.

'I'm afraid I don't see—'

'That splodge there,' Rudley said, tapping the building. 'Whatever it is, it weren't there yesterday.'

'Really?'

'Really. I took Queenie out on that pasture. It's just for cows normally – no structures.'

That was interesting. Lethbridge-Stewart studied the photograph closer. Not a building then – but what? A spaceship, perhaps? It looked a bit boxy and clunky, but he recalled Anne had mentioned once that spaceships didn't have to be saucer-shaped, as they always were in popular literature. This definitely wasn't round – it looked as if somebody had stuck a bunch of mis-matched shapes together. The graininess of the picture made it difficult to distinguish any features.

'How large would you say it is?'

Rudley shrugged. 'Hard to say. A couple of hundred feet, maybe. How could anyone build something like that overnight?'

'I don't think it was built,' Lethbridge-Stewart said slowly. 'More like *dropped.*' He tapped his swagger stick against his leg thoughtfully. 'Will you excuse me, please?'

He put in a call to Air Marshall McMillan.

'One of the locals has confirmed to me that there's an intruder.' He reeled off the photo number and grid reference. 'Can you get a better picture of it for me?'

'Not sure how low the Canberra can go, Brigadier,' McMillan replied. 'But I'm sure we can do better than last time. I'll get back to you.'

Lethbridge-Stewart nodded to himself. Well, once again, it was time to simply wait...

Major Grigoriy Bugayev narrowed his eyes and glared at the trees, as if defying them.

He hated Siberia at the best of times – too many people he'd known had ended up here – but with the onset of winter so close, it was particularly unpleasant. Especially when there was a mystery to be solved. And this strange barrier was taxing his imagination. And he had an exceptionally good imagination. That was his job.

He was General Timarov's problem solver, which was both a great honour and a great risk at the same time. One of the hazards of being known as a problem solver was that you were handed things others had already tried to deal with – after they had failed. The more obvious solutions had already been tried and found wanting. Now it was time for the department of dirty tricks to take over, and dirty tricks were what he excelled at.

So – the problem to date. A considerable portion of this mountain and the next had been enclosed in some sort of force shield. The shield had not been breached, and there was no indication of its cause. Whether it was designed to keep people out or to keep something else in was unknown. A spy plane had been diverted and taken surveillance photos, but they didn't show very much that made any sense of the situation. And – naturally! – one general had brought in an anti-aircraft gun and fired it at the barrier. The shell had exploded against it, without any obvious effect. General Timarov had then been ordered to deal with the situation, and the order had eventually reached Bugayev.

And now he stood here, smoking illegally imported American cigarettes and casting about for ideas. And they were about as visible as the cause of this mess. Failure – needless to say – was not an option. But success appeared elusive at the moment.

One of his men, Chernov, approached him cautiously and waited. He was trained well enough not to speak first. Bugayev nodded to indicate his approval, and his underling handed him a sheet of paper.

'There is an English officer who wishes to communicate with you.'

Bugayev glanced at the paper. 'Lethbridge-Stewart?' He scowled. 'And what does he want?'

'The woman calling didn't say.'

He was impressed that Lethbridge-Stewart's team had managed to track him down – he deliberately sought to make it difficult to find him. Knowing Lethbridge-Stewart, this would not be a simple social call.

He glanced at the emptiness in front of him. And it was highly likely to be unconnected with this barrier problem, though how the Englishman knew of it was impossible to explain.

'He is an old… friend,' Bugayev informed Chernov. 'It would be rude not to return his call – especially since he went to all of the trouble of tracking me down. Please, have me connected.' He waited a few moments, as Chernov hurried off to arrange this, and spent the time smoking and staring at the growing thickness of snow on the far side of the barrier, and comparing it to the lack of snow outside.

The temperature within the barrier had to be at least ten degrees lower than it was out here – though he could not imagine how that had been accomplished, or what the purpose was.

Chernov came hurrying back, carrying a radio handset that he passed over to his boss. Bugayev nodded his dismissal, and his agent retreated to a safe distance so that Bugayev could speak without being overheard.

'Alistair,' he said, with all of the joviality he could muster. 'It's been a while. How are you? Are you a father yet? Do you have the son you desire?'

'Let's get straight to the point, shall we?' Lethbridge Stewart replied. 'Is that barrier you're looking at frustrating you?'

'Ah! You seek to impress me with the evidence of your intelligence.' He smiled, enjoying the battle of wits. 'Should I ask how you know what I am doing?'

'It's very obvious, I'm afraid, Major. I am similarly frustrated as I gaze upon a barrier of my own.'

That was news. 'You English seek to copy not merely our technology and literature but also our mysteries?'

'Bugayev, let's not trade barbs, but information. I know that you have an invisible, impenetrable barrier; we have one of our own, and so, too, do the Americans.'

'Bah. They copy the Soviets in everything – a step or two behind us.'

'Let's forget the propaganda stances for the moment,' Lethbridge-Stewart suggested. 'We have a common… problem. Why should we not have a common solution?'

Bugayev raised an eyebrow. 'You are proposing an exchange of information?'

'No; what would be the point of that, when none of us knows anything yet? I'm proposing an exchange of personnel between the three of us – England, Russia and America. Two men each to the other two sites.'

'You must know I don't have the authority to authorise such a thing,' Bugayev protested. But he was already starting to get ideas.

'No, but you know who to speak to who does. This is a problem we all share, so it's no longer a political or provincial matter. We should cooperate to attempt to analyse and solve it. And it isn't as if there's anything you wouldn't want us to know about in that section of Siberia, is there?'

Not this section, no…

'True enough,' Bugayev conceded. 'Your suggestion is worth considering. But I cannot guarantee my superiors will accept; they do not trust you as I trust you.'

'I wasn't aware that *you* trusted me. But there is one more item that might convince them.'

'Ah. That would help. What is it?'

'The American… event is occurring at Groom Lake.'

Groom Lake… His superiors had been attempting to penetrate the secrecy around that place for a decade. If *he* could offer them an opportunity to get agents inside it…

'As you say, that might help to convince them.' He made his mind up. 'I'll call you back shortly and give you their answer. And I suggest in the meantime you had better discuss this proposal with Captain Kramer at the UN in New York – Department of Peacekeeping Operations. She will have to make all of the necessary arrangements.'

'Thank you.'

Bugayev gestured to Chernov, who hurried over. 'Have you ever considered a trip to England?'

Lethbridge-Stewart glared at the radio before setting it down. Did *everybody* know he was an expectant father? Or was it simply that he was of interest to everyone these days because of the activities of the Fifth?

He tried to put it out of his mind, and realised he hadn't been worrying about Fiona since this business had started to unravel. It might be an idea to give her a call, just to check that everything was fine…

No. He didn't want to annoy her by constantly checking up on her condition. If there was any development, then she was more than capable of dealing with it. He had to concentrate on the issue at hand, this blasted barrier.

He was pretty certain that Bugayev would be able to sell this matter of co-operation to his shadowy superiors – they would not be able to resist the lure of Groom Lake. It was highly unlikely that the Yanks would allow them to get anywhere close to anything connected with the national security, but the Reds weren't likely to allow that to dissuade them. But it meant that he could now tell Dougie to prep for Siberia.

Siberia and Nevada – opposite ends of the temperature spectrum… Lethbridge-Stewart was glad he was here on the Isle of Man, with decent temperatures and the possibility of a good old British drizzle.

He just wished he had some idea of how to handle this situation. Or even an idea what the situation actually *was*. Alien minds thought differently than human minds, but he could think of no connection between Man, Siberia and Groom Lake. And yet there had to be one.

There was an incoming call, this time from Maddox.

'We have a couple of updates, sir,' she reported. 'The RAF informs us that their Canberra will be over the anomaly in approximately ten minutes, and that they'll get pictures to you as soon as they're developed. And the Navy says that the *Agamemnon* is now in position just outside the southern edge of the barrier, and that they're conducting surveillance.'

'Thank you, Sergeant.'

Well, that was good news, of sorts. Maybe now he'd get some useful information on what was happening.

Captain Carstairs swept the choppy surface of the sea with his binoculars and sighed.

He turned to his first officer, Breckhurst. 'Talk about a fool's errand, Martin,' he complained. They were both standing outside the bridge where they couldn't be overheard. The spray from the Irish Sea was cold but gentle. 'How are we supposed to keep an eye on an invisible something?'

Breckhurst grinned. 'Maybe it's some sort of service joke, sir?' he suggested. 'You know, like sending somebody for a left-handed screwdriver.'

'The Admiralty isn't noted for its sense of humour. Or sense of pretty much anything, it seems. Damn it all to hell, Martin

– this is a bloody waste of time and manpower.'

'They also serve who stand and wait?'

'Damn it all, Martin, don't go quoting Milton at me.'

'Well, there *is* something to this, sir,' Breckhurst pointed out. 'There's some sort of an invisible fence there, where it shouldn't be. Even if we can't see it.'

'Yes, but what can *we* do about it? Just chug up and down like a bloody tugboat and stare at bloody nothing?'

'Orders is orders,' his first pointed out.

'I know that. Ah, don't pay any attention to me. I've always hated doing something stupid just because somebody sailing a desk thinks it's a good idea.'

'Yes, sir.'

Carstairs scanned the empty sea again. He could see the coast of Man clearly in the distance and almost wished he could be on shore having a pint instead of shunting back and forth here on this silly-assed duty. But he loved the ocean, one of the main reasons he'd become a sailor in the first place. Its capricious moods and constant air of brooding mystery had always excited him, and there was nothing like the swaying of the deck beneath one's feet. Whenever he was ashore, he counted the minutes until he was back afloat. Even when being afloat meant ending up doing half-baked patrols like this.

'Better enter it into the logbook, I suppose,' he grumbled. 'Even if there is nothing to report.'

Breckhurst grinned. 'Well, if you need to report *something*, sir, I just spotted a whale breaching off to port – maybe a mile.'

'Minke, I suppose?'

'Probably,' Breckhurst agreed. 'They're reasonably common in these parts.'

'Savour it, then, Number One, that's probably the most exciting thing that's going to happen to any of us today.' Carstairs turned and went back into the bridge to make his entry.

Breckhurst smiled gently to himself.

The Old Man was in a grouchy mood today. He hated these kind of orders, ones that left him traipsing back and forth without any real chance of seeing or doing anything. He was a good captain, but didn't suffer fools gladly – and this certainly had every evidence of being a damned fool's errand.

Breckhurst raised the binoculars he was holding and scanned the surface for any other evidence of that whale. The captain was right – make the most of what little excitement there might be. Besides, it wasn't that often that he got to do a spot of whale watching, and he always felt a certain shiver of awe whenever he saw one of those wonderful creatures.

He scanned from where he had seen the last sweep of a fin, and then around.

There! A spout. As the whale breathed. With a little luck, it might show a fluke before diving again. It seemed to be enjoying itself, if that wasn't anthropomorphising it a bit much… Yes, there was a flash of a fluke, and then—

All hell broke loose.

The water churned, as if it were somehow suddenly boiling. Spouts, huge waves, and then the minke was half-visible in the spray. It wasn't jumping smoothly as it would in a breach – it looked more like it had been backhanded by some unseen giant and sent flying. There was nothing else visible yet, though.

Were they in the presence of some kind of invisible giant, as well as an invisible wall?

And then the wave surge hit the ship, crashing against the side and sending a shockwave throughout the vessel.

Breckhurst grabbed the rail to steady himself and called out – very late! – a warning. The blow wasn't enough to damage the *Agamemnon*, but it had been completely unexpected. It must have sent anything loose flying down below. The mess hall probably would be a mess. He looked in at the bridge, and saw that papers and instruments had gone flying, and a couple of the crew were on the deck.

'What in seven hells is happening, Number One?' Carstairs yelled.

'I don't know, sir,' he answered. 'Still trying to make sense of it. *Something* seems to have swatted the whale.'

'Make sense, Number One.'

'I can't, sir.' He recovered the binoculars – thank goodness he'd slung the cord around his neck, or they might have gone flying – and scanned the sea. The whale was nowhere to be seen, but the waters were still quaking and shivering. 'I don't know—'

The water exploded again. The whale was in the air, this

time looking for all the world as if someone had dealt it an uppercut. It crashed down into the sea again with an audible crack.

'Incoming!' Breckhurst yelled. 'Brace for heavy waters!'

The second crash of the waves against the ship was worse than the first.

The deck seemed to leap ten feet to the side, and, even gripping the rails tightly, he was thrown to his knees, painfully. The entire ship rang like a bell from the impact, and for a second he feared that the *Agamemnon* was going to go over. Somehow, though, the good old girl managed to stagger back upright.

The whale was clearly in serious trouble. Tough as it was, it wasn't built for an attack of the kind it was facing. Slamming down onto the surface of the sea had clearly injured its back. It was struggling to right itself, but it didn't get the opportunity.

Something surged out of the ocean, and grabbed hold of the whale.

Breckhurst couldn't make it out exactly, but it was huge – at least thirty feet long – and had several powerful tentacles that wrapped around the doomed minke. Then a head that seemed to be a mix of the worst parts of a crocodile and a sabre-toothed cat emerged and fastened onto the whale. Even at this distance, he heard the crack as the whale's spine snapped and its struggles stopped.

The whatever-it-was ripped a huge chunk from the freshly-dead whale, and the huge jaws started chewing. Four impossible eyes turned towards the ship, and the monster suddenly stopped in mid-crunch.

It stared at the naval vessel.

Were they going to be the next target? What the hell kind of warning could he give? Monster on the starboard bow? As Breckhurst struggled to try and frame some kind of an alert, the tentacles folded about the dead whale. The difficult-to-make-out head of its killer peered at the *Agamemnon* once again. Then it slowly slipped beneath the shivering waters, and the waves started to die down.

Would it return? Was it getting set to attack the ship next? This was like some really bad Hammer film. He tried to call out a warning, but managed only a croak.

The door to the bridge opened, and Captain Carstairs

staggered out. He was bleeding from a gash on his forehead that he didn't even appear to have noticed.

'What's going on out here, man?' he demanded.

'I… I don't rightly know, sir,' Breckhurst admitted shakily. 'Some sort of…' He struggled to find the right word, but was forced to settle on one that he knew would get him into trouble. 'Monster. Came out of the sea and killed the whale. Then went back, taking the whale with it.'

'Monster?' Carstairs glared at him. 'Are you aware of what you're saying?'

'Unfortunately, yes, sir.'

'Is it gone?'

Breckhurst shrugged. 'Hard to say, sir. It could be below us right now. What does sonar say?'

'Nothing – the operator was knocked unconscious with the first wave. I've ordered his replacement to run a scan, so that may tell us something.' He glared at Breckhurst. 'Monster, Number One? You want *that* in the log?'

'No, sir. But I'm afraid it will have to be…'

The second officer popped his head out of the bridge door. 'Sonar on the phone, sir. There's some sort of echo he can't identify heading towards land – *through* that barrier.'

Carstairs looked unhappily at Breckhurst. 'Well, Number One, it looks like we're going to have to report a monster after all…'

CHAPTER FOUR
X *the Unknown*

LETHBRIDGE-STEWART'S DAY suddenly became a lot busier.

The report from the *Agamemnon* was forwarded to him almost immediately from Admiral Hennessey's office. 'So now we have a sea monster on the loose,' he groaned.

'That's our life in a nutshell, isn't it?' Wright muttered.

Lethbridge-Stewart didn't reply, but he had sympathy for the man's attitude. Well, this was what the Fifth had been formed to deal with, wasn't it? Still, it was clearly time to call in reinforcements. He could hardly deal with a monster that killed and ate whales for a snack with just seven men. He'd probably need a couple of big guns, too – just in case. Hennessey had informed him that he was sending in two further ships, but cagily didn't identify them further.

Then the updated recon pictures arrived from Air Marshall MacMillan – along with another note saying that fly-overs would take place hourly from now on. He checked the pictures of the area that Rudley had pointed out to him. There *was* something clearly there, but it was difficult to make out precisely what it was.

He estimated it to be several hundred feet long and almost as wide. Judging from the shadow it cast, it was at least twice that tall. The outline was vaguely pear-shaped, but with bits and pieces sticking out at bizarre angles. Definitely looked alien to him.

The most disturbing point, though, was that there were several structures close by this thing that weren't there in the earlier photo. It was clear that something was being constructed – but what? Some sort of a weapon, perhaps? And then there was that monster on the loose in the Irish Sea…

It wasn't adding up to a very nice picture.

On the positive side, Major Bugayev called back to say that his superiors had spoken with the Americans and an agreement had been worked out. Each side would exchange a single liaison officer, and both would send representatives to the Isle of Man. Lethbridge-Stewart could send a single officer out to Siberia.

Albert and Elsie Rudley had cheerfully agreed to let him use their back parlour – closed off temporarily to the public – as his operations room for the time being. He could hear the pub beyond the door come to life as the evening wore on. He didn't know what the locals were thinking about his men in the place, but there didn't appear to be much concern. Thank goodness for small mercies, at least. Peel might be one of the largest towns on the island, but it was tiny in comparison with the mainland villages, and apparently the natives weren't as curious. And not a reporter in sight, thankfully. Lethbridge-Stewart didn't enjoy making up stories to keep the Fleet Street johnnies out of his hair, and here there didn't appear to be any need. It certainly made a change.

There was a tap at the side door, and Elsie popped in. She was a cheerful, plump woman of late middle age – precisely the sort of person you'd think of if somebody said *barmaid* (and you didn't have Julie Christie in mind).

'Here you go, love,' she said, holding a tray with a glass of whisky on it. 'You look like you could do with this.' She winked. 'On the house.'

He briefly considered refusing, but then realised that she was right, and he could probably enjoy a drink right now. 'Thank you, Mrs Rudley.' He accepted it and sipped. Mmm – Glenfiddich, fifteen-year-old.

'Call me Elsie,' she instructed him. 'Everybody else does.' She studied him frankly. 'You married?'

'Married?' He set the drink down on the table. 'Good grief!' He'd been so occupied that he hadn't worried about Fiona all day… 'Can I borrow your phone, Mrs Rudley? I'd better call my wife. We're having a baby – ah, well, *she* is, do you see?'

'Of course, love.' She jerked her head towards the door she'd entered by. 'It's back there. I'm sure she'll appreciate a call. Set your mind at ease.'

Fiona answered on the third ring. Yes, she was fine, no, the baby wasn't causing any problems. And how was his day?

'Strange,' he informed her. 'And probably going to get stranger.'

MacMillan had laid on a Bristol Britannia for Anne and Bill.

It had flown into Edinburgh, picked them up and then shot off towards Newfoundland. It was scheduled to do a couple of fuel stops and then land them at Las Vegas mid-morning. The Yanks would pick them up from there and transport them the rest of the way to Groom Lake. It was all a bit of a whirl, but a reasonably efficient one.

Anne hadn't known what to pack, and had finally settled on just clothing. If she couldn't scrounge up lab space from the Americans, she'd be rather surprised, and it seemed to be silly to take scientific equipment with her when they'd probably have the same stuff – and maybe even better – at the Ranch.

Bill had taken mostly the same attitude to packing, but – as a serving officer – he had included his pistol. The idea of borrowing an unfamiliar sidearm from the Americans didn't appeal to him. 'Besides,' he'd added, 'we don't know if we'll need weapons. They've not made any offensive moves. Yet.'

'And we don't know how much use that popgun would have, anyway,' Anne added. 'We tend to need the bigger guns when we need anything at all.'

'Pessimist.' He kissed her nose.

'Realist.' She pushed him back a bit. 'And don't start getting frisky in here, Mr Bishop.'

'Why not?' He swept his hand about. 'We have the whole cabin to ourselves.'

'A stewardess might pop in at any moment to ask what refreshments we'd like.'

'It would be a hairy sergeant major and he'd be serving tin cups of blazing hot tea.'

'Do they have sergeant majors in the Air Force?'

'They have sergeant majors *everywhere*,' he assured her. 'They just have different names.'

'All the more reason for you to behave yourself.' She kissed his nose in return and then grinned. 'Wait till we get to Vegas.'

'That's what all the girls say.' Bill sighed. Then he glanced forward as the door to the cabin opened, and a young flight officer hurried back to them. 'Uh-oh… Speak of the devil…'

'He's not *that* hairy,' Anne muttered, stifling a giggle.

The young man looked like he couldn't make up his mind whether or not to salute her.

'Something wrong?' she asked.

'Captain's compliments, ah, ma'am. There's a radio call for you.'

'How did your Aunty Kathy track us down?' Bill muttered.

Anne tried to keep a straight face and frowned at him. Then she followed the young man into the rather cramped cabin. The radio operator handed her a set of earphones.

It was Lethbridge-Stewart, of course, updating her. Once the call was over, she returned to her seat, mulling over what she'd been told. Bill saw her concentration, and dropped all joking.

'Further trouble?'

'Yes. This time a sea monster off the coast of Man. And from what Alistair tells me, the aliens are building something behind that barrier of theirs. No idea what, I'm afraid. They're very busy little creatures, it would seem.'

'And the monster? Still at large?'

She shook her head. 'It went back behind the barrier. It didn't seem to have any problem penetrating it – unlike us. On the positive side, that means there *is* a way through. On the negative, I still don't know what it might be.'

'You think it was released deliberately? You know – keep out; trespassers will be eaten? That sort of thing?'

'Hard to say, but it's certainly a real possibility.' She sighed. 'Bill, something big is going on here, but it's not following any sort of pattern that I can see. Wouldn't it be lovely if the answer stared us right in the face in Nevada?'

He grunted. 'Come on, with our luck? What are the odds of that?'

'Low. But we *are* going to Las Vegas – the town built on poor mathematics and long odds…'

Colonel Walter Douglas shifted slightly in his seat to ease his aching muscles. 'You'd think with my rank I'd get better transport,' he muttered.

The Lightning's pilot in the seat beside him replied, 'You

said something, sir?'

Douglas glared back at him. 'Nothing worthwhile. It's just a bit cramped in here.'

'Not a lot of elbow room. But you wanted fast transport, and—'

'Be careful what you wish for. Yeah, I get that.'

True to its name, the English Electric Lightning was fast indeed – but it wasn't meant as a transport plane. This was a two-seater trainer, really, pressed into service for this trip. But he'd make it to Siberia hours faster this route, and there was no telling how precious those hours were. He'd spoken briefly with the comrade in charge there – Major Bugayev – and though nothing seemed to be happening at the moment, that was hardly likely to remain the case. Whatever was hiding behind that barrier, it was up to *something*. But, why in Siberia, of all places? Because it was so isolated, perhaps? The Nevada site, too, was out in the middle of the desert, away from most of civilization.

But the one outside Peel wasn't. It was literally walking distance from a decent-sized town.

So, what did they have in common?

This wasn't his area of expertise, really. Give him a physical problem to solve, and he was in his element. All this science fiction speculation was beyond him – he usually left it to Anne. Still, Alistair was relying on him, and he'd better be on his toes when he met this Bugayev.

Alistair knew the man slightly, but could offer little advice. The Russian lurked and worked in the shadows; his boss was unknown, as was the extent of his authority. He appeared to be willing enough to work in co-operation with his (technical) foes, both Brits and Yanks, but that was likely to be because he hoped to get more than he gave.

Damn all of this political interplay. If only there was some sort of way that they could all put aside politics and differences and focus on simply protecting the entire planet. Menaces like the Great Intelligence, the Dominators, the Grandfathers, and the rest didn't threaten just England but the whole world. It would be very helpful if the entire planet could fight back as one, and not as splintered countries all trying to out-do, out-think and out-play the others. But that was just him being an idealist again – such international co-operation was remote in the extreme. There might be a United Nations building in New York, but the earth's nations were still far from united in anything.

Except mutual mistrust.

Ah, well, enough ideological speculation. Maybe he could get a little kip in before they landed to refuel…

Morning came, and Lethbridge-Stewart made another call to Fiona, with the same response: nothing happened, nothing to worry about and get on with his job. If only it was that easy! But he felt comforted from merely hearing her voice.

After a hurried breakfast, he dashed back up the hill to the observation post. He was pleasantly surprised to discover Wright there, sharing a cuppa with the sentry. The Welshman's days of shirking off seemed to be well behind him now.

'Morning, sir,' he greeted Lethbridge-Stewart. 'Nothing to report. Whatever these blighters are up to, they're awful quiet about it.'

'So it would seem, Corporal.' Lethbridge-Stewart stared into the trees behind the barrier, but Wright was correct – neither sight nor sound of anything happening.

There had been another packet of photos waiting for him at breakfast, and they showed that the area inside the barrier under construction had tripled in size overnight. The aliens clearly didn't have problems with unionized labour. But there was no immediate evidence of any of this. You'd think with all of that fabrication going on that there would be some noise – but nothing. There were birds trapped inside the barrier, of course, and the larks and whatnots were happily chirping away in there. He could hear them plainly. But of the construction less than a mile beyond – nothing.

'There's a squad arriving in a couple of hours, Evans,' Lethbridge-Stewart informed him, and inwardly kicked himself. 'Sorry.'

'It's okay, sir. I sometimes have to remind meself, too, like.'

Lethbridge-Stewart continued, before the subject of Sally was raised. 'You should be able to post three men at a time – spread them out a bit.'

'Righto, sir.' Wright brightened up. 'Oh, the American liaison officer is on his way out, sir. Should be here any time.

He landed at Jurby about forty minutes ago.'

'Thank you, Corporal, that's good news.' He glanced at his digital watch. 07:42 – still quite early. There was likely to be a long day ahead. He was frustrated, knowing that there was activity on the other side of the barrier that he could neither understand nor access. He rather wished he hadn't sent Anne off to the States – he relied an awful lot on her, and it was irritating not to have her on hand.

'Oh – here's the Yank now, sir,' Wright said, pointing down the hill.

Lethbridge-Stewart took a look and saw a chap in a US Army uniform striding up the hill.

The officer stopped, waved heartily and yelled, 'Hi, Al!'

Lethbridge-Stewart couldn't believe it. 'Izzy? Is that you?'

'Sure is, Al. Master Sergeant Isidore Rivkin at your service,' the man said, pointing at the rank insignia on his arm.

Good Lord, is that what Izzy is short for…? Lethbridge-Stewart never thought to ask back in the day, and he supposed he just accepted *Izzy* as a proper noun. Thankfully, before he could put his foot in it and say something out loud, Izzy reached Lethbridge-Stewart and pumped his hand heartily.

'Stu and I were tasked with this mission – one to Siberia, one to dear old England. We played dice to see who'd go where.'

'And you won, eh?'

'No, I lost. Stu picked Siberia – we heard that the weather was better there.' Izzy was grinning hugely. 'Gee, Al, it's good to see you again. How long has it been since Korea?'

'Quite some time.' He studied his old friend from his National Service days. 'What happened to you? Didn't you always tell me not to get myself promoted?'

'Yeah, and just look at how much attention you paid to that…' He shrugged and grimaced. 'Stu and I did something dumb – we kinda saved a Korean village from the Chinese.'

'That doesn't sound dumb to me,' Lethbridge-Stewart said gently.

'Well, no, that weren't the dumb part. The dumb part was we did it in front of a visiting colonel, and he insisted on promoting us.'

'All the same, I'm glad to see you, Master Sergeant.' He indicated Wright. 'This is Corporal Wright; just let him know if there's anything you need.'

'Pleased to meet you, sir.'

'You're Welsh, eh?'

'Yes.' Wright was clearly puzzled by this strange foreigner.

'We'll get along great, boyo. I'm a Brooklyn Jew myself – used to being in a minority. And I was a corporal for years.' He leaned in and said in a softer voice, 'You guys like the Scots and the Irish? Make your own brews?'

'I make a mean cup of tea.'

'Tea?' Izzy shook his head in mock sadness. 'No wonder you Brits never win any wars, Al. Didn't you learn *anything* from the War of Independence?'

'If you're *quite* done making fun of my country…'

'Nah, but I'll knock it off for now.' Izzy grinned again. 'And the driver did tell me we're bivouacked in a pub. Smart move that… *Brigadier.* I dropped my kit off there. Got some holiday snaps for you, too – Maggie sent them from Nevada for ya. Kinda dull, so you'll love 'em.'

'We can go over them later. I'd better give you an idea of what's happening here.'

'Or *not* happening,' Wright muttered.

'Or not,' Lethbridge-Stewart agreed. He pointed his swagger stick toward the trees. 'The invisible barrier starts there, goes back a couple of miles and swings out to sea.'

'I don't see nothing.'

'That's because it's *invisible.*'

'Then how d'ya know it's still there?' Izzy asked. He reached out and walked forward like that until he was stopped. 'Yeah, guess it's still there.' He frowned. 'So, it's a one-way sorta thing then?'

'One way?' Lethbridge-Stewart scowled. 'What do you mean?'

Izzy pointed at a bird overhead. 'Well, that little guy just flew *out.* And both air and light seem to get through it just fine… I can feel a slight breeze; can't you?'

Now that Izzy had pointed it out, Lethbridge-Stewart realised he was quite correct – there *was* a gentle breeze blowing through the barrier. 'Well, that might explain how the monster got out… Though not how it returned.'

'A *monster*?' Izzy's face lit up. 'They didn't brief me about *that.'*

'Probably didn't want to scare you off.'

Izzy shook his head. 'Wouldn't miss this for the world. So, is it Godzilla? Frankenstein? The Wolf Man?'

'Some kind of sea-serpent, according to the British Navy.'

His face fell. 'So, they're getting all of the fun then?'

'If it's fun you want,' Wright piped up. 'Then you're in for a ton of it.' He pointed into the trees.

Something was moving back there.

Lethbridge-Stewart's eyes narrowed, and he shaded them from the glaring morning sun. In the trees and shadows, something was clearly there, moving towards them. He couldn't make details out, thanks to the glare, but it clearly wasn't human. It looked to be about eight feet tall and incredibly thin. It was walking with a kind of loping motion, and it was heading straight towards them.

His hand moved automatically to the pistol at his waist.

Anne had managed to doze a little on the long flight, though she was shaken from sleep every time the plane landed to refuel.

Eventually, though, they touched down for the last time at the airport in Las Vegas, and taxied off to a small hanger. She and Bill emerged to radiant early morning sunshine.

Bill handed her sunglasses. 'I was warned,' he informed her.

She accepted them gratefully and stared about her.

Even from here, on the edges of the town, she could see that it lay firmly in a desert. She knew that there was an oasis of sorts here, which is why the original town had sprung up – well, maybe not *sprung* so much as crawled. It wasn't until organised crime moved in that the place really grew. Nevada had never passed the laws against gambling and prostitution that surrounding states had, so the gangs had seen great opportunity here. Casinos and brothels alike proliferated until the US Government had finally managed to crack down on the more obvious crime syndicates. Theoretically, what was now left was honest and open. Theoretically.

But the gangs had managed to build various things that stayed – like headline singers doing shows at the various casinos. Sinatra and the Rat Pack, and, more recently, Elvis, stood out, but there were plenty of others happy enough to trudge out into the desert to encourage people to lose their money and still get entertained.

Not that she and Bill would have the time or opportunity to take in the local sights, of course. In the shade by the hanger was a US Air Force jeep, along with a uniformed corporal and a young woman relaxing in the vehicle. She and Bill hurried over.

The young airman saluted Bill, and then held out his hands for their bags. 'Welcome to Vegas, sir, ma'am,' he said politely, as he stored their luggage. 'We'll be on our way shortly.'

The young woman unwound herself and studied them with a grin. She was quite a stunner – long dark hair, flawless skin, dark eyes that glittered with humour, and a shape that could have made her a model. 'Tanya Tolstoy,' she introduced herself, holding out an elegant hand. 'No relation.'

Anne shook it. 'Is that your real name?'

The Russian shrugged. 'A name is merely a label.'

Bill laughed. 'Maybe yours should be *handle with care?*' he suggested.

'I will consider it,' she said, with a flash of perfect teeth.

'I'm William Bishop,' he said, taking his turn with her hand. 'This is my wife, Anne.'

She studied them archly. 'Welcome, Captain Bishop… Mrs Bishop.'

Anne prickled. 'Dr Travers,' she said firmly.

'Ah.' Tanya nodded. 'You have an identity of your own.'

'Mine is earned.' Anne was starting to get annoyed.

'So is mine. I have not been sent here simply because of my looks. Though in America, looks are considered a good thing, no?' Tanya's voice had a slight accent – just enough to sound sexy and intriguing. Anne wondered how much of it was real and how much merely an image.

'You must have made good time to beat us here from Russia,' she said.

The driver had finished stowing their gear and had vanished into the hanger, leaving the three of them alone.

'That's because I came from Cuba,' Tanya explained. 'I am technically on vacation.' She shrugged. The short skirt she was wearing rose an inch or so at that gesture. 'That is why I am dressed for pleasure and not work.'

'You separate the two?' Anne asked, keeping her face as impassive as she could.

'Sometimes. But I do enjoy my work, which is why I am here now.'

'And what exactly are you qualified to do?'

Tanya gave a slow smile. 'Whatever the situation calls for. Which, at the moment, is to enjoy the view.' She looked off at the towers of the casinos. 'Do you know if Elvis is in town? I should *really* like to attend one of his shows.'

Bill managed to inch into the conversation. 'Isn't he considered decadent in Russia?'

'Oh, yes. But we are not in Russia, are we?' Again that impish grin. 'And I feel like being a trifle... decadent.'

Not with my husband you don't, Anne thought savagely. She glowered at Bill, who didn't seem to notice at all. Typical!

'Here's our driver now,' Anne said, breaking the mood.

The corporal hurried over. 'All cleared now,' he informed them. 'We can be on our way. Colonel Hickenlooper is expecting you all.'

Tanya nodded, and then glanced at Anne. 'You will wish to sit with your husband together, I imagine? I'll take the front.' She hopped in beside the driver, showing a good deal of her long legs as she did so.

'Eyes front, soldier,' Anne growled at her husband.

He hastily pretended he hadn't noticed the long flash of flesh and helped her into her seat before plonking down beside her.

'Is it far?' she asked the driver.

'Hour or so, ma'am,' he replied, as he started the vehicle. 'Hope you brought sun-screen – it gets kinda hot out there.'

Anne hadn't. 'We're British,' she admitted. 'The sun is a stranger to us.'

Tanya had an oversized handbag she'd stashed in the jeep. She rummaged into it and produced a bottle. 'Use mine,' she said, cheerily. 'I was on holiday, remember? I came prepared. Rub it into every exposed area.' She raised her leg slightly to show some of her own exposed areas. 'Or get your husband to help.'

She managed to somehow make even a kind gesture into a way to rub Anne the wrong way. Was it feminine competitiveness – or something else? Whatever it was, it made it very difficult to like the woman.

Though neither Bill nor the driver appeared to have any trouble whatsoever liking Tolstoy…

Douglas was rather surprised to discover that it wasn't as cold as he'd expected it to be in Siberia. Not that it was warm, mind, but there was snow only on the mountain tops, and not several feet deep everywhere. He mentioned this to Bugayev, who grunted.

'Wait until winter returns,' he suggested. 'Or the barrier.'

Alistair had said that Bugayev was deep and enigmatic, and that certainly appeared to be the case. The man had the look and style of an eagle – tall, imposing and indifferent. It was impossible to gauge what he might be thinking, as his expression never changed. He said little, even to his own men, and appeared to be dwelling in a world inside his own mind, and visiting the real world only from time to time to make a pithy observation, or to cast his hooded eyes about as if they somehow absorbed whatever he glanced at. Douglas – more used to working with Alistair – found him rather off-putting. But, then, he imagined that was how the Russian wished to be perceived.

The mountains, too, were not quite what he'd expected. They were lushly forested, a vast swath of greenery against the background. Siberia looked to be more liveable than some of the places he'd skied on holiday…

They walked the final distance to the barrier. He could see the wrecked lorry, looking as if some huge, monstrous foot had stomped on the engine. Bugayev caught his surprised look and almost cracked a smile.

'I leave it there to remind my men that this is potentially dangerous,' he offered.

That made sense. Since nothing appeared to be happening, the soldiers might get a little complacent – and that could be deadly if something actually did occur. Like the sea monster back home.

As they approached the force field, Douglas whistled.

It was snowing inside the barrier. A foot or more had fallen and piled up inside the invisible edge, and the wind was whipping it about, snowflakes swirling in the breeze. It wasn't quite a blizzard on the other side, but the snow was still falling.

'Must be ten or twenty degrees colder inside there,' he said, softly.

'Eighteen,' Bugayev corrected him.

'How is that possible?'

Again, that almost-smile. 'How is *any* of this possible?'

'Good point.' Douglas couldn't resist a slight needling. 'Beyond even Soviet technology.'

'Slightly, perhaps.' Bugayev remained impassive. 'And further from American know-how. And furthest from British potential.'

'Touché.' Douglas considered the matter for a few moments, walking slowly up and down the barrier. 'Do you have any idea what's inside there?'

'Snow.' Bugayev shrugged. 'We've tried taking pictures, but the conditions are not optimum.'

'It makes no obvious sense. Why put an impenetrable barrier in the middle of Siberia and simply fill it with snow?'

'The same is not happening in England or America?'

'No.' He hesitated for a moment at the thought of sharing intelligence with a Russian, but realised it was counter-productive to withhold information. 'The one on the Isle of Man and the one in Nevada have unchanged conditions inside them. Well, except for the sea monster that came out of ours.' He shook his head. 'None of this is making any kind of sense to us.'

Bugayev hesitated, and then shook his head slightly. He was obviously having the same qualms about sharing data. 'Nor to us,' he finally admitted. 'Something – *someone* – is expending a lot of power on creating this, and it appears to have no purpose.'

Douglas sighed. 'But there must *be* a purpose,' he reasoned. 'And it's worrying that none of us can see it.'

One of the Russian guards stationed around the edge of the barrier suddenly called out. Douglas didn't understand Russian, but he *did* understand fear. The man was pointing into the enclosed area, into the swirling snows, and he'd raised his rifle.

Bugayev said something sharply, and then leaned forward to stare into the falling snow.

'There!' he exclaimed, pointing.

There was a shadowy shape inside the downfall. It was impossible to discern just what it might be, but it was *big* – ten or twelve feet at the very least. It was more of a form than anything definite, and then there were others, too, of varying sizes. They appeared to be on the move, approaching the barrier.

Every moment their vague shapes started to become slightly more distinct. They weren't people – or even humanoid-like creatures. They were bulky, plodding, walking with a swaying motion. They appeared to be carrying scimitar-like weapons in front of them, and the other Soviet soldiers immediately raised their rifles.

Bugayev gave a curt command, and nobody tried to fire. Well, it wouldn't have been much use anyway – bullets would simply splat against the barrier, after all.

The shapes moved on. As they drew closer to the barrier, the snow thinned out and their forms became more and more distinct. And more and more unbelievable.

They weren't carrying weapons – well, at least not *artificial* ones. The scimitars were tusks, long and curved and dangerous. The shapes were resolving into a small herd of elephant-like creatures, only huge and covered in a thick, greyish fur. They stomped forward as if unaware that there was a barrier ahead of them.

They were mastodons, or mammoths…

At any rate, creatures that hadn't existed on Earth for thousands of years.

And they were marching intently onwards, straight at the startled soldiers.

CHAPTER FIVE
The Thing from Another World

GROOM LAKE turned out to be slightly disappointing at first.

It looked like any other Air Force base Anne had ever seen. There were a dozen or so large hangers – most of which, she noted wryly, were firmly closed. She wasn't sure whether it was to keep the visiting Russian or the visiting Brits from seeing what was inside. There were barracks buildings, and then the central section that was obviously for the technicians and brass. There was also the inevitable flight tower, and several rotating radar dishes.

The entire area was surrounded by a heavy security fence, and the main entrance was through an impressive guard post. Each of them had to show their IDs in three different places to equally impassive guards who took their time waving them on. Tanya seemed to find the whole thing vastly amusing, and spared no opportunity to flash her long legs or cleavage. Anne felt downright dowdy next to her. And she was annoyed with herself for feeling like this was some sort of a competition.

Finally, though, they were cleared by security, and their driver took them over to the command centre. Almost immediately a female officer stepped out of the doorway to greet them.

'Colonel Maggie Hickenlooper,' she introduced herself, shaking hands all around as the others greeted her.

Anne had been intrigued to meet this one-time flame of the Brig's. She'd personally known two so far, and she could see why he'd dated Hickenlooper – she was slim and attractive, with a mass of dark hair (unlike Sally's and Fiona's blonde) under her cap. When she removed her sunglasses, Anne could see the colonel had bright blue eyes. She looked intelligent, capable – and unhappy.

'Feinman will see to your things,' Hickenlooper said. 'You need to freshen up?'

'I'm fresh enough,' Tanya offered.

'Yeah. You look pretty fresh.' Hickenlooper glared at their driver. 'Eyes back inside your skull, Feinman. Take care of their things.'

'Yes, ma'am,' he agreed, and drove off.

'How about you two?' Hickenlooper asked.

Bill glanced at Anne, raising his eyebrow slightly, and placing the onus on her. 'Fine for now,' she said, briskly. 'And raring to get to work, Colonel.'

'Yeah, we'll probably beat that enthusiasm right out of you.' Then Hickenlooper softened slightly. '*Colonel* is fine in public, but what's say you call me Maggie when we're all alone and cosy like this, hey?'

'Fine by me,' Anne agreed. 'Call me Anne; any friend of Alistair's is a friend of mine, and all that. I do get a little overpowered by all of the military atmosphere, though.'

'Me too,' Tanya agreed. Then she grinned. 'But I do like a man in uniform.' She eyed Bill as she said this. He flushed slightly.

'That's *my* man in uniform,' Anne said firmly.

Tanya smiled. 'Of course he is. There are plenty to go around.'

'Yeah, well, this isn't *The Dating Game*,' Maggie growled. 'We've got transport laid on to get us out to the site, but I thought you might like to take a quick side trip to see the Artefacts.'

'The what?' Bill asked blankly.

'It's what we call the alien crap we've gathered over the past couple of decades,' she explained. 'Frankly, it's mostly wreckage and junk, but it's what everybody wants to see when they come here. It doesn't add up to much, and none of it works. But it's alien, and that somehow makes garbage seem special.'

Anne immediately thought about what she had squirreled away in the Warehouse, but decided that co-operation with the Yanks didn't need to extend to revealing what they had secreted. 'Can't wait to see it.'

'Me either,' Tanya agreed. 'I do hope I'm included in this invitation.'

Maggie looked as if she wished the Russian were anywhere else and anybody else's responsibility. 'Just this once, yeah, you are. Just don't get your hopes up too high.' She glared at them all. 'No cameras, though.'

Tanya laughed. 'I have no cameras,' she promised. She raised her arms to accentuate her slender figure. 'Unless one of you wishes to search me?' She looked hopefully at Bill.

'I don't think that will be necessary,' Maggie commented. 'If you can conceal *anything* under that dress, you're a better woman than I am.' Tanya laughed delightedly. 'Okay, stick together kids. No wandering off.'

The storage area for the Artefacts was rather disappointing – merely one of the hangers.

They all had to show their passes again to gain entrance – even Maggie – and then they walked into the large building. It was mostly empty. The Artefacts were stored about half-way down the left-hand side. There were six large metal shelving units, a couple of what looked like barrels.

And a spaceship.

This was about twenty feet long, and looked like an alien concept of a drag racer. It appeared to be mostly engines, with a two-man (two alien?) cabin at the front. It was badly burned and corroded, but relatively intact.

'What happened to this?' Anne asked, walking up to the bullet-shaped craft. There were bumps and protuberances all over it, some of them clearly melted.

'It crashed,' Maggie replied. 'Near Roswell, New Mexico.'

'Student driver?' Tanya suggested with a grin.

'For all we know,' Maggie answered, seriously. 'Our brains' best guess is that they had some sort of artificial gravity in this thing, and it failed somehow. We scraped up the remains with teaspoons. The ship itself is relatively intact – and completely inert. We haven't managed to get any information at all from it.'

'Can we look inside?' Anne asked, eagerly.

Maggie shrugged. 'Be my guest. It's not like there's anything worthwhile hiding about this piece of junk.'

Bill laughed. 'Yeah, but it's *alien* junk.'

'Whoop-de-doo,' Maggie muttered.

There was a hatch into the ship, and it looked like it had been forced open. No doubt by the Americans when they found it. There was a stepladder beside it, and Anne stood on it, peering inside. That was more impressive – the controls definitely looked a lot more high-tech, and they were gathered about two seats. She tried not to think about what had caused staining inside the cabin. The seats were certainly not built for humans – they were angled awkwardly, and too broad and short to be comfortable. There were some sort of helmets attached to the back of the seats that presumably were meant to go over the pilots' heads.

There was a gentle tap on her leg.

'May I?' Tanya asked.

They exchanged positions, and the Russian peered into the ship in fascination. 'I've seen nothing like this even in Russia,' she admitted.

'It's definitely alien, but nothing I've seen before,' Anne said.

Tanya glanced down at her. 'You have seen alien technology before?'

'Once or twice.' Anne saw Bill frown slightly, clearly worried she was revealing more than she was supposed to. 'What? You don't think Miss Soviet Union 1972 here doesn't know that?'

Tanya attempted – and failed – to look contrite. 'Am I the cause of marital discord?'

'No,' Bill replied firmly. 'It's just a slight collision of military and scientific minds.'

'Ah. Good.' The Russian looked at Maggie. 'What is that space on the control panel?'

'That?' Maggie shrugged. 'One of the boys thought it was a radio set of some sort. He managed to get it out, but couldn't get it to work.' She jerked a thumb over her shoulder. 'It's on one of the shelves over there now.'

'Let me have a look,' Anne said, frowning. She was annoyed that she hadn't seen the gap. She and Tanya exchanged places again.

'To the left of the main panel,' the Russian said helpfully.

'Down about a foot.'

Now Anne could see the space. It was in shadow, which is why she hadn't spotted it herself. 'What sharp little eyes you have.'

'I have a few sharper body parts,' Tanya said, chuckling.

Anne was thinking. There were *two* pilot's chairs, so… She examined the right-hand side of the panel, and saw that there was a small device in a similar position. There was definitely the look of some sort of a communication device about it. There was a small speaker grill, and a couple of knobs, obviously for some sort of tuning. It actually looked depressingly commonplace. And then something caught her eye…

'You say this ship is completely dead?' she asked Maggie over her shoulder.

'As a dodo, yeah.'

'That's interesting. Because I can hear a very faint hum.'

'What sharp little ears you have,' Tanya murmured.

'You're not the only person with a fully functioning body.' Anne wiggled her way into the cockpit and managed to slide uncomfortably into the right-hand side seat. Tanya joined her in the other, along with a fine display of naked legs, undoubtedly for Bill's benefit. Anne tried to ignore her theatrics, but it was difficult. The Russian was rubbing her the wrong way, and likely by intent. She wasn't going to give Tanya the pleasure of seeing her get annoyed, though. She focused on the issue at hand.

The hum was louder now, though still very soft. And it was clearly coming from the remaining radio. Anne bent forward to examine it, and was rewarded by a stabbing pain to her backside.

'Damned chair,' she growled, and shifted. Who the hell built a spike into a seat? Or maybe it was something that had happened in the crash? She touched the radio very gently, and felt a minute vibration in her fingertips. 'The radio is working,' she stated, softly.

'I'll be damned,' Maggie said. She was on the stepladder, peering into the cabin. 'Why the hell has it come to life now?'

'Only one reason I can think of,' Anne answered. 'There's now somebody here on Earth that it can talk to…' She grinned abruptly. 'It's been dead for an obvious reason – you've had only one end of the phone here. With nobody to talk to, it's been dormant. But now that its buddies have arrived, it can finally complete the circuit.' She stroked the panel almost lovingly. 'I think we can now talk with your visitors.'

'Mastodons,' Douglas breathed, staring in awe at the great hairy forms on the far side of the barrier.

They had come to a halt, clearly spooked by the difference in weather that they were seeing. It was a small herd, seven individuals of varying size and appearance. One was clearly a juvenile, only about half the size of the others.

'Mammoths,' Bugayev corrected him gently. 'And they have been extinct for about ten thousand years. Certain corpses have been found, frozen in the tundra, but…' His voice trailed off. He seemed to be as impressed as Douglas felt.

He was vaguely aware of a car engine behind him. The vehicle drew to a stop and then somebody elbowed his way to join him and Bugayev close to the barrier.

'Holy Toledo, what have I been missing?'

Douglas glanced at the American soldier. 'First Sergeant Stuart Reiss?'

'The same,' he admitted, staring in awe at the mammoths. 'Although Stu is fine, Colonel.' The mammoths were standing, swaying slightly, and staring at the cordon of troops in front of them. He whistled softly. 'Wow – Barnum woulda loved one of these guys. Talk about mammoth…'

Douglas shook his head. 'What do you think is going on?' he asked. 'Obviously these creatures couldn't have created the barrier.'

'It makes little sense,' Bugayev agreed. 'If it were not impossible, I would say that these mammoths must have somehow been dragged from the past.'

'Maybe these aliens are some sorta conservationists?' Reiss suggested. 'You know, like the Wildlife Fund? And this force field whatzit is like a cage in a zoo?'

Douglas shrugged. 'It's as plausible as anything else. But why mammoths? I mean, there are a lot of other animals that are still alive that the aliens could have picked.'

'Maybe they think these guys are cute. Don'tcha think

they're sorta cute? In a sort of don't-get-under-their-big-feet kind of way?'

'I don't know,' Douglas admitted. 'But it's rather worrying.'

Reiss scowled. 'Why? When you Brits say something is *rather worrying*, that translates to *it's time to panic* in American.'

'Well, if whoever is behind this can resurrect mammoths – what else are they capable of bringing back? Sabre toothed tigers? Dinosaurs?'

'Great. Now I'm going to be scared stiff the rest of the day. Thanks a lot, fella.'

Douglas frowned at the level of informality coming from Reiss, but said nothing, deciding it was merely one of many differences between the British Army and its American counterpart.

'You do have a point,' Bugayev said reflectively. 'The scale of power that is being used here is colossal. It is beyond anything that any human can manage.' He smiled bleakly. 'Even the Soviets.' He stared at the snorting mammoths. 'Depending upon the motivations of these beings, we may be facing a threat to our entire planet.'

Lethbridge-Stewart watched the approaching figure cautiously.

Wright made a move to raise his rifle, but Lethbridge-Stewart gave a slight shake of the head, and the corporal subsided.

'Let's see what this gentleman wants first, shall we?'

'How'd ya know he's a gentleman?' Izzy asked.

'Well, it could be a female.'

'No, I meant the *gentle* part.' The American scowled. 'There *is* a sea monster involved in this scenario, remember?'

'Let's just wait and see,' Lethbridge-Stewart suggested. 'There's only the one of him-her-it, so that either means *friendly* or *overwhelming power*.'

The being was closer now, and they could start making out details. It was certainly not human, but there was enough of the human about it to make it seem vaguely familiar. Two arms, two legs, torso and head… That was a relief, and at least a reference point.

Lethbridge-Stewart was certain that Anne would have

made several pertinent observations by now, but he could only think of one: the creature was over eight feet tall, and appeared to be walking with a loping gait that suggested it was uncomfortable; so, it was probably from a world whose gravity was rather less than that of Earth. Not a lot less, clearly, but less.

He couldn't make out smaller details, but the being had a face that was vaguely human – there were eyes, large and blinking. The creature wore some sort of tinted glasses, and that suggested another point: its home world had a lower level of light than Earth. The brightness of even an English sun was clearly too strong for it.

There was no obvious nose, but the central section of its face was pushed forward slightly, like some sort of primitive beak. And it had a raised ridge of some sort starting between its two eyes and running backwards across its skull. Reading a face like that was completely impossible, of course – its expression could mean anything from *prepare to die, Earth scum* to *hello, what's playing this week in the West End?*

The alien came to a sudden halt at the other side of the barrier, and then gave a giddy bow of sorts.

'I present my apologies,' it said, in perfect, unmodulated English.

'For what?' Lethbridge-Stewart asked, curiously.

'For the misbehaviour of my employee,' the alien answered. 'He has been admonished. I present also his abject apologies.'

Well, if he's apologising, Lethbridge-Stewart thought, *that's a good sign.* Even if he had no idea what the being was apologising for.

'Ah – we thank you for your sincere apologies.'

'Appreciated,' the alien said, and then turned to go.

'Wait a minute. Can I ask what you are apologising *for?*'

The alien blinked rapidly, but turned back to face them again. 'For the hunting of the indigenous species.'

Oh.

'The attack on the whale.'

'Correct. Thank you for your understanding.' It turned away again.

Izzy whistled. 'The *thing* that attacked and munched the

whale – that was one of your workmen?'

'Indeed. His performance report has been duly marked with the reprimand, I assure you. I assume that this is acceptable response to his infraction?'

'Oh, absolutely,' Lethbridge-Stewart replied, managing to look as though he knew what he was talking about. He *really* wished Anne were with him at this moment.

'Then we are finished.' The alien turned to go again.

'Wait, wait,' Lethbridge-Stewart called. 'You can't just walk away.'

'I cannot?' The being blinked rapidly again. 'Forgive me, I do not know the customs of your planet. How am I required to retreat? I do not wish to be rude.'

'No, that's not what I mean.' Lethbridge-Stewart struggled for the right words. 'There is so much we need to talk about.'

'Contact with you has been forbidden,' the alien said. 'I am breaking protocol with this meeting, but it was necessary to issue our apology. Now the contact must be terminated.'

'Look,' Lethbridge-Stewart said urgently, 'I can understand if your rules say you're not supposed to contact us, but you must understand that there is a great deal that we wish to know.'

The being's head wavered from side to side. 'Those are not *my* rules. They are *yours*. I would greatly prefer to converse, but you have forbidden it.'

'Is it just me,' Izzy demanded, 'or does the more he say tell us less and less?'

'It's not just you, boyo,' Wright muttered.

'I don't understand,' Lethbridge-Stewart said to the alien. 'This is the first time we have spoken to you.'

'And it will be the last. Your instructions will be followed.'

'They're not *my* instructions!' Lethbridge-Stewart snapped.

'Forgive me; I struggle with making my meaning clear.' The alien was certainly full of apologies. 'These instructions came from your king.'

'My *what?*'

'Your king. And we have vowed to obey the instructions.' It inclined its head. 'Technically, I have abrogated his command, and will, of course, issue him an apology.'

This conversation was incredibly confusing.

'We don't *have* a king,' Lethbridge-Stewart said. 'We have a queen.'

'Ah, forgive me – I was not aware that your race was gender fluid. Your king has become your queen.'

'No, no.' This conversation would be ridiculous if it were not so important to establish communications here. 'You don't understand… We haven't had a king for some years. The Queen has ruled the land for the last twenty years now.'

'Your words are confusing me,' the alien admitted. 'They do not mesh with my instructions. I shall have to return to clarify my instructions.'

'*We* are confusing *you*?' Izzy exclaimed. 'Jeez, guy, *my* head is spinning.'

The alien was moving back now the way it had come. It seemed that the conversation was over, and all they had achieved was total confusion.

Lethbridge-Stewart called to its retreating back, 'Who are you going to speak to?'

'To your monarch. To the King of Earth.'

'The *who*?' Izzy demanded.

'It would appear,' Lethbridge-Stewart said drily, 'that we have a ruler of whom we were completely unaware…'

CHAPTER SIX

Them!

ANNE FELT her excitement rising.

She stared at the alien radio as she stroked the cold metal. Finally – a breakthrough! Whoever was out there in the desert was presumably the party on the other end of this device. If she could just talk to them, find out why they were here…

'Hands off,' Maggie ordered abruptly, glaring at her from the doorway. 'That's technically US property. Co-operation only goes so far, young lady.'

Anne stared back at her. 'You have got to be kidding,' she said, deflated. 'You're going to start getting all proprietary *now?*'

'You're damned right I am. That's *American* property there, and *we'll* be the ones to use it.'

Tanya arched a shapely eyebrow. 'A moment ago it was American *junk,*' she pointed out. 'If it were not for Dr Travers, it would *still* be junk.'

Anne was surprised and pleased at this support from the other woman, but she realised that the Russian was probably simply playing politics, and attempting to score points.

'That's as may be,' Maggie retorted. 'But we have our own brains trust here at the base, and they ain't gonna be excluded.' She scowled at Anne again. 'So, out of there until they arrive, *capiche?*'

Extremely reluctantly, Anne complied. Tanya clambered out first, past the spectacular scowl on the colonel's face. Once she was certain that they'd obeyed her order, Maggie strode to the door and spoke with one of the soldiers on duty.

'Damn the military mind,' Anne muttered.

'Hey – you're *married* to one of those military minds,' Bill reminded her.

'Don't tell me you're on her side.'

'Well, no, but I can see her point. They've kept a sleepy eye on this *rubbish* for decades; now it's finally proving to be of potential use. Surely you can see that they feel they have a right to exploit it?'

'Don't expect me to be reasonable all of a sudden.' It was bitterly disappointing – to be *so* close to contacting the minds behind whatever was happening, only to have the rug pulled out from under her feet at the last second…

'Okay, our guys should be here shortly,' Maggie said, rejoining them. She eyed Anne suspiciously. '*They* will be in charge here, but I'm sure they'll share information with you.'

'How generous of them.'

Maggie glared at her again. 'Yeah – it *is* generous of us. I could just throw you and that Russian babe outta here, you know. Come to think of it, that's probably what the Pentagon would want me to do.'

Bill jumped in. 'I'm sure there's no need for that,' he said, hastily. 'After all, your government did agree to co-operate with us in this matter…'

Maggie subsided a little. 'Yeah, I guess you're right. But I don't want any more attempts by any of you to take over here. Understand?'

'I am sure that is the last thing we intend,' Tanya said placatingly. 'Dr Travers was merely… over-excited at the prospect of talking with aliens. Aren't we all?'

Anne had to bite back her immediate thought, that she'd spoken with more aliens than possibly anyone on the planet, other than Lethbridge-Stewart. Bill looked relieved that she managed to remain silent.

'That's understandable, I guess,' Maggie agreed. 'But just remember – this is a US base and a US project, and keep your fingers to yourselves.' She marched back to the sentry at the hanger door to check on where the American boffins were.

'I'm starting to see why Captain Kramer isn't her biggest fan,' Bill murmured.

'Neither am I,' Anne confessed. 'Can you believe that Alistair once dated her? What did he see in her?'

Bill's lips twitched. He didn't want to speak out against

his commanding officer, and Anne supposed she could respect that.

'Americans feel that they must always be in command,' Tanya suggested. 'You may have figuratively emasculated her.'

'She isn't masculine,' Anne pointed out.

'Everyone else is.' Tanya looked actually sympathetic for a moment. 'The Americans are not as enlightened as we Soviets – they do not admit the equality of the sexes. She may have difficulty maintaining her authority.'

Anne was about to grouch, and then reconsidered. The Russian woman might well have a good point – Maggie *was* the only woman of rank they'd seen here, and she probably did have a tough job as a result. It had been hard enough for Anne to be respected among her peers in the scientific community, and still was at times. Yes, she could relate to Maggie on that point at least. 'You could be right,' she grudgingly admitted to Tanya. 'It's just so frustrating – so close to finding answers.'

'We are *still* close,' Tanya pointed out. 'At least we are allowed to remain and observe. It might be as well not to provoke her again.'

Much as it pained Anne, she had to admit that the other woman was correct again. She hated to take a back seat here, but it *was* the only seat that she was being offered…

'I'll behave,' she promised.

Tanya gave her a cheeky grin and Bill offered an encouraging smile.

A jeep roared up outside, and two men jumped out and ran to salute the colonel. There was a brief huddle at the door, and then Maggie brought the two men over to them.

'Our top brains here,' she announced. 'Drs Swift and Bradley.'

The older of the two held out his hand to Anne. He couldn't have been more than forty, but his hair was greying at the temples, and was on the long side for a soldier.

'I'm Thomas Swift,' he said. 'So glad to finally get to meet you, Dr Travers. I've read several of your papers.'

'And I yours,' Anne admitted, shaking his hand. 'I had no idea that they had someone of your calibre at this base.' She was honestly impressed.

He smiled, a trifle shyly. 'To be honest, I'm not here for *that.*' He jerked his thumb at the spaceship. 'We'd just about given up all hope of discovering anything from it. I'm here for—' Maggie gave a conspicuous cough. 'Ah – something I'm not supposed to talk about.' He gave the shy grin again. 'Ah, and this is my assistant, Andrew Bradley.'

Bradley was a younger man, and he looked like a career soldier – well-toned and trim, with regulation short hair. He hesitated for a moment, clearly unsure if he was to salute or shake hands, and then settled on the latter. 'Pleased to meet you, ma'am.'

'My name's Anne,' she informed them. 'You make me feel old, calling me *ma'am.*'

'They call *me* ma'am,' Maggie grunted.

'Well, that's out of respect for your rank, I'm sure,' Bill said hastily.

Good catch, Anne thought. 'You two gentlemen have heard what's happening?' She nodded at the spaceship.

'Indeed,' Swift said, enthusiastically. 'It's been a solid lump of nothing for so long…We never expected anything like this, eh, Andy?'

'Gave up on it years ago,' Bradley admitted.

Swift rubbed his hands together. 'Well, let's get started, eh? First contact, and all that.'

'Do you think that's a good idea?' Bradley asked.

'I think it's the *only* idea. What's wrong, Andy – cold feet?'

'No.' Then the younger man shrugged. 'Well, yes, maybe. It's just that this is a huge responsibility – there are *aliens* out there. What if we say something that offends them, and they get mad and want to blow up the earth or something. I'm not sure we should be doing this. We should contact the Pentagon… the President… *Somebody.* Somebody trained for this kind of thing.'

'We're as close as it gets to *somebody trained for this kind of thing,*' Anne said. She could understand his fears – hell, she *shared* them. It *was* a huge responsibility, talking to aliens for the first time. And first contacts were always unpredictable and scary. Who knew how an alien species might think, or what might offend them? 'Look, there are two possibilities here. First, that the aliens are friendly. In that case, they'll *want* to talk to us. The second, that they're hostile. In that case, it really doesn't matter what we say, does it? They're already intending to invade us.'

'Maybe they just broke down?' Maggie suggested. 'The junk we have here tends to suggest that happens a fair amount of times.'

Anne shook her head. 'Unlikely in this case. There are *three* landing sites. It's highly improbable that they all broke down at the same time. And if they had, surely they'd have landed close together, rather than at extreme ends of the earth?'

'Good point. So, are we going ahead or not?'

Anne looked at Swift, and saw her own impatient enthusiasm mirrored in his eyes. 'Oh, we're going ahead, right?'

'Absolutely,' he agreed. He waved his hand at the craft. 'Ladies first.'

'I'll stay outside,' Tanya offered. 'There's only room for two – cosily.' She grinned at Bill. 'There's more room out here.'

Is she doing this just to irritate me? Anne wondered. Or was it that she simply couldn't help herself? Well, she trusted her husband to behave himself, and she'd simply put it out of her mind.

Right…

She clambered back into the cabin, catching Maggie's scowl as she did so. Obviously, Maggie was none too happy with this turn of events, but it had been her idea to call in her own scientists, and she could hardly forbid Swift to allow Anne along.

'Careful with these seats,' Anne advised the other scientist as he folded his own lanky form to settle in. 'They have strange and uncomfortable contours.'

'That's one way to put it,' he muttered, grimacing. 'You know, I've never actually tried sitting here before. Maybe the chairs are uncomfortable to keep the pilots focused on their work and getting out of here again as soon as possible.'

She grinned at the thought – but, then, you couldn't always be sure that it really *was* a joke when it came to alien mentality. 'The radio is on my side,' she said, gesturing.

He leaned over to examine it again. 'It *is* live. This is definitely something new.' He frowned. 'Do you think you can turn it on?'

'It shouldn't be too difficult. The designers wouldn't want to have the pilots be too distracted by operating it. I'm guessing it would be as simple as possible.'

'Makes sense,' Swift agreed. 'So, where's the *on* switch?'

Taking another guess, Anne simply tapped the device. It started to glow softly, a light lilac colour. 'I think I found it.'

He grinned. 'Say something,' he suggested.

'What, historic first words?' She laughed, and then bent toward the panel. 'Uh – hello – is there anybody there?' There was no response. 'Maybe it's not tuned in?'

'Maybe nobody's listening right now?'

'Maybe they do not understand English?' Tanya called from outside the craft. 'Try Russian instead.'

Any of those were possibilities, of course; they were dealing with the alien, the unknown. It could be any of a hundred reasons… There was that knob on the side of the panel, as well. Perhaps this was like an old-fashioned radio, and you needed to switch it one way to transmit and another to receive? Or maybe it was a tuner of some kind, and it needed to be adjusted? She tried it gently, but it seemed reluctant to move.

'Give it a good twist?' Swift suggested.

'No,' she said, thoughtfully. 'This ship crashed, right? Well, if it had been *me* in this cabin, I'd have been on the radio, calling for help until the bitter end. So, I'd guess the device is set to whatever the aliens use for an emergency call.'

Swift inclined his head slightly. 'Exquisite thinking, Anne. So, why aren't they answering?'

'Maybe they weren't expecting an emergency call?' Bill suggested from outside.

It was as good a possibility as any. Maybe they were being routed to the 999 operator, so to speak…

There was an electronic squeal from the radio, and then a voice – clearly on the verge of losing its temper – snapped, '*Now* what do you want?'

Anne and Swift exchanged startled looks.

'Uh – hello,' Anne said, a little lamely.

There was an audible sigh. 'Oh, very well, if you *insist* on the formalities… Hello. How are you? How are your offspring? What is the weather like where you are? *Now* can we get to the point of this call? I thought we'd cleared everything up ten of your minutes ago. You're damned impatient, if you ask me.'

Anne stared at her companion again. He seemed as confused as she was with all of this.

'I'm sorry,' she said, 'but I don't understand what you're saying.'

Another heavy sigh. 'Oh, very well. I'm sorry about the incident with that indigenous creature that was slaughtered. I do hope it wasn't a beloved pet. The technician involved has been reprimanded, and it won't happen again.'

Well, this was finally something she could understand. 'You're talking about that incident with the whale off the Isle of Man?'

'Well, I don't know the technical names for any of these things, but I suppose so. Are you happy now? Will you let me get back to work, or do you have another ridiculous demand to make?'

'He's clearly not a diplomat,' Swift murmured softly.

Anne had to restrain an urge to giggle, because he was quite right.

'Who do you think you're talking to?' she asked, cautiously.

'Oh, you're going to be like *that* about it,' the voice growled. 'Yes, I *know* you're King of Earth, but don't expect me to grovel like those blasted bureaucrats. You're just lording it over this far-flung ball of dung in a very big universe, and it doesn't amount to much in my estimation.'

'King of Earth?'

'If you expect me to say *yes, your majesty* or *no, your majesty,* you've got another think coming. I'll fulfil my commitment, but it doesn't include bowing and scraping to any second-rate monarch of a flea-pit planet.'

'Somebody got out of bed on the wrong side this morning,' Bill commented from the outside.

'If their beds are anything like their chairs, I am not surprised he is in a surly mood,' Tanya said.

Anne waved them both to be quiet. Things were going poorly enough without them setting Mr Grumpy off again.

'Ah,' she said, slowly, 'we don't know anything about this

King of Earth you've mentioned.'

There was a brief pause, and then a sound like a walrus gargling with a tub of tuna. 'Oh, crap – you're the *rebels*? How did you get hold of a communicator?'

Swift leaned forward. 'Again, we don't know what you're talking about. Rebels? We are representatives of the United States Government.'

'The *what*?'

'We appear to be suffering from a good deal of confusion,' Anne said. 'Can we meet face-to-face and talk about this?'

'Your king has forbidden us to meet with rebels.'

'Well, it doesn't sound to me like you enjoy taking orders from this so-called king.'

There was a pause, and then a sound like a million insects screaming. 'You are right,' the voice admitted, wheezing. 'At least you have the virtue of being entertaining. Very well, I will agree to meet with you. Where are you located?'

'Well, if you're in the spaceship behind the force shield in the desert,' Swift said. 'Then about twenty minutes away.'

'Well, that's convenient, at any rate.' There was a pause. 'I'll let three of you in. If you come unarmed, I'll even allow you to live.'

'Too kind,' Swift muttered. 'See you soon.'

The radio went dead, and Anne and he exchanged glances again.

'Well, *that* was bizarre,' she commented.

'We'd better get busy. I've a feeling that joker is a stickler for timing.' Swift heaved his lanky frame out of the seat and to the ship's hatchway. 'Colonel, you'd better lay on a jeep for us.'

'And who,' Maggie asked, 'is *us*?'

'Well, Anne and I, obviously. And I guess we'd better bring the Russkie along, so we're all represented.'

'I should be included, to represent the military.'

'He said no weapons,' Swift said. 'I suspect that also means no soldiers.'

'And what if this… being decides to kill you all?'

'I expect a state funeral. Look, if he does decide to simply wipe us out, your being there won't help. But if you're outside, maybe you can avenge our deaths? We'll take along a radio, and keep it on, so you can hear everything that's said. Will that make you happy?'

'No,' Maggie admitted. 'But you'd better not stand here jabbering about it. You've less than twenty minutes now.' She glared at Tanya. 'I don't like the idea of including you, but I guess Moscow will complain if I don't. And I've got enough strikes against me as it is.'

'Thank you,' Tanya said. 'I will speak favourably about you when I make my report.' Her lips twitched slightly. '*If* I survive this meeting, of course.'

'Get the hell out of my sight, all of you,' Maggie snapped.

Bill jogged along beside Anne as they headed for the waiting jeep. 'Take care of yourself,' he said. 'That's an order, and I out-rank you.' As she paused to climb into the vehicle, he kissed her briefly. 'Seriously.'

'I will,' she promised. 'Don't worry too much – you know I can talk myself out of almost anything.'

'It's the *almost* that bothers me.'

'Do I get a kiss goodbye also?' Tanya asked. She'd already taken the seat beside Swift, who was at the wheel.

'No,' Anne and Bill said, simultaneously.

Douglas became aware of other movement around him. He wrenched his eyes away from the mammoths.

One of them had discovered that there was food to be found, and was tearing at the snow-laden branches of a tree. Clearly, whatever force had brought them here hadn't worried them too much; they could still concentrate on the essentials of their lives. He saw to his amazement what appeared to be a film crew setting up. There were five men and two women working on getting a film camera onto a tripod, and setting up sound recording equipment.

'You're making a movie of this?' he asked Bugayev.

'A record, certainly,' the Russian admitted. 'It will not be for general theatrical release.' He sighed. 'A pity – it could well be an Oscar contender.' He saw Douglas' expression of surprise and smiled slightly. 'The Central Committee wishes to be kept updated on progress here; this seemed to me to be the best way of doing it.'

'It's not that. I'm just surprised that neither Lethbridge-

Stewart nor the Yanks thought of doing it as well.'

'Another example of Russian efficiency.'

'In this case, I'd have to agree with you. I'll suggest that Lethbridge-Stewart get in a BBC Outside Broadcast unit.'

'See if you can get Raquel Welch in her fur bikini in, too,' Reiss suggested. 'Hollywood never dreamed up special effects like these.'

'I think she'd freeze – even if we could get her in there.'

Reiss grinned widely. 'I'd offer to keep her warm…'

'You and the rest of the male population of the world.' Douglas laughed. He went back to staring at the mammoths. 'You know, those critters really are sort of cute. They'd probably be a huge hit on *Zoo Time.*' There was movement in the distance, its exact cause blurred by the falling snow. 'Looks like another one of them arriving.' The shape looked smaller and a bit different than the gigantic beasts. 'Maybe some other sort of animal…'

'These guys don't seem bothered by us,' Reiss observed, still studying the mammoths.

'I shouldn't think that there's much they'd be scared of,' Douglas said.

'Perhaps why humans could hunt them to extinction,' Bugayev observed. 'They thought themselves too powerful to be harmed – but the power of the proletariat overcame even them.' He gave the other men a bleak stare. 'That may be a parable for the forces of the West.'

Trust the Red to make everything a political statement, Douglas thought. He elected to ignore the bait, and glanced at the shape in the distance.

It had resolved itself slightly, and he realised that it was bipedal, and heavy-set.

'It looks as if your proletariat may be arriving,' he said, softly.

Reiss whistled. 'We gonna see a prehistoric hunt?'

'Could be.'

The shape was moving closer. It was still unclear, but obviously smaller than the mammoths and more human.

'That is not a person,' Bugayev stated. He glared over his shoulder at the film technicians. 'Hurry! Get that camera recording!' They started to work faster, knowing the potential consequences if they failed.

Bugayev was right, Douglas realised – the advancing figure wasn't human. It had the same basic body form as a person, but it was taller, and stockier. There was no sign of any weapons, but there seemed to be evidence of long hair.

And then it started to run towards the barrier, and it came into sharp focus. It was leonine in features, with a fanged mouth, and it had large, powerful hands that ended in sharp claws. There was no evidence of a tail, but there was a mass of mane-like hair over its head and down its back. It gave a loud roar, and the mammoths finally seemed to notice it. The large male trumpeted a response, and raised its trunk and long, curved tusks, shuffling in the snow to attempt to turn and face the attacker.

The lion-being ignored the larger mammoths, targeting instead the half-grown youngster. The smaller – but still massive – animal attempted to hide behind the males, but it moved ponderously slowly. One of the mammoths roared a response, and attempted to swing its trunk to slam against the attacker. The leonine being slipped lithely under the blow, which missed it by several inches, and then sprang for its target.

With a squeal of pain, the smaller mammoth bucked, but the creature latched onto it, digging deeply into the bulk of the terrified prey with its claws. The adult mammoths were panicking also now, and instead of attempting to defend the attacked youngster, they gave bleating cries and lumbered away from the battle scene.

The youngster was in serious trouble. Blood was spraying in all directions from its wounds, but they clearly weren't fatal. The leonine creature had dropped off, and was standing in the snow, watching carefully for its opening. It wasn't long in coming. The mammoth threw back its head, and trumpeted wildly. The attacker leaped in nimbly again, and this time its target was the exposed throat. The lion-thing roared, and then ripped out the victim's throat with its powerful fangs. Blood spilled everywhere, drenching the attacker, who merely laughed in that steaming shower of blood.

The mammoth attempted to move, but it was already dying. It stumbled to its knees, hesitated for a moment, and then collapsed. The lion-alien leaped atop its victim and roared out a very satisfied howl. The mammoth gave a final shudder, and that was it.

Now the leonine alien seemed to notice the startled observers. Douglas was briefly thankful for the impenetrable barrier between them and this killer. The alien grinned.

'Good hunt,' it declared. 'Like some?' Douglas saw that it was dressed in some sort of an abbreviated leather gear, and that there were tools hanging from a belt. The alien removed one and triggered it. It was some sort of a laser device, and a blade of light sprang from it. Using this, the alien hacked off the trunk of the dead mammoth. 'Good eating,' it stated. 'Enjoy.' It flung the trunk towards them.

It went through the barrier and sloshed down at their feet.

Douglas stared at it, unbelieving. *It passed through the barrier!* He reached out a hand, but the barrier was still in place. Did this mean the barrier was only one way? But the mammoths had halted when they reached it… But was that because there was no snow beyond the barrier, or because they couldn't cross?

While he'd been considering all of this, the lion-thing had severed several huge hunks of mammoth meat. Not at all bothered by the blood, it turned off its 'knife' and then slung the meat across its shoulders. 'Good eating,' it repeated. 'Much enjoy!' Then it started jogging off, back the way it had come.

Bugayev turned to the camera crew. 'Assure me you filmed that!' Terrified, they nodded frantically. 'Good. Process the film and send it to Moscow immediately.' They started to obey.

Reiss glanced at the steaming, severed trunk at their feet, and then at the remnants of the corpse, and then at the rapidly vanishing alien. 'Generous sort of a cuss, ain't he?'

Lethbridge-Stewart stared off where the alien had vanished, and then shook his head.

'If this is an invasion, it's being conducted by mental patients,' he finally decided.

'Yeah.' Izzy scratched his head. 'Trust you Brits to have such polite invaders. I'll bet ours are howling, screaming and firing off death-rays galore.'

'I'm not so certain that this is an invasion,' Lethbridge-

Stewart mused. 'You don't generally apologise to people you're attempting to conquer.'

'You English would.' Izzy put on a very bad fake English accent. 'Excuse me, old boy, would you mind awfully surrendering? This bally gun gets so hot when I fire it…'

'Very droll.' Lethbridge-Stewart shook his head again. 'I wish that some of this would just start making sense. I got the strong impression from that whatever-it-was that it doesn't mean to upset us.'

'Yeah, I got those vibes, too. You reckon this is some sort of an attack by space hippies? Love and peace, man, and all that?'

'I don't think that they actually mean us any harm. Of course, that doesn't mean that they *won't* cause a great deal of harm. Sometimes things done with the best of intentions cause the greatest hurts.' He made a sudden decision. 'I think we'd better see how our other two teams are doing. Maybe they're having breakthroughs that we aren't.'

'Plus,' Izzy said brightly, 'we're staying in a pub with an almost unlimited supply of scotch… I always think better with a snort inside of me.'

'Yes,' Lethbridge-Stewart said. 'I recall that pertinent fact about you.'

Back at the pub, the latest batch of RAF photos was waiting. They examined these first.

The area that the aliens had under construction had tripled in size. They were obviously being very industrious, but there was still no way to know just what was being built. Frustrated, he had Maddox connect him with Douglas in Siberia and then with Bishop in Nevada.

'Well, there's some hope,' he said, relaying their reports to Izzy. 'It appears that Dr Travers has managed to contact her batch of aliens and engineered a face-to-face meeting.'

'Smart fella, this doctor?'

'Smart lass,' Lethbridge-Stewart corrected him. 'One of the best. I'm sure we'll learn something at last.' He sighed. 'And now mammoths in Russia…'

'Al,' Izzy said slowly, 'there was an alien hunting those critters there. And a very different alien hunting whales here… You don't think that we're dealing with some kind of alien hunters, do ya? And that these force whatsits are some kind of hunting preserves?'

'You mean that these beings are coming here to hunt our wildlife?'

'Yeah. Kinda like a safari – taking trophies, ya know.'

He hadn't thought of that. 'I suppose it might be possible,' Lethbridge-Stewart admitted. 'Two of the three sites have had aliens killing animals… But there's nothing for them to hunt in Nevada, is there?'

'Not *now*,' Izzy agreed. 'But these guys have some sort of time technology, right? And there's an awful lot of dinosaur fossils out west…'

The thought definitely worried Lethbridge-Stewart. Dinosaurs brought into the modern age…? He shuddered at the thought. *That* would certainly cause a great deal of trouble.

'Let's hope that you're wrong,' he said.

'Oh yeah,' Izzy agreed. He stared at his empty glass. 'I definitely need another splash of scotch…'

The jeep roared across the almost flat desert.

Dr Swift was hunched over the wheel, looking grim and determined. Tanya, next to him, was holding onto a large, floppy hat and grinning wildly. She was clearly a fan of speed – or thinking of the impending possibilities. Either way, she was obviously enjoying herself. Anne, in the back, held on for grim life, and tried not to worry. She was not successful.

There wasn't actually much to see – scrubby grass, a few stunted bushes, lone trees few and far between. There wasn't even a road, just the sun-baked desert earth. The sun hung hot and high in the sky, creating a shimmering haze on the horizon; she was glad for her hat and sunglasses.

Tanya saw her studying the landscape and laughed. 'It's like Siberia, only without the snow,' she commented.

'Interesting you should say that,' Anne said thoughtfully. 'Maybe there *is* a link between our three sites, after all.'

'How do you mean?'

'Well, they're all completely different environments, aren't they? Hot, dry desert, cold, snowy waste, and ocean view. They've all clearly been selected in advance somehow… Have these aliens been to Earth before and done a survey? I mean, it's unlikely that they chose these three sites purely by accident, is it?'

'They've obviously been in contact with *someone* on Earth,' Swift pointed out. 'They call him the King of the Earth, after all – maybe he selected these locations?'

'Good point. What I can't figure out is *how* anyone could have contacted them…'

Tanya shrugged. 'Surely, the same way that we did – only first.'

'The radio in the spaceship?' Anne frowned. 'But we were the first to see that it was working. Nobody else saw it first.'

'Nobody else *said* they saw it first,' the Russian corrected her.

'It was inside the ship,' Swift said. 'You couldn't simply see that the radio was live if you walked past, could you? You had to be inside the craft. And, until today, nobody's been inside it for – well, a long time.'

Anne suddenly felt stupid. 'Nobody could have seen *that* radio,' she agreed. 'But Maggie said that there was another one, and that it had been removed from the ship and stuck on a shelf somewhere…'

'I wonder if it's still there?' Tanya mused.

'Right…' Swift shook his head. 'People do go in and out of that hanger…' He gestured to the jeep's radio. 'Give the colonel a buzz and ask her to have the shelves checked.'

Tanya complied. When Maggie responded, the Russian made the request. There was a short, sharp expletive from the other end and Maggie hung up. Tanya grinned. 'It seems that this thought had not occurred to her before.'

Swift looked grim. 'I'm willing to bet that the radio's been *misplaced.*'

'Like everything in Vegas, that's a sucker bet,' Anne said.

'Who has had access to the storage unit?' Tanya asked.

'Too many people,' Swift replied. 'While everything inside it is considered restricted material, security isn't strictly enforced, I'm afraid. A determined person could smuggle out something as small as that radio.'

'If it's missing, that will tell us that there's somebody leaking official secrets,' Anne said. 'If we can discover who that is, then maybe we can track down our so-called King.'

'It may not be easy,' Swift warned. 'As I said, there's a lot of potential suspects – including me. I've been in and out of that hanger a good deal.' He gave the two women an abject look. 'It's just so frustrating, having all of that incredible technology, and not being able to understand it.'

Anne thought about what the Fifth had in the Warehouse; Swift would go crazy if he saw some of the things they had in storage. But, of course, there was no guarantee that he'd be able to make anything of that, either. But, as a scientist, she could certainly empathise with his feelings of frustration.

Tanya stroked Swift's arm, gently. That certainly caught Swift's attention. Anne rolled her eyes – the Russian agent didn't seem to be able to turn off her Mata Hari attributes. They appeared to be almost instinctual in her.

'Are we there yet?' Anne asked, to divert attention.

'Very nearly,' Swift said, jerking his attention back to the non-existent road. 'You can see one of our observation posts up ahead.'

Indeed she could. It consisted of another of the ubiquitous jeeps and three soldiers, who jumped to attention when they saw the arrival of others. Rifles moved to cover them as they drove up and stopped.

'Papers,' a sergeant demanded. He was clearly simply following procedures, as the guards had been alerted to their arrival. But bureaucracy reigned everywhere, even in the desert... After a cursory glance at their three passes, the sergeant saluted and moved aside.

It wasn't as if they couldn't simply have driven around him if they had wanted... Oh, well, boys had to play, Anne supposed. And she knew that Alistair would have approved of their actions.

'How are we to get through?' Tanya asked, thoughtfully.

'I'm assuming the aliens know we've arrived,' Swift replied, 'and that they'll open some sort of a doorway for us.'

'And if they haven't and don't?' Anne asked.

'Splat,' Swift answered, smiling.

Not exactly encouraging... But what else could they do? They couldn't contact the aliens directly. She supposed that they could ask Maggie to contact them to be sure.

Anne expected to hit the barrier at any second, and braced herself for impact.

Nothing happened. The jeep moved ahead unhindered. She felt a sense of relief, and glanced behind them. One of the guards had pushed out with his hand, and had clearly met the barrier. Obviously, as agreed, only they themselves were being allowed inside.

To meet what…?

CHAPTER SEVEN
Star Wars

WHILE LETHBRIDGE-STEWART was busy studying the reports, Izzy took the opportunity to take his freshly filled glass of scotch for a walk up to his room.

He glanced back to ensure that he hadn't been followed, and then closed his door. After a moment's thought, he decided to lock it. He didn't want to have any visitors for the next few minutes.

He had stowed his gear when he'd arrived, and he checked the bags carefully to make certain they hadn't been tampered with. He felt faintly ridiculous with this cloak and dagger stuff, but his orders had been quite explicit: Lethbridge-Stewart was not to know anything about this.

That bothered him, because he did consider Al a friend. They might not have seen one another face-to-face for a dozen years or so, but that didn't matter. He liked the stiff-upper-lip Brit, and he felt more than a little guilty doing this. But his orders left him no choice.

The radio transmitter was disguised inside a can of shaving cream. The spy guys were really up on things, he reflected – the can actually could dispense the foam for his shave, but that was just from the top half. Inside the rest of the can was a very miniaturised radio. It was kind of cute, actually. But it was fully operational, and that's what mattered.

He switched it on, and waited for the tell-tale hum. He gripped the tiny microphone.

'Echo Two to IntOps. Echo Two to IntOps. Come in, IntOps.'

He glanced guiltily at the door, but all was quiet back there. In one way, he'd almost have been relieved to see Al standing there, moustache bristling. But, on the whole, he was glad his friend hadn't managed to somehow materialise.

It was bad enough having to betray his confidence as it was…

The landscape beyond the barrier was completely unchanged from the one they'd been driving through.

Whatever the aliens were doing here, it was still limited to a smallish area. Dr Swift drove the jeep through the scrub desert, heading in the direction surveillance photos pinpointed as the base of operations. Anne was silent, her eyes scanning for any signs that the aliens were doing something – anything. Tanya and Swift were also quietly looking around.

After about ten minutes of seeing nothing but desert, there was finally a glimmer of light in the distance, reflecting off some kind of surface. All three of them hunched forwards, as if that would somehow help them to discern details. It didn't, of course, but it was a subconscious reaction they couldn't avoid.

There was a stirring excitement in Anne's stomach as there was finally evidence of the aliens. She had no idea what was to happen, or quite what their reception would be, but she still felt a thrill each time she encountered the unknown.

As they drew closer, she could begin to make out details that solidified as they kept driving. This was the alien construction, what they had come to Earth for, it seemed. It was centred about what was clearly the spaceship these beings had used.

It was unlike any she had previously seen, especially unlike the tear-drop shaped craft back at Groom Lake. This one was massive and vaguely zeppelin-like in shape. Well, a zeppelin that had been sat on by some immensely overweight creature, so that it was wider at the bottom than the top. Aerials and other protuberances broke up the smooth shape of the craft, and there were huge pods at what presumably was the rear of the craft. There were several openings in the otherwise smooth surface, and there were smaller craft zipping in and out and back and forth to the construction areas.

These spread out from the central craft like the arms of a starfish. It was clearly a work in progress, with random-looking walls and cubes, vast cables and deep trenches all being worked on by small figures. At the end of each arm, construction was in progress on what appeared to be vast domes.

'It looks a little like *Gagarin Base*,' Swift commented, referring to the international lunar research base.

'Possibly for the same reason,' Anne guessed.

'I don't like the look of this,' Tanya confessed. Her voice was strained.

'Whyever not?' Swift asked, surprised. 'It's very impressive, and it's going up so fast.'

'That's exactly why not. It *is* impressive, and it's going up fast. Look at the size of it. How many... beings is it being designed to hold?'

She had a good point, Anne realised. There would be room in there for an awful lot of aliens – a good site for a colony. She was immediately reminded of the first white colonies in this country...

'They look like they're planning to settle down,' she observed.

'Exactly,' Tanya said. 'And do we have the power to tell them that they can't? And if we try – will they listen?'

It was a very unsettling thought. She might look and act like a man-hungry vamp, Anne realised, but there was a lot more depth to her than that. Well, obviously, or her masters would never have assigned her there in the first place. Anne made a mental note not to underestimate her in the future.

The closer they got, the more detail became apparent. Tanya was right – this was going to be an immense complex when it was finished. And all of this had been constructed in not much more than a single day. It was highly impressive – and extremely worrying.

'They can't have carried all of this material in one ship,' Anne said slowly. 'It's simply not large enough.'

'They must be sourcing the materials locally,' Swift suggested. 'These deserts are quite metal-rich, if you have the power and will to extract it. Which would mean that they have to have furnaces and casting equipment to shape the raw materials...'

'It looks as though they aim to settle in,' Tanya finished

for him. 'And if the same kind of construction is going on in Siberia and in England, I would say that these beings have every intention of colonising our world – if we let them.'

'If they have technology on this level,' Anne said, 'I don't honestly think we could stop them.'

'Then this may be the beginning of the end of the human race. When two cultures meet, the more advanced one inevitably wipes out or absorbs the lesser.'

'Then we had better be very careful what we say and do.'

They were fast approaching the closest of the half-constructed buildings. Anne could make out more detail now. As walls were being raised, wiring and ducting was being added by robotic welding machines that scurried across surfaces like spiders. The aliens doing the work were of varying species, clearly. They seemed to come in many varieties – tall, short, angular, stocky, blue, red, avian, reptilian… There were hundreds of them, all working feverishly, none of whom seemed to pay the human arrivals any attention.

'Where do we go from here?' Swift asked, baffled.

'The spaceship, I'd guess,' Anne said. 'These guys are the construction workers – they don't have the authority or inclination to talk with the locals. The ones we want are those in charge, and they aren't going to hang around the worksite.'

'The bourgeois do not fraternise with the proletariat,' Tanya observed.

'Something like that.' Anne stared about them as they drove on.

This was all amazingly impressive – and deeply disturbing at the same time. It looked as if these aliens were planning on staying – was there any way to persuade them to leave? Or – if it came to a worst-case scenario – force them to leave? With technology like this at the intruders' disposal, Anne was starting to very much doubt it. Was this Plymouth Rock, and was that ship an alien Mayflower? Even the boisterous Tanya seemed subdued and lost in her own thoughts – probably very much like Anne's own.

Swift drove up to the immense spaceship. It was incredibly impressive, a massive vessel. There were no obvious guns or other weapons, but the aliens probably didn't feel any need to be blatant about their power – after all, the humans couldn't even get through the barrier unless the aliens unlocked it for them.

The spacecraft was abuzz with activity. There was a large being in some kind of a flying chair – or bed – who was barking orders and answering queries in some guttural alien tongue Anne couldn't understand. The being was about ten feet tall (or long), and looked like a greyish octopus or squid, with large eyes, a small mouth and a booming voice. Its tentacles were in constant motion – gesturing, signing, or simply rippling. One huge eye rotated to glance at them (which was rather unsettling, as the other was fixed on a small group of aliens). 'I'll be with you in a moment,' the creature said in perfect English, and then went back to yelling at cowering underlings. One of these timidly replied, and a single tentacle wrapped itself around the being, hauled him off the ground, shook him and then thumped him back down. The victim wavered dizzily for a moment, and then they all fled.

'I really, really hate all of this bloody paperwork,' the octopoid grumbled. 'Damned bureaucrats and all of their benighted forms!' Both eyes swivelled to focus on the waiting humans. 'Look at me! I'm a sea-based being, but do they assign me to the watery section of this damned planet? No! That would be too simple and logical, wouldn't it? They prefer to take me out of the water and slap me down in a bloody desert! I ask you, where's the sense in that, eh?'

Anne stared at the alien. Obviously, this was the same being that she had talked to earlier – his foul mood proved that. Their chances of achieving anything here didn't seem very good.

'I guess we came at a bad time, then?'

'Bad time? When is there ever a bloody *good* time?' The creature's tentacles curled and whipped about in annoyance. 'I'm a being of action, so it makes no damned sense to throw me here, where I'm mired in inefficiency and interruptions. Speaking of which, what the hell do you humans want now? If it's another complaint, file a form and I'll defecate on it as usual.'

'Ah. We want to know what it is you're doing here,' Swift said, in a rather apologetic voice.

'What am I doing here?' the creature yelled. 'I'm having a goddam heart attack, that's what I'm doing here! You never saw such inefficiency in your lives!'

That was clearly a touchy subject.

'No, he means – what *is* all of this?' Anne waved her hand to encompass the construction site.

The two huge eyes stared coldly at her. 'It's a bloody constructions site; what did you think it was? Stop wasting my valuable time with stupid questions.'

Anne sighed inwardly. This was not going to be easy. 'Can I ask your name?'

'Want to report me, is that it? Well, go ahead, and see if I damned well care! There's nothing I'd like more than to be reassigned out of this place. It's Kwith – with a long...' And here he made a sort of raspberry noise.

'Well, Mr Kwith—' Swift began.

'*Mister* Kwith?' the octopoid yelled. 'That's Captain bloody Kwith to you, and don't you forget it. I didn't study and work all of those decades simply so you could insult me.'

'No offense was meant,' Anne said, hastily. 'We didn't know. My name is Anne Bishop, and these are—'

'I don't give a damn what you humans call yourselves,' Kwith snapped. 'Are we done now?' A couple of tentacles waved. 'As you can see, I've got a lot of damned work to keep me busy, and I can't lay here and exchange pleasantries with the natives all day. And, yes, offense *was* taken.'

This was not going at all well.

'We are simply trying to find out what it is that you're doing here,' Anne said, as calmly as she could. 'Why are you doing all of this?'

'Why? Because I've been *ordered* to do it, of course.' Kwith shivered all over. 'Do you think I'd come here for my own pleasure?'

'But what is the *purpose* of all of this? Why have you aliens come to the earth in the first place?'

Kwith's eyes focused on her again. 'Oh, I get it. It's more damned bureaucracy, isn't it? It's as bad here on this ball of heat, filth and sand as it is back in the Galactic Centre. You've not been filled in on the details, and they've tossed you in at the deep end, just like me, eh?'

Tanya piped up. She'd been very quiet for a while, probably at a bit of a loss. She clearly used her body and looks to get what she required, and this being was totally indifferent to her charms. 'That is *exactly* it,' she said, firmly. 'They have shafted us, as they have you, and left us to flounder, too. How can we be expected to do our jobs properly if we are not fully updated?'

Amazingly, this seemed to calm Kwith down. His tentacles stopped twitching about, and his bellowing dropped several decibels. 'Some things are the same the universe over,' he moaned. 'Bloody inefficiency! Nobody does their jobs properly – except for me. It's a damned shame the way they treat us, eh?'

'Abso-bloody-lutely,' Anne agreed, following Tanya's inspired lead. 'If only you would help us out of this quagmire we're in, it would be *so* helpful.'

Kwith nibbled at the end of one of his tentacles. 'It sounds like you really do need help.' He heaved and gave a great sigh. 'I wouldn't want anyone to suffer the way I've suffered. What can I do to help?'

'You could tell us why you've come to Earth in the first place and why you're building this... this...' Anne groped for words.

'Impressive edifice,' Swift suggested.

Kwith quivered a little, and Anne was afraid that they had upset him again. But it seemed that he was just trying to get more comfortable in his floating chair/bed.

'You may not be able to grasp this,' he said, 'but out there in the galaxies, there are many, many aggressive species. A lot of them take out their aggression on backward planets, attacking and invading them. It's bloody stupid, of course, but it happens.'

'We have a certain... familiarity with that kind of situation,' Anne commented.

'Really?' Kwith waved a careless tentacle. 'Well, all of this fighting and invading is horribly messy – not to mention distressing.'

'Especially if you're on the receiving end of such an invasion, I should imagine,' Swift muttered.

'Precisely. Well, it invariably ends with lots of death and

destruction, and the inevitable seizing of planetary homes by the victors. And it also results in refugees from the invaded planets – lots of refugees. Well, the galactic community sympathises with them, and wants to help them – as much as their damned bureaucracies allow – and it needs places to settle these tragic victims, where they can attempt to get their lives back in order, and stay away from constant warfare.'

'Understandable, and very commendable,' Tanya said, approvingly.

Anne could see where this was going. 'Hang on,' she said. 'Are you telling me that you're resettling them *here*? On the earth?'

'Of course. Why the hell else would I endure this slagheap of a planet? We're Engineers, and it's our job to build the camps they'll be assigned to.'

'Well, you can't do it!' Anne exclaimed.

'Why the hell not?' Kwith was back to bellowing. 'Don't tell me that there are *more* damned forms to fill out, and ecological surveys or whatever to endure? I've got a blasted deadline for this job, you know!'

'No, no, that's not what I mean.'

'Good, because if there are any more problems, I'm going to regurgitate my food over this entire benighted desert – so I'm warning you to stay clear. You probably wouldn't enjoy being vomited upon.' Kwith blinked. 'Then again, aliens are crazy, so maybe you would.'

'Let's not test that,' Tanya suggested, hastily.

'What I mean,' Anne said, 'is that you shouldn't be building your refugee centres here on Earth at all.'

'Of course I should!' Kwith growled. 'Those are my orders, and – no matter how bloody stupid they are – I always finish my assignments, despite the lack of skills, brains and co-operation of my damned staff!'

'You have no right to do this,' Anne protested. 'This is *our* planet, and you shouldn't even be here. You're acting like one of those invaders yourself.'

'What are you talking about? We have all the correct permits, and your king has signed off on all of the required papers. You've obviously simply been bypassed by the chain of command. Don't stand here complaining to me – go away and sort this out and let me get on with my increasingly irritating job!'

'What king?' Swift asked, scowling. 'We don't *have* a king.'

Kwith's tentacles twitched wildly. 'Oh, stars and novas,' he muttered – in a soft voice for once. 'Don't tell me you people are the *rebels*...'

'We can't,' Anne said firmly. 'Because we don't have a clue what you're talking about. Earth doesn't have a king – we never have had, and probably never will. And we can hardly be rebels if there isn't anyone to rebel against, can we?'

'Of course you have a king,' Kwith said. 'We negotiated a treaty with him, and he granted us the lands for our refugees. It's all signed, sealed and filed.'

'It sounds to me as if you've been conned,' Swift said.

'Conned?' Kwith was back in anger mode again. 'It was all conducted legally! We negotiated with him, and gave fair trade. We do not cheat, and we are not cheated.'

'Hang on,' Anne said. '*How* did you negotiate with him? How did you even contact him in the first place?'

'The same way you contacted us – by radio,' Kwith said. 'We Engineers had a scout ship in the area, looking for likely places to build the refuges, and your king contacted them. A treaty was negotiated and signed, and then we were sent to build. I don't want to hear any more of your complaints – this is all above-board and proper.'

'Just a moment,' Anne said. She turned to Swift. 'It *has* to be that other radio, the one Maggie is checking on.'

'I am willing to wager that she is still looking,' Tanya said. 'And that she is unable to find it.'

'It's the logical explanation. Someone stole it, and is posing as Earth's king, and has made a deal of some sort with these aliens.'

Kwith made a rather disgusting noise that Anne took to be his equivalent of clearing his throat; thankfully, it wasn't accompanied by regurgitating semi-digested fish. 'That sounds like some sort of internal problem, and nothing to do with me,' he stated. 'Not my fault, not my problem. Deal with it yourself.'

'It would help if we knew who this so-called king might be,' Anne said.

'Probably,' Kwith agreed.

There was a significant pause.

'Are you going to tell us?'

'No,' Kwith said. 'And that for two reasons.' He checked them off on a couple of twitching tentacles. 'First – as I said, not my problem. Second – I don't have a clue who he is. And if you want to know *why* I don't know, I refer you back to number one.'

'Great.' Anne sighed.

'I've never spoken to him myself,' Kwith offered. 'A couple of his flunkies, sure. But who cares about flunkies, right?'

'You're saying it is our problem and we should fix it?' Tanya asked.

'For an upright ape with too little hair, you're quite perceptive.'

'But *how* do we fix it?' Anne mused.

Tanya grinned. 'Well, *this* hairless ape would suggest we use the same method we used to contact Kwith – the radio.'

'You mean just call up the king and ask for an audience?'

Tanya shook her head. 'It might be better if we didn't make an appointment, and alert him to the fact we know about him.' She gave Swift a warm smile. 'I was thinking that it should be possible to tune into his radio's carrier wave and locate his palace that way.' She shrugged. 'I am not a scientist myself, but you two are…'

'It should be possible,' Swift agreed. Anne could see his mind was racing. She had to admit that Tanya could be pretty effective at times. 'I'll just need to be back in my laboratory…'

'Well, there you are,' Kwith said. 'Go and sort out your own stinking problems, and leave me to solve mine.'

'One moment,' Anne said sharply. 'We've just told you that this so-called king has absolutely no authority or right to conduct this deal with you. You can't just carry on as if nothing's happened.'

'Nothing *significant* has happened,' Kwith barked. 'Your dispute with this king or non-king of yours is an internal problem, and none of my concern. *My* concern is to follow my orders and to build this bloody refugee centre. Now, you go off and gibber with your friends and enemies, and let me get on with my miserable career.'

'You're just going to carry on, then?'

'Yes; I just told you.' Kwith's tentacles shivered. 'Until my orders change – well, more than they are normally botched up – I have to carry on with my job. I'm an Engineer, and I've a project to complete. So, sod off and let me get on with it. My headache's bad enough as it is.'

'Not bloody likely,' Anne snapped. 'How do we go about getting your orders changed?'

'Oh, sure, I'll just up and tell you how to make my life more miserable than it already is…'

'Come on, Kwith,' Tanya added. 'Just think – if you tell us and we can get your orders changed, then you can stop this horrible job and go somewhere more pleasant…'

Kwith's tentacles stopped writhing, and he actually appeared to perk up. 'You may have a point there…'

'Well?' Anne prompted.

'You could always file a restraining order,' the octopoid said slowly. 'I'd be forced to cease operations while it's ruled on…'

'Brilliant,' Anne said, happily. 'And how do we file a restraining order.'

'Oh, it's a simple matter of filling out a few forms.'

'That is wonderful,' Tanya said.

'And then handing them in.'

Anne was starting to feel a little less happy. 'And that's a problem?'

'Well, not really,' Kwith said. 'They just have to be delivered in person, that's all. In case the authorities have questions. And they *always* have questions, trust me.'

'Fine. So, where do we do that?'

'On Dulkis.'

'Where is Dulkis?' asked Tanya.

Kwith quivered again. 'It would be easier to tell you at night, when the stars are out. But…' He gestured with a tentacle. 'About there, and seventy-four light years straight ahead.'

Anne's heart fell. 'How are we supposed to get there?'

Kwith shrugged his tentacles. 'Not my pro—'

'Yes, you said!'

'What about that spaceship back at Groom Lake?' Tanya

suggested.

'Would you want to fly seventy-four light years in *those* seats?' Anne growled.

'I wouldn't try it in that piece of junk,' Kwith commented. 'You'd be lucky to make it to Jupiter before it fell apart.'

'Junk?' Swift asked, appalled.

'Why do you think we never asked for it back? Its warranty expired decades ago.'

'I guess we were lucky that even the radio was still working,' Swift muttered.

'Is there any *other* way of doing this?' Anne asked. 'Because if we go back to our *real* rulers with this information, it's not likely to go very well.'

Kwith shrugged again. 'Sorry if you lose your jobs over this, but better your loss than mine.'

'No, that's not the kind of *not very well* I was thinking of,' Anne said carefully. 'Don't you find the sun awfully bright?'

'I absolutely loathe it,' Kwith admitted. 'So what?'

'If we can't come up with a *peaceful* solution to this issue,' Anne informed him, 'then the next thing our bosses will try is a military solution.'

'Yes, well, good luck with that one,' Kwith said. 'You've seen that the barriers we've erected are pretty near impervious. Shoot as many guns off as you like.'

'Oh, I'm sure that would be of no use. And I certainly wouldn't suggest it. But an atomic bomb, on the other hand…'

'Would not get through, either,' Kwith said.

'Of course it would,' Anne snapped. 'Sunlight gets through – so *radiation* would get through, too.' She eyed him carefully. 'You don't look like a heavy dose of radiation would do you much good.'

Kwith went absolutely still. Then his tentacles all started to twitch at once. 'I can have the shields set so that no radiation can get through,' he growled.

'No infra-red? It would get awfully cold in here quite quickly. No light? You might have trouble building things. Just imagine how many more accidents and setbacks there would be. It would *really* screw up your schedule.' She grinned maliciously. 'But I don't have to do that… *If* you co-operate…'

'You would make a very good Russian,' Tanya murmured,

approvingly.

'Ah… What did you have in mind?' Kwith alien asked, cautiously. He seemed to have lost a bit of his bluster.

'We need a way to get to Dulkis, obviously.'

'And back again,' Tanya added, quickly.

'Right,' Anne agreed. 'So – can you help us out here?'

Kwith cleared his throat again, in an even more disgusting manner. 'As it so happens,' he admitted, 'I'm due to have my Project Inspection tomorrow. Some interfering busy-body will be arriving from Dulkis to make sure I'm using the correct percentage of workers from each allied planet, and only approved materials. I'm sure you know the kind of thing that people who don't actually have to do the work dream up to piss off those who do have to do it. Once he's interfered to his satisfaction and disrupted as much work as he can, he'll be heading back to Dulkis. I can't see any reason why he shouldn't take you back with him to present your appeal. Just promise me that you'll annoy him as much as you have me, and I'll be happy.'

'And getting back?' Tanya persisted.

'Oh, irritate the politicians back on Dulkis enough, and they'll be glad to get rid of you again. I know *I* shall be.'

'So,' Anne summarised, 'we return here tomorrow, and you'll see we get aboard that ship?'

'Believe me, it will be a pleasure not to have to share the same planet with you. And the thought of all the trouble you'll cause up there…' Kwith wheezed out his pleasure. 'Incidentally, if you're looking for a new job, I could use you. You're a very good negotiator, and I could always use someone like that.'

Anne laughed. 'Thanks. But I like the one I have.'

'Stuck on this disgusting little slimeball of a planet?' His tentacles quivered. 'I can offer you so much more.'

'All the red tape I can swallow, eh?' She shook her head. 'I'm happy here. Besides, I have a husband.'

'Just the one? I can fix you up with twenty.'

Anne laughed again. 'Thanks, but I have modest tastes; I'll stick with just the one.'

'Provincials,' Kwith muttered. 'Well, if you should change your mind…'

Swift tapped Anne on the shoulder. 'Perhaps we had better head back now,' he suggested. 'I'm sure our superiors would like to hear what we've discovered, and I'd like to get started on tracking down our self-proclaimed king. Plus, there's bound to be a great deal of discussion over who goes along on this trip tomorrow... to another planet...' There was a far-off, dreamy look in his eyes that Anne was certain was probably matched in her own.

Another planet... Her colleagues in the British Rocket Group would be incredibly jealous of her. Then reality struck.

What if she wasn't one of those picked to negotiate? To be so close to a journey to the stars, only to lose out to some political hack... Unthinkable!

'Yes, you're quite right,' she agreed. She turned back to Kwith. 'You *will* let us back in tomorrow?'

'Of course,' he promised. 'The thought of getting a little revenge on all of those paper-pushers by setting you onto them is far too amusing for me to muck up.'

As they prepared to leave, a sudden thought struck Anne. 'Just a minute. There's just one last thing...'

Kwith groaned. 'There's *always* just one last thing.'

'Let's say we can't talk these politicians of yours into stopping this project...'

'Believe me, they're not *my* politicians.'

'And you get to finish it...'

'That's starting to look like a distant, far-off dream...'

'Just how many refugees are we talking about here?'

Kwith stared at her with his huge eyes. 'How many?'

'Yes,' she said, firmly. 'How many?'

'Well, just a few...' Kwith was clearly stalling.

'*How* few?'

'A couple of million.'

Anne stared at him in shock. 'A couple of *million?*'

'Well, six or seven million, tops,' he assured her.

Her companions couldn't seem to think of anything to say. All Anne could do was to repeat, '*Millions...*'

Kwith gave another of his shivery shrugs. 'Well, I did say that there were a lot of wars in space. That means a lot of refugees.'

'Yes,' she said, weakly. 'But...' She shook her head and

tried to get a grip on her overwhelmed emotions. 'We'd better get back,' she said, as firmly as she could. 'I have a feeling that this is going to be one long, headache-inducing nightmare discussion…'

'Welcome to my world,' Kwith said, glumly.

CHAPTER EIGHT
Night Creatures

MAGGIE MET them back at Groom Lake and led them into her office, refusing to allow them to speak.

'They gossip here worse than in a hair salon,' she complained. 'Let's not give 'em fuel.'

Bill was waiting in her office, and Anne gave her husband a grateful hug.

'How did it go?' he asked her.

'Let's have the quick and dirty report first,' Maggie said. 'We'll save the formal report for afters.'

Dr Swift glanced around. 'I was expecting to see a five-star general at the very least.'

'There's one sitting in the base office right now. I get to go brief him after this. But I've been placed in charge of this whole affair.'

Anne was surprised. 'I guess they have a great deal of confidence in you.'

'Guess again.' Maggie scowled. 'What it means is that they don't think there's any good outcome from this, and not one general will place his career on the line to try and resolve it. *My* career, on the other hand, they're real willing to risk. So, what are my chances of coming out of this intact?'

'Better than you might think,' Anne said. 'But not as good as you'd wish.'

She and Swift gave a precis of their alien encounter of the first kind. Tanya said nothing, and spent most of the time batting her eyes at Bill. When Anne wound up the narrative, Maggie sighed.

'Yeah. Well, I had a spot inventory done in the artefacts store. Turns out that there's lots of little crap missing – alien nuts and bolts and what have you. Probably taken by souvenir hunters, and none of it really worrying. But that second radio *has* gone missing, and we don't know when it was last seen. So, your guess about this self-styled king looks to be about right.' She glared at Swift. 'Tell me you can track it.'

'Well, not at this very moment,' he admitted. 'But I think that with Andy's help I should be able to build a detector. I'd hazard a guess that it's somewhere in the US still, and in the hands of a major league souvenir hunter. There's a handful of film stars, pop stars and other millionaires who'd go into ecstasy just knowing they had some alien tech in their grubby little paws. I figure somebody on this base wanted to make a small fortune for himself and sold it.'

'Makes sense. Go build me a doohickey then.' Maggie waved her hand in dismissal, and Swift went cheerfully off. Once the door was closed behind him, Maggie gestured for the others to take seats. 'I wanted him outta here because I figured he'd throw a tantrum over this next part.'

'Which is…?' Anne prompted.

'This proposed visit to – what the hell was the name of that planet again?'

'Dulkis.'

'Yeah, sounds like the ending of most of my dates.'

'Including with Alistair?'

'I don't kiss and tell. Back to the point. I figure you're aiming to go on this ride?'

'The chance to visit an alien planet?' Anne said. 'After the last few years dealing with aliens… I most definitely am not passing up the opportunity.'

'It could be kinda risky,' Maggie pointed out.

Nothing could dampen Anne's spirits. 'It's an *alien planet*,' she stressed. 'As a scientist, how could I possibly not go?'

'Uh, because they're *aliens*, and they don't think like we do. Who knows what they might do to you? There's no guarantee you won't end up on the wrong side of a banquet. Don't you limeys get *The Twilight Zone?*'

'I don't think there's much chance of that. Kwith – for all of his bombast and bluster – seemed a likeable sort of chap, just weighed down by his workload.'

'Yeah, well, I can sympathise with that. But he's just one

alien, and he'll be here and not there with you, so what he means don't necessarily apply to what the rest of those bug-eyed monsters might feel.'

'Anne is right, though,' Tanya said, speaking for pretty much the first time. 'I, too, shall go along. The technology these beings possess is far beyond our capabilities. I do not believe that we can defeat it here. And we *must* defeat it. These beings are not invaders – at least, not *intentional* invaders – but what they are proposing is completely unacceptable. Millions of alien refugees would disrupt our world drastically. They cannot be allowed to arrive here.'

'I agree,' Anne said. 'Much as I sympathise with these poor wretches, settling such a number of them here on Earth would be a massive disaster. Just look at the shape our world is in, with so many nations at each other's throats, with so many conflicts and so much prejudice. Then just imagine the effect of dumping millions of aliens in the midst of this.'

'It might actually unify the world,' Bill suggested. 'Of course, they'd be unified *against* the refugees...'

'Exactly,' Tanya agreed, giving him a warm – almost incandescent – smile. 'Just knowing that they *exist* might create mass panic.'

'You sound like every meeting I've ever had about the UFO problem,' Maggie growled. 'But my orders are to keep this under wraps – as much as possible. I assume Al has given you the same instructions?'

'That's the official policy,' Anne agreed.

Maggie gave her a thoughtful stare. 'You're taking this very much in your stride. Well, I'm gonna have to assign one of my men to go with you. Can't let you Brits and Russkies have all the fun.'

Anne frowned. 'I thought Dr Swift...'

'Yeah, I'm sure you did. And I'm sure *he* did, too – which is why I sent his butt outta this room. I'll break the bad news to him later, when he can scream at me in private.' Maggie scowled. 'I need him to track down this king of ours; it's time we kicked another royal backside outta this country. And if this royal guy has some alien tech, then I'm gonna need Swift to deal with it. So, I can't spare him. I guess it had better be Bradley in his place, then.' Abruptly, she grinned at the two women. 'Damn, but I wish I were going with you. What a gal's night out, eh? But there's no way the Pentagon would agree to that; they want me here, in charge, so they got someone to court-martial when it all goes balls-up. So, *don't* let it go balls up, okay?'

'I'll do my best,' Anne said, drily.

'I, too,' Tanya promised. 'For an imperialistic war-monger, I find you oddly likeable.'

'Don't ever tell my troops that,' Maggie grumbled. 'Now, get the hell outta here and go get some food and sleep. If those alien beds are anything like their chairs, you're not gonna get much rest while you're gone. Speaking of which, did they tell you how long this little jaunt of yours is gonna take?'

Anne blinked. 'Uh… I never thought to ask. The thought of going to another planet sort of blew all questions clear out of my mind.'

'That's a scientist for you.' Maggie glowered at Tanya. 'I don't guess you thought to ask, either?'

The Russian shrugged. 'It is my job to go along; it will take whatever time it takes. I am in no hurry.'

'Yeah, well, I am.' Maggie sighed. 'The sooner we can stop those Engineers of yours in their tracks, the better. So, no sight-seeing while you're gone, and get the hell back as fast as possible. Provided it's with the news that the aliens are all packing up and going home. Otherwise, you might as well stay there.'

'Maybe I'd better bring Bill along with me then,' Anne said, clutching his arm.

'Yes, please,' Tanya murmured. 'We Soviets are always in favour of sharing limited resources…'

'Sorry to disappoint both of you,' Bill said. 'But I have to stay with my feet planted firmly on the ground. The Brig would never approve of both of us going, love, and I have to liaise with the colonel here.' He glanced at the clock on the wall. 'And she's right – you two had better eat and sleep. You've a very big day ahead of you tomorrow.'

Anne and Bill went to the base canteen to get food. Tanya, naturally, tagged along with them.

Anne wished she could have time alone with her husband,

but she couldn't very well tell the other woman simply to get lost – satisfying as that might be. Who knew how long they would be together on this journey to another star? She didn't want them to start off on an antagonistic note.

Canteen food was pretty much the same the world over (though here it was heavy on the fried chicken) – vaguely unsatisfying but filling.

'Some last meal on Earth,' she said.

'Perhaps we should pack some sandwiches for the trip?' Tanya suggested. It didn't sound like she was joking. 'And I am getting quite addicted to these… potato chips.'

'Crisps,' Bill corrected her. 'Americans love to rename foodstuffs they steal from us.' He picked up a thin chip. 'French fries…' He grimaced.

'I wonder what they call *borscht*?' Tanya mused.

'It's bad enough having to eat this,' Anne said. 'Let's not dissect it as well, eh?' She pushed her plate away. 'Well, I'm going to try and get some sleep. Are you coming, Bill?'

'I'll have to be up early, though; the Brig's going to want an update as soon as he's awake, and they're five hours ahead of us in England, don't forget…' He glanced at Tanya. 'Sorry to eat and run, but…'

'Go and have fun. I'll find something to occupy myself.'

'I'll bet she will, too,' Bill murmured to Anne as they headed for the quarters that they had been assigned. 'Something… or someone.'

'I'm glad she's coming with me and not staying here,' Anne informed him. 'I wouldn't like to think of her alone with you…'

'Relax,' he replied. 'I've been trained to withstand all forms of torture.'

The room that she had been assigned was perfectly fine for Tanya.

It was sparse and utilitarian. She enjoyed her creature comforts as much as anyone, but she never expected or demanded them – except when she was on assignment. She never forgot her childhood in Leningrad after the Great Patriotic War, growing up in poverty, amid all of the wreckage left by the German invaders. After those privations, anything was a luxury to her, even the quarters of an American soldier.

Not as enjoyable as the grand hotel she'd been staying at for her assignment in Cuba, of course. Still, it was relatively private and comfortable.

She checked for microphones, of course; not that she really expected to find them, but you didn't neglect the training. She didn't find any; the Americans were so trusting... More fool them.

She checked her one suitcase, and realised that it had been opened – well, they weren't *that* trusting, clearly. It made her smile. She hoped that whoever had searched it had enjoyed seeing her lacy underthings and short skirts – and that they had distracted attention away from the other items in the case.

She removed her hairbrush, and clicked the hidden catch to reveal the small transmitter hidden within. It appeared to be untouched. She removed the other sections of the radio from their hiding places and assembled it swiftly.

Bugayev answered her signal very swiftly. The call was routed through HQ in Cuba, and the major had been awaiting the call. She brought him up to date as quickly and simply as she could.

'Tomorrow, I accompany the English scientist and an American back to the aliens and then on to their world,' she finished.

'Good. You must always be certain of doing what is best for Mother Russia – not merely what is best for Mother Earth.'

'I know my duty, Major,' she said, a trifle stiffly.

'Which is why I had you assigned to this mission. If you did not have my complete trust, you would not be there.' Then he added, thoughtfully, 'You would not be anywhere. I merely wished to remind you that there are greater purposes behind simply aiding the Americans to save the world. I should very much like to see something of value to the State out of this.'

It would not hurt your career... Naturally, she did not say this aloud. 'I understand, Major.'

'You feel, then, that these aliens are not a threat?'

'On the contrary,' she answered. 'They are not *consciously* a threat – the one we spoke with seemed to be almost sympathetic. But there is immeasurable danger in what they naively plan to do to our world. Introducing several million alien refugees would be disastrous – especially the ones in

Siberia.'

'Quite. They must, therefore, be stopped – in any way possible. You understand my meaning?'

'Of course, Major.'

'And at any cost – including your life. And those of your companions.'

'That is understood.' She had always known that her own life could be required at any time in the service of the State; and she had killed before, under orders. Mostly. She rather liked Anne Bishop, and it was amusing to provoke her by flirting with her husband – but she would have no hesitation in killing her, should that become necessary.

'There is no way on earth that the Americans and the British would allow you to lead in this mission to Dulkis,' Bugayev mused. 'But you will not be *on* Earth for much longer. It might be better for you to take command once you are spacebourne.'

'I do not feel I have the qualifications, Major. Dr Travers appears to have dealt with alien beings in the past, and has some experience with them.'

'Well, if you feel that it is best she remain in charge, perhaps you could make yourself... invaluable to her.'

'I shall endeavour to do so.'

She signed off and disassembled the radio and stowed it away.

Anne awoke, sleepily, as Bill shook her gently.

He was fully dressed. 'It's three in the morning, and the Brig will be eating breakfast now, so I'll have to go and report progress to him. I just wasn't sure I'll have a chance to say goodbye properly before you... go. So I thought I'd do it now.' He gave her a big hug, and kissed her. 'Take care of yourself out there, love, and come home safe.'

She hugged him tightly back. 'I will – I promise.'

'Good girl.' He ruffled her hair, and pushed her back down. 'Now, get your rest.'

She heard him cross the room to the door and leave. She pulled the thin blankets a bit tighter around herself, and settled back for a few more hours' rest.

Maybe it was because the base was in a desert, but the air

conditioning here seemed to operate only at full blast. Even in her thick English nightie she felt a bit cold. Still, she was starting to drift off again when she thought she heard the door open again.

'Bill?' she murmured.

Had he forgotten something? She started to sit up when a strong hand pushed her back down again, and a shadowy figure bent over her. She felt the pillow jerked out from under her head, and then her attacker pressed it down over her face, and pushed and pushed.

She couldn't breathe. She tried to cry out, and struggled, but her assailant was too strong. She made to grab at whoever it was, but couldn't get a purchase. All the time, she couldn't breathe. She was being slowly asphyxiated. She struck out, and hit something, but it wasn't her attacker. She could hear noises rushing in her ears, and she couldn't breathe... couldn't breathe... Lights flashed in the darkness, and she could feel her strength waning.

And then – nothingness.

CHAPTER NINE
Twenty Million Miles to Earth

TO HER intense surprise, Anne gasped her way back to consciousness.

She managed to open her eyes, and the first thing she saw was Tanya bending over her in a black negligee. The second thing she saw was the knife in the woman's hand, dripping blood. She gasped, and struggled to sit.

'Stay still a moment,' Tanya ordered. 'Are you all right?'

Anne struggled to breathe and stared at the knife. She couldn't manage a reply.

Tanya followed her gaze. 'Don't worry, it's not your blood – it's his…' She gestured at the floor. Anne leaned over slightly and saw a crumpled body, face-down in a pool of blood that was leaking from a knife wound in his back and into the carpet.

'That's not going to come out easily,' Anne muttered weakly. Then she realised she was suffering from shock, and sat abruptly up. 'What happened?'

Tanya scowled. 'I was having trouble sleeping, thinking about our mission, and I heard a crash from this room. I came to investigate, and saw Dr Bradley trying to smother you with a pillow. I didn't know how close he was to succeeding, so I simply threw my knife…'

'You wear a knife to bed?' Anne stared at her. 'Where the hell do you hide it?'

Tanya grinned. 'A girl has to have some secrets…' Then she looked at Anne with some concern. 'I only had time to recover my weapon when you awoke. I haven't had a chance to alert anyone yet. Will you be okay while I do?' Her eyes lingered a moment on the body.

It wasn't the first body she'd seen, and Anne was afraid it

wouldn't be the last. 'Yes. I just need a few minutes, and I'll be fine.'

Tanya nodded, and left the room. Anne breathed slowly, deeply, glad to be alive.

It had been a really close thing, and she'd been so sure that she was going to die. She was shaking a little, and strove to pull herself together.

'This is no time to lose your nerve,' she chided herself. She was suffering from the shakes, but she forced herself to fight them. Then she clambered out of bed on the far side, away from where the corpse lay. She stood there, uncertainly, until she was sure she wouldn't collapse, and then grabbed her nightgown and wrapped it around herself.

Then she collapsed into the wooden chair by the desk, exhausted.

It seemed only moments later when people started to pile into the room. A couple of armed soldiers were first, and they went over to the body, ignoring her totally. Tanya was back, and she came to comfort Anne. There was a medic, who started to take her vitals, and then Maggie, who started to yell orders in all directions. Anne couldn't quite take any of this in.

Thankfully, Bill arrived, looking ashen. He grabbed her and hugged her tightly.

'Are you okay?' he demanded. And then, to the medic, 'Is she okay?'

'If you'd let me finish examining her,' the man snapped, 'I might be able to tell you.' He returned to his ministrations, pushing at Bill. Anne refused to let him loose, though. Holding him was the best medicine she could think of.

'What the hell happened here?' Maggie demanded, coming over. Tanya repeated her account. 'Bradley? Why in hell's name would he attack Anne?'

'It would appear obvious to me,' Tanya replied. 'He was trying to prevent us going to Dulkis.'

'But *why*?'

'That's easy,' Bill said. '*He* is the one working for our mysterious king. He stole the missing radio, and has been helping this scheme to go ahead. His boss wouldn't want us to sort this mess out with the aliens, so he ordered Bradley to stop it.'

'And he tried to smother Anne,' Tanya added. 'He was probably hoping he could make it look like she'd simply died in her sleep. But I heard the struggle…' She pointed towards the bed, and Anne saw that the bedside lamp had smashed on the floor. She could recall that she'd struck out in her struggles and hit something, so that made sense.

'And you killed him before he could kill Anne.' Maggie sighed. 'It's a damned shame – if he had remained alive, we could have questioned him.'

Anne noticed that Maggie was fully dressed, even at this early hour. Was that a little odd, or had she aimed to talk to Alistair as well?

Tanya – now wearing a heavy robe over her negligee – shrugged, and then had to grab the front of the robe closed before she revealed too much. 'I had no time to think, I'm afraid.'

'Course not,' Maggie agreed. 'Anne's life was the priority.' She bent to look at Anne. 'How are you feeling, honey?'

'Terrible. But glad to be alive. I didn't think I would be.' She looked at the medic. 'What's your verdict?'

'Oh, somebody's interested in the opinion of the expert?' He glared at everyone. 'She'll recover. I'd suggest a sedative and lots of bed rest, but I'm sure nobody cares what I think.'

'I haven't the time for that,' Anne said. 'I have travel plans.' She giggled a bit at the thought, and realised her nerves were still very frayed. Abruptly, she felt exhausted. 'Though I might agree to a few hours' rest.'

'I'll getcha another room,' Maggie promised. 'This one's gonna need some cleaning.' She glanced again at the body. 'It's a damned shame he's dead, though. We could have had our questions answered.'

'He might still help us,' Bill said, slowly.

'Son, he ain't talking.'

'Well, not aloud, maybe. But he was presumably paid for his work for the merry monarch. His bank statements might tell you something.'

Maggie's eyes lit up. 'You got something there,' she agreed. 'And, right now, nothing much would give me more pleasure than rousting a bank manager outta his bed at this ungodly hour to do some checking for me…' She started out of the door, and then hesitated. 'Take your wife two doors down thataway;

the room's not in use yet, so you should be able to get some rest. But if you're not up to it, you ain't going flying.'

'I'll be up to it,' Anne promised. 'I'm not going to miss this for anything.'

She leaned on Bill as they moved. Tanya smiled slightly, and waved as they left. Anne stumbled a little as they headed for the new room.

'Did you speak to the Brig?' she asked Bill.

'Not yet. It can wait. I'm going to sit with you while you rest.'

'I don't think there's any need,' Anne said. 'Bradley's dead, so I should be safe. *If* he was my attacker…'

His eyes narrowed. 'What do you mean?'

'Shut the door,' she instructed. As he did, she sat heavily on the bed. He joined her and hugged her again.

'Now, what did you mean by that?'

Anne licked her lips. 'We only have Tanya's word that it was Bradley who attacked me. I didn't see who it was – just that it was somebody strong. And I'm not certain that I knocked that lamp over in my struggles. But I was a bit unfocused at the time and I might have done it…'

'Why would Tanya lie about it?'

'What if it was *her* who attacked me?'

Bill shook his head. 'I'm afraid you've lost me, love.'

'All I know is that I was attacked and blacked out. When I came to, there was Tanya, her bloody knife and her story of saving my life. But…' Anne struggled to get her thoughts into order. 'Bill, she's a *spy*. I'm sure she's had training in killing people, for all of those smiles of hers. She could have been my attacker, and then framed Bradley for it, and killed him so he couldn't contradict her tale.'

Bill considered her idea for a moment. 'Okay, I'll grant you that it *could* have happened like that. But… Well, how did she get Bradley into your room?'

Anne rolled her eyes. 'If you'd seen what she was wearing, love, you wouldn't have to ask *that* question. Any male would have followed her anywhere with what she was promising.'

'But why kill Bradley and not you?'

'Well, you answered that one; because she'd have a ready-made suspect for the theft of the radio. He'd be a great fall guy.

It's obvious that I couldn't have taken that radio, but he had the opportunity. So, she could set up Bradley as a scapegoat *and* make herself out to be a hero at the same time.'

'Even if that is what happened, we don't have an answer to *why* she would do all of that. Surely not just to make us trust her?'

'Why not?' Anne asked. 'She's Russian, so she knows that the Americans certainly don't trust her, and she probably thinks we don't, either.'

Bill smiled slightly. 'Well, we *don't*, do we?'

'No. We don't.' The stress was catching up with her. 'Look, Billy, I have to get a little rest. I want to be in shape for the flight later.'

He pushed her gently down. 'Sleep, my love,' he murmured. 'I'll be here, watching over you.'

That was extremely reassuring.

She was out in minutes.

She felt a lot better when she woke again a couple of hours later.

The memory of what had happened was still upsetting, but seeing Bill watching over her gave her a surge of comfort and love. He was one person she could always depend upon.

A very smart corporal caught up with them as they were having a quick breakfast in the mess hall, and gave them 'compliments' before informing them that Maggie would like to see them 'at your earliest convenience'.

'That's military slang for *get your arse over here right now,*' Bill translated for her.

Anne caught the corporal's grin as he hurried off. Anne took a final swig of rather insipid tea, and they followed along.

Maggie was in rare form when they arrived. Anne had noticed that her 'down-home' accent tended to get broader when she was under stress. She wasn't sure what the American's accent had been originally, but it varied now between mid-West, Texas and New York. She wondered how much of it was consciously done simply for effect.

'How you feeling, hon?'

'Better,' Anne assured her. 'I'm fine to go on.'

'Glad to hear it. I rousted Bradley's banker outta bed, and it's paid off – slightly. Turns out he had an account with a coupla hundred thousand in it; regular payments from some Swiss account.' She scowled. 'Seems as if the Swiss like aiding and abetting crooks to launder money, and our guy says there's no way to trace it further without their co-operation. Which we won't get. I've tried siccing DC onto 'em, but even they don't hold out much hope.'

'It certainly looks like he was the one who sold the radio, then,' Anne said.

'Was there any doubt? Anyhoo, that looks to be a dead end, so we're relying on Swift getting his act together. He's supposed to be on his way over here to bring me up to date on progress. He'd better have good news, 'cause I need some.'

'I'd better go and check in with Lethbridge-Stewart now,' Bill said. 'If I see your doctor, I'll tell him to hurry up.' He gave Anne a quick kiss on the cheek. 'Have a nice trip. Send me a postcard.'

'Well, the *wish you were here* will be sincere,' she assured him. He laughed and left.

Maggie gave her an almost friendly stare. 'Gal to gal here,' she said, softly. 'How do you *really* feel?'

'Gal to gal,' Anne answered, 'I'm raring to go. If somebody wants me stopped badly enough to try and kill me, then they're clearly afraid I can do something dramatic. I just hope their fears are justified.'

'Attagal,' Maggie said, approvingly. 'Damn, I *really* wish I could go along with you. We'd show those aliens and this damned so-called king a thing or two, eh?'

'On which subject, have you decided on a replacement for Bradley yet?'

'I've one or two possibilities in mind. I guess I'd better settle on a victim soon, eh?' There was a rap on the door, and she yelled for the rapper to come in.

It was Swift. He looked dishevelled, and there was five o'clock shadow on his face that he kept scratching. Clearly, he had been working all night. 'Morning, Colonel,' he said, yawning. 'It *is* morning, right?'

'Tell me you got good news,' Maggie growled.

'I got good news,' he said, and then grinned. 'Actually, I *do* have good news. I managed to cobble together a detector for you.'

'So? What does it tell you?'

'Nothing.' As she was about to explode, he held up a hand. 'And it won't tell us anything until the other radio is switched on. *Then* it will track the signal.'

'Oh.' She settled back. 'So, we gotta wait?'

'Yes.' He shrugged. 'I wouldn't imagine it will be for long, though. Once we show up to complain to this alien inspector about him, somebody's bound to start sending messages in his direction.'

That prospect made Maggie smile. 'Glad to hear it.' She eyed him distastefully. 'You'd better go grab some sleep so you'll be in shape to start tracking.'

'The hell I will,' he growled. 'I'll sleep on the trip.'

'What trip?'

'The one to Dulkis.'

'That? Ah, well, I have some bad news for you there. You're too valuable to me here to spare you.'

Swift leaned forward, fists on her desk. 'You're not damned well keeping me out of this, Maggie! An alien planet...' He shook his head firmly. 'You don't need me now; any idiot can use that machine of mine.'

'Even me?'

He hesitated. 'Well, I wouldn't go *that* far,' he admitted. 'But any of the techs in my lab. It's very simple. Besides, you don't have any other candidate for the job. I heard that Bradley got himself killed last night.'

'Gossip travels fast in this goddam high security base!' Maggie roared.

Swift grunted, and then glanced at Anne. She held up a hand. 'I'm fine, before you ask, and I'm going.'

He smiled. 'Good; you're a smart cookie, and I'll enjoy comparing notes with you.' His eyes held a far-off look. 'And examining Miss Soviet Union's... credentials... Speaking of which, where is she?'

'I thought this meeting would go smoother without her distracting some folks,' Maggie said drily. 'I'll haul her in later. Now, about this dumbass idea of you flying off into interstellar space and leaving me in the lurch...'

'Who else do you have in mind?' Swift demanded.

'Well, there's Kleinman—'

'He's a damned idiot.'

'—and Chun.'

'Okay, not too bad,' Swift conceded. 'But not in my class.'

'Modest, aintcha?'

'No – realistic. Come on, Maggie, you *need* me to be on this mission, and you know it. Don't make me beg.'

'Don't make me throw you in the brig,' she countered. Then she threw up her hands. 'I'm just too meek and mild, and anybody thinks they can walk all over me. Go and get yourself cleaned up. I wouldn't want any aliens thinking that all Americans are as goddam filthy as you are.'

'You're a sweetheart,' Swift said, grinning. He shot for the door before she could change her mind.

'Don't go spreading lies like that around, you hear?' she yelled after him. Then she shook her head and looked at Anne. 'They take advantage of my good nature.'

'If it's not one thing,' Lethbridge-Stewart muttered, 'it's another. And here's another.'

He'd been disturbed enough by Bishop's report that morning. The attempt on Anne's life was extremely worrying, and now she was going off on some sort of jaunt into space! He wished he could order her not to go, but he knew her well enough to realise that such an order would end up being disobeyed anyway, and she'd point out, quite rightly, that she wasn't officially a member of the Fifth anymore. Of course, she *had* to go. She was their best chance to get this whole affair straightened out.

'I'd offer you a penny for your thoughts, Al,' Izzy said, barely glancing up from his chair in the pub's otherwise empty lounge. It was too early for Albert to open up, so they had the room to themselves. 'Only from the look of you, I'd say they're worth a helluva lot more than a penny.'

'Oh, sorry, Izzy.' He filled his friend in on the report he'd just received. Izzy whistled. 'Yes, it's a bit of a mess, isn't it?'

'That's like calling Korea a spot of bother.' Izzy grinned. 'Which, knowing you, is exactly what you do. Whaddya think? Is this brain dame pal of yours thinking on the right track?'

'Anne? Undoubtedly. She's got a very good head on her shoulders.'

'A looker, huh?' Izzy gave a wolf whistle.

'I mean she's extremely intelligent and competent.' Lethbridge-Stewart glared at Izzy.

'Yeah, right.' He mused a moment. 'Ya think she could be right about this Tanya babe setting the whole thing up?'

'That woman is an agent for Bugayev, and he has the resources to fix almost anything. The question, though, is: *did* he fix it? Or are we simply being overly suspicious?'

'On the subject of shady Russkie operatives, wasn't he supposed to be sending us some kinda liaison guy?'

'Yes indeed. But Wright tells me that there's been some sort of unexpected delay, and he'll be arriving later.'

Izzy scowled. 'Should we be looking for some sort of masterplan in that, or is it a simple SNAFU?'

'Who can say?'

'Oh, it's a simple life you live, Al ole pal.' There was a rap on the door. 'And I suspect it's about to get even more complicated...'

It was Corporal Wright. He saluted – smartly, for him. 'Beg pardon, sir, but Mr Bryden is on his way.'

Lethbridge-Stewart had to restrain himself from rolling his eyes. 'You had better bring him to see me directly he arrives.'

'Shouldn't be long,' Wright remarked, and disappeared again.

Izzy grunted. 'I get the impression this isn't your favourite guy, Al.'

'He's... a trifle too focused,' Lethbridge-Stewart said, carefully.

'Got his own agenda? Not a team player?'

'Oh, he's certainly on our side. I have no doubt of that. But that doesn't preclude him also having his own agenda.'

'Great. Want me to sit this one out?'

'Actually, it might be helpful if you didn't. He might be a little more... circumspect with an audience.'

'Gotcha.'

Wright had been perfectly correct. In less than five minutes there was another knock on the door, and Wright entered and saluted.

'Mr Bryden – and guest.'

What's this? Lethbridge-Stewart nodded, and Wright ushered Bryden and a second man into the room before leaving.

The businessman started to speak, saw Izzy lounging carelessly to one side, and paused. Then he plunged ahead.

'Brigadier, I understand that Mrs Bishop is in America.'

'For the moment, yes.'

'Then I've brought you some help in her absence.' He gestured to the man beside him – tall, bespectacled and looking uncomfortable in his suit. 'This is Dr Fisher, one of my top lab boys. He's brought along some equipment, and can't wait to take a crack at analysing this energy shield of yours.'

'Yeah, he looks like he's eager to be outta here,' Izzy commented. 'Raring to go, eh?'

'I'm sorry,' Bryden said stiffly. 'And just who might you be?'

Izzy slowly unfolded himself. 'I might be just about anyone,' he said, lazily. 'But I'm your friendly neighbourhood American liaison. Howdy.'

'Master Sergeant Rivkin represents the US interests in this matter,' Lethbridge-Stewart added. 'He's been fully briefed on the matter.'

'How's about I take the brain here up to the site?' Izzy suggested. 'I can brief him on the way. I'm sure you Brits want to talk about me behind my backs.' He grinned, and draped an arm over Fisher's shoulder. 'Come on, old son, let's go do some science, eh?'

They were actually out of the room before Bryden's surprise wore off. 'Typical American,' he spluttered. 'Trying to take over everything.'

'He's just trying to help out,' Lethbridge-Stewart said. 'Speaking of which, thank you for the loan of your man. I'm sure he'll prove to be most useful in Dr Travers' absence.'

Bryden looked annoyed, but there was nothing he could actually object to. 'I'm glad to help out,' he said, rather lamely. 'Is there any further progress?'

'Yes. There appears to have been an inside man at Groom Lake selling alien artefacts on the black market. You wouldn't happen to have heard any rumours of such things, would you?'

'Why should I hear things like that?' Bryden growled.

'You have... access to information that authorised channels don't. An opportunist might consider approaching you with items for sale.'

'Well, nobody has.' Bryden sounded like he was annoyed that he hadn't been approached.

Lethbridge-Stewart nodded thoughtfully. 'Well, if you could keep your ears and eyes open, it could prove to be very useful. We don't know if this man worked alone, or as part of a team.'

'I'll bear it in mind,' Bryden promised.

Lethbridge-Stewart was certain that he would – he was probably itching to get one of his American contacts to put feelers out and find out if there was anything he might be able to purchase. It probably wouldn't amount to anything, but it might divert Bryden's attention for a while.

As Lethbridge-Stewart had more than half-expected, Bryden abruptly held out his hand. 'I'd best look into that,' he said, shaking his goodbyes. He scurried off.

Well, that was one less problem, at least.

Stu was rather surprised to discover that the Russians stopped mid-morning for a tea break. He'd thought only the Brits did that.

He tasted the brew he'd been handed – strong, black and bitter, kind of like the Ruskies themselves. But he seized the chance to wander away from the barrier with the mug. Nobody paid any attention, which he hadn't been expecting. Still, they could hardly be worried that he'd be spying on anything in the Siberian hinterland. Aside from the barrier, there wasn't anything of interest to be seen.

When he was certain he was alone, he put his mug on a tree stump, and took his miniaturised radio out of his pack. It was time to check in.

'Grey Twelve to IntOps,' he called. 'Grey Twelve to IntOps. Come in, IntOps…'

Anne, Tanya and Swift found that their jeep was allowed back through the barrier without a problem, but their faces fell when they arrived at the construction site.

It was twice the size it had been the day before. And the work crews were out, adding to the buildings at a frantic pace. None of them were as yet complete, but the walls were growing, and the acreage covered was spreading.

'That's not a good sign,' Swift muttered.

'And it's not as if they could just roll it up and cart it away – assuming we can get this council of theirs to agree to stop,' Anne added.

'It looks as if a military solution might be our only option,' Tanya said. 'Peace-loving as the Soviet Union is, we may have to consider aggressive action.'

It was a depressing situation, not helped when they had to wait for Kwith to show up. An assistant – looking like some sort of orange-furred gorilla in a three-piece suit – apologised for the delay, but informed them that the captain was showing the delegate around the worksite. They had no option but to wait.

'It looks like that's our ride,' Swift said, pointing to a ship that hadn't been there yesterday. 'Talk about a sweet jalopy…'

Anne studied it, and found she agreed with him – *this* looked more like her idea of a spaceship. It was sleek and needle-like, with a burnished bronze outer skin. It was horizontal, resting on what looked to be landing skis, and about two hundred feet long. At the rear were six fins, three of them attached to what looked like rockets, but without visible exhaust nozzles. It was beautiful, in a Dan Dare kind of way.

'It looks fast,' Tanya observed.

'*Fast* is a relative term, I'm afraid,' Anne said. 'Wherever this Dulkis is, it's a long, long way away.' Her spirits were not high. 'Even if we can convince this alien convention to stop building, how soon can they cease? What will be built by then? Will we ever be able to return to normal?'

The Russian woman laid a gentle hand on her arm. 'I know the odds appear against us, but we *must* try. I fear the outcome if we must resort to force of arms. My father died in the Great War and so many families I grew up with lost loved ones. My home town was mostly destroyed – and, even now, is in poor state. I would not wish the same to happen to any further families.'

Anne was surprised and touched by the vulnerability in the spy's voice. But was that how Tanya *wanted* her to feel?

God, she hated all of this mutual distrust and suspicion.

'If it comes down to a war with these aliens,' Swift agreed, 'the outcome is both uncertain and frightening. The devastation that could result might well cause the collapse of all human societies.'

'Then we had better not fail,' Anne said, as forcefully as she could. 'Too much rests on our shoulders.'

'That gives me motivation – and fears, at the same time,' Tanya admitted. Anne couldn't disagree with that summation.

Kwith showed up a short time later, skimming the sands on his chair/bed. Accompanying him in a smaller, but similar, unit was another alien – though he looked at first glance to be almost entirely human. Kwith waved a couple of tentacles in what Anne imagined was a gesture of greeting at them.

'This is Examiner Brond of Dulkis,' he said. 'For a damned interfering busybody, he's relatively likeable.'

Brond climbed out of his vehicle and bowed slightly. 'I am… intrigued to meet you.' He wore a loose, flowing robe of some rich, blue-hued material. He had a white goatee and receding hairline, and could have passed without comment anywhere in the world.

'And we are glad to meet you,' Anne said. 'I'm sure you can imagine how concerned we are.' She gestured around her. 'We need to get this all stopped as soon as possible.'

Brond regarded her wryly. 'You do understand that my *official* job here is to ensure that this refugee centre gets built, don't you?'

'Of course,' she agreed. 'But *you* do understand that the peoples of Earth know nothing about this, and certainly haven't authorised it?'

'I wouldn't know. To the best of my knowledge, we have a completely legal and binding agreement with the monarch of your planet.'

'Whoever that person is,' Swift broke in, 'he's a damned liar and a fraud, because this planet doesn't have a king.'

'Please, please,' Brond said, throwing up his hands. 'I am not the person you need to convince of that. Kwith has informed me of your claims – probably to distract me from examining his work too closely – but I have no authority in this matter. I am simply a building inspector. You will have to take this case up before the Assembly of Worlds on Dulkis.' Then he smiled slightly. 'Kwith also informs me that you will need transportation.' He sighed. 'I have room for you on my ship, so I suppose you'd better accompany me back.'

'May I ask how long this journey will take?'

Brond shrugged. 'Far too long for my liking – a good day and a half of your human time.'

A day and a half? Anne felt her hopes rising. She'd been afraid it would be *months* – or even years! A day and a half…

Clearly, Brond could see the relief in her face. Alien he might be, but so much about him seemed so human. 'Conditions will be a trifle cramped,' he warned her. He eyed the supplies that they had packed in the back of the jeep. 'You will not be able to bring much of that with you. And you will have to share a cabin. I hope this does not violate your rules of hygiene or morality, but we were not expecting… visitors.'

'It will be fine, I'm sure,' Anne said. 'I'll just bring some clean underwear and such.'

'What about food?' Swift asked, clearly not wanting to delve into the clothing issue any further. 'Should we bring our own?'

'There is no need,' Brond said. 'Our synthesizers will analyse your metabolic needs and provide appropriate nutrients.'

Kwith wheezed a laugh. 'But it's bloody bland, so don't imagine you'll feast,' he warned. 'I can't stand it myself.'

'You could do with losing a few pounds,' Brond snapped. 'They will survive.'

'If you can call eating that muck *survival*,' Kwith muttered. His huge eyes turned to Anne. 'For what it is worth, I send my respects and wishes with you. And it's worth absolutely nothing, to be honest. Still, for humanoid vermin, you're less detestable than most.'

'Yeah, I like you, too. Thank you for all your help.' Anne studied him. 'So, on your planet, do they shake tentacles to say goodbye?'

'Not if we can help it.' He made another of his hooting, disgusting noises that could mean just about anything. 'No offense, but I don't care to actually *touch* you…'

To be honest, Anne wasn't certain she'd like to touch him, either – his skin looked rather slimy… 'Hopefully, we'll see you soon – and with orders for you to pack up and go.'

'Yes, please. I can't wait to get out of this horrible heat and into somewhere pleasantly fetid again.'

'If you will accompany me…?' Brond said, and set off towards the waiting spacecraft.

Anne hung back a moment until she thought he was out of hearing range, and then turned back to Kwith. 'How did the review go?'

Kwith gave one of his noisy responses. 'As well as they ever go,' he replied. 'Pick, pick, pick… But it's all minor crap, so I aim to give the list to one of my subordinates to eat. But thank you for caring – if you do.' He waved a tentacle. 'I'd better look busy, or that busybody will think I'm not taking him seriously. Which I'm not, of course.'

Anne left him to it and caught up with her companions. She had her clothing bag with her, as the others had. They'd left the food in the jeep, and Anne could only hope this was a smart decision, given Kwith's opinion of the food synthesizers. Then again, Kwith had a very low opinion of pretty much anything that he didn't run, so he was likely exaggerating the problem. She hoped…

Inside the ship, Brond turned them over to an aide, who took them to a smallish cabin.

It took a while, as the three of them were staring at everything they passed. To be on a real spaceship, soon to head to an alien world… It was incredibly exciting for them all, even if there wasn't much to see in the corridors. It felt like being on a very high-tech submarine – slightly claustrophobic, and in an almost sterile atmosphere. There was no attempt at art or style – the walls were simply metallic, a silvery hue. There were touch pads by some of the doors, but little else to see until they reached the room assigned to them. There the aide showed them how to operate the lock-pad so that they could access the room.

It was absolutely generic. There were two bunks set into one wall, four chairs growing like mushrooms from the bare floor and a table. The aide demonstrated how to open small doors in the wall for storing their packs, and then gestured at the only other door.

'Hygiene chamber,' he said. 'It should be reasonably suitable for you.' He didn't offer any suggestions in case it wasn't.

Tanya stared at the chairs. 'I trust these are more comfortable than the ones in the other ship.'

'They're adjustable,' the aide explained. 'See this small lighted panel on the side? Tap it once, and the chair becomes fluid. Sit in it, and it will accommodate itself to your form. Tap the panel again and it will retain that shape.'

'I wish we'd known that *before* we tried those other seats,' Anne muttered. She glanced at the beds, and saw similar panels, which was a relief.

'We shall be taking off shortly,' the aide informed them. 'Please do not attempt to run all over the ship; it will only interfere with the crew performing their duties.' He started for the door.

'Hang on a minute. There's not even a window – or porthole, or whatever you call it in here.'

'There is no need for one.'

'No need?' Anne glared at him. 'We'll be leaving Earth and heading into space for the first time in our lives, and you think there's no need for us to watch?'

'Oh, yes,' he said. 'I forgot how primitive you are. You wish to observe the process, is that it?'

'Yes, that is it. It may be old-hat to you, but it's new to us.'

'I'll see what I can do. Just wait here – we can't have you traipsing all over the ship, can we?' He left the room.

Swift snorted. 'Well, he's put us in our places proper, hasn't he?'

'Petty bureaucrats abound,' Tanya said. 'Even in Mother Russia.'

Anne glanced around. 'Well, I guess we're going to have to take it in turns sleeping, as there are only two beds.'

Tanya grinned at Swift. 'Or we could get to know one another better…'

'As appealing as that sounds,' he said, somewhat regretfully. 'I *am* married.'

The Russian shrugged. 'So am I, I think. Unless he's managed to get himself assassinated by now. What has that to do with anything?'

Anne cut Swift off from replying. 'It might take a bit longer than we have to explain Western morality to you,' she said. She looked at the other door. 'Do we dare check out the hygiene chamber?'

Tanya grinned. 'Let us brave it together.' She tapped on the pad, and the door slid open.

She and Anne peered in, while Swift started stowing his clothing away in one of the wall hatches.

To Anne's relief, it didn't look completely alien in the bathroom. There was a hand sink, though no obvious taps. There was something that clearly operated as a toilet – thankfully with one of the glowing pads. It would obviously adjust to their backsides. And there was a transparent tube in the corner of the room, large enough for them to stand in together, if they wanted.

'I do hope that's the shower and not the emergency exit,' Anne murmured.

Tanya giggled. 'I shall let you try it first.'

'How kind.' They returned to the main room. 'It looks – functional, if not overly comfortable. There's no mirror, though.'

'No towels, either,' Tanya said. 'I imagine there may be further hatches in the walls that would contain them. It is going to be… interesting adjusting to this craft.'

There was a pleasant musical tone from the door, and then the aide reappeared. 'I have obtained permission for you to witness events from the observation lounge,' he said. 'Please, though, remember not to interfere with crew members, and not to leave the room and go wandering.'

'We'll be good,' Anne assured him, refusing to take offense at his arrogant assumptions. This was going to be so much fun, she couldn't even get mad at him. Space… 'Come on,' she said, happily. 'Let's go get seats!'

CHAPTER TEN
Atomic Monster

DOUGLAS HAD been brought up to date by Lethbridge-Stewart, and he'd passed the information along to Bugayev.

The impassive Russian remained as unreadable as ever. He merely grunted, but then offered the information that his operative had reported much the same news.

'I do not like the idea of them going to this alien world,' he confessed.

'You don't think that we can trust these aliens?' Douglas asked, wondering if he was going to get some real information at last.

'To be frank, I trust them more than I trust the Americans. They seem to be candidly open. That is not my issue with this arrangement. I dislike being relegated to the sidelines.'

'I'm sorry?'

'It is important that I retain control of this situation,' Bugayev explained. 'I cannot do that if my agent is on some alien world. I must then rely on her intelligence and performance.'

Ah. Control freak with his reins cut… That made sense. 'Isn't she reliable?'

'Very. But these are extraordinary circumstances we find ourselves in, would you not say? It irks me to be out of communication with her.'

'That's reasonable. I'm a bit worried about Dr Travers myself.'

'I am not worried about *Tanya*,' Bugayev corrected him. 'I am worried that she may not do the… optimum response when she does not have my guidance. She is expendable, but the mission is critical.'

Charming. But, Douglas had to admit, the Russian was correct about the importance of this mission. If Anne and the others couldn't convince the aliens to stop building, then who could say what shape the world would be in tomorrow?

'It is frustrating not to be able to take action,' Bugayev admitted. 'It is tempting to suggest bombing the three sites and thus removing the problem entirely.'

That was an alarming idea.

'It doesn't strike me as the best solution,' Douglas said hastily.

'It may end up being our *only* solution if this mission of peace does not work out.'

'There's no guarantee it *won't* work,' Douglas pointed out. 'These barriers have resisted everything you've fired at them so far and shown absolutely no weaknesses.'

'But would they stand up to an atomic blast?'

'I don't think it would be a good idea to find out. At least, except as a really last resort.'

Bugayev stared at him with hooded eyes. 'I did not expect such cowardice from a military man.'

'It's not cowardice,' Douglas snapped. 'It's practicality. Look, first off – there's no guarantee it would have any effect on this force screen. So far these aliens have shrugged off our attempts to penetrate the barriers. They seem to be treating it like we're children throwing stones at it. But they might get upset if we chuck a nuclear bomb at them. And if it *doesn't* do anything to these force fields, it will certainly do something to the surrounding countryside. The fallout would be lethal – to *us.*'

Bugayev shrugged. 'This is Siberia – nothing important would be affected. And the Americans are always setting off their provocative atomic tests in their Nevada deserts.'

'Well, the one *we're* dealing with in England is smack dab in the middle of an inhabited area.'

'Evacuate it, then, if you feel you must.'

'Hardly a practical solution – we'd have to evacuate the entire island – thousands of people! – and that's not going to be easy. It would cause chaos and panic.'

'You British are undisciplined. We could remove that many people easily here in the Soviet Union.'

And have… Douglas didn't say that aloud, though. 'But it's not the possibility that it might fail that bothers me,' he explained. 'That would be bad enough – but it would be *worse* if it succeeded.'

'How so?'

'Well, think about it. So far, the aliens have been – well, not *friendly*, but at least tolerant and indifferent. But if we succeeded in blowing up the three sites, we'd be killing hundreds – maybe even thousands – of them. I can guarantee their attitude towards us would change considerably. They would undoubtedly feel the need to retaliate. I don't know about you, but I don't like the thought of what these highly technological beings might be able to do if they got mad.'

'So, you would have us just roll over on our backs like puppy dogs?' Bugayev asked. He shook his head. 'That would not sit well with the Supreme Soviet – and it does not sit well with me. We are nobody's puppy dogs – not the West's, and certainly not some creatures that do not even belong on this earth.'

'I get what you're saying,' Douglas said, sweating a little at the implications of what Bugayev was proposing. He hoped that it was nothing but thoughts. 'But we have to tread gently in this very sticky situation. This mission to Dulkis is our best bet to resolve this peacefully. If our agents can convince the aliens to abandon their plans, it will all turn out fine.'

I hope!

'And if they can't? We have to have alternative scenarios ready to engage.' Bugayev shook his head. 'I can see your points, and they are valid. But a full-scale attack may well be our only viable option. We have no choice but to start to plan such an assault – and hope that it will never become necessary. But it must be prepared and ready to be implemented. Kindly pass that along to your brigadier, and warn him that if you English are not willing to bomb your island site – then the Soviet Union will have to do it for you.'

Dear God…

Douglas stared at the man. 'You're considering bombing the Isle of Man? You do realise the consequences of such an action?'

'Of course. You British will feel a desire and need to

retaliate. It would be a foolish action.'

Douglas' mouth was dry. 'You're talking about setting off World War Three...'

'To stop these aliens, it may be necessary, yes.'

Lift-off was actually rather disappointing in some ways.

Anne, Tanya and Swift were given seats (which they promptly adjusted) in a room – cabin? – with a virtually 360-degree view. One of the aliens (who looked and smelled like a green-skinned warthog) handed them devices the size of an overly large coin.

'Translator,' he grunted when each held one. 'Put it in a pocket or body orifice and you'll be good to go. Works on brain waves – as long as you have any.' He shuffled off.

'Charming,' Anne remarked.

'He did not go to finishing school,' Tanya commented, grinning. Her device had somehow vanished, even though her clothing had no obvious pockets. 'But it clearly works, since I am now speaking Russian and you appear to understand me.'

Anne chose not to inform Tanya that she could have understood her no matter what language she spoke. Just as she'd been privy to all the small-talk from the various aliens in the lounge. Some secrets were best kept.

'Well, one thing you have to say about these aliens,' Swift said. 'Their technology is useful.'

There was a soft tone that sounded from the air, low and mellow. 'Departure,' a disembodied voice said.

And the view began to change. There was no countdown, no blast of rockets, no flames or even a lurch. The ship simply started to ascend. Anne felt rather let down; she'd been expecting huge blasts and gravity pinning her to her seat – but it was smoother than taking a train, and just about as exciting. She could see the land below dropping away and that was about it. As she watched, she saw Las Vegas in the distance come into view and then shrink back into obscurity. The ship entered the cloud layer, and then popped out of the top of the clouds. Sunlight was behind them, thankfully, as it appeared to be more intense. Earth below started to recede.

The sky grew darker, turning deep blue, then purple and finally a star-sprinkled black. She could see the edge of the world below her, intensely blue and shining against the darkness of eternal night, and her heart sang. To be looking back and down at Earth...

Her emotions were almost overwhelming her, and she could feel tears in her eyes, partly from the feeling of leaving home for the first time and partly simply because of the sheer beauty of it.

She watched as Earth fell away, shrinking into a globe, and then a ball.

And, beyond the horizon, the moon slipped quietly and majestically into view. It was glowing a silvery grey. Her heart caught in her throat as she saw it, like a marble above the small ball that was Earth.

'Amazing,' Tanya murmured beside her. Her voice sounded awed.

'Indeed,' Anne said, just as softly. 'This is astounding.'

There was a snort from the warthog. 'Seen one planet, seen them all. Your first time, eh?'

'Oh, yes.'

'You can always tell the neophytes. Is that place your home?'

'Yes.'

'Ah, that explains it. Only a native could love that dump.'

Anne felt she should defend the honour of her home world, but she really didn't want to break her tranquil mood. All she wanted to do was to sit and stare into interplanetary space. To be out here, amid all that staggering wonder...

It lasted about five minutes of staring into star-speckled blackness before she started to feel restless. Once Earth had vanished into the distance, there was nothing else to see. She looked around the room and saw their crotchety alien companion doing something with a wall panel.

'Would it be all right if we looked around the ship?' she asked.

Warthog grunted again, and scratched his snout. 'Why ask me? I'm only the cleaner.'

'The what?'

'The cleaner.' He held up what looked like a sponge attached to a transistor radio. 'You don't think this ship cleans itself, do you?'

Anne felt guilty. 'Uh, I hadn't really thought about it, but, yes, I rather supposed I did.'

'Oh, aye? Well, we're having none of that, you know. We have a right to our jobs, you know – even though these snobs want to automate everything. Over my dead body, that's what I say – and I don't care who hears it.'

'Um, quite,' Anne agreed weakly. She appeared to have made a rather sensitive comment. Alien warthog looked like he was all set for a good rant.

'Power to the people!' Tanya said loudly. 'You have a right to your job and your dignity – as much as the captain of this ship.'

'Darned right I do,' he answered, apparently pleased with this response.

Tanya grabbed Anne's elbow. 'I'll set her straight, don't you worry,' she promised the alien. Then in a low voice, she muttered to Anne, 'Let's get out of here, quickly, or he'll bend our ears for hours.'

They hurried from the room into the corridor, with Swift right behind them. When the door closed, Tanya leaned against a wall and giggled. 'That was a lucky escape. I do find idealogues so dull, don't you?'

'I thought you were supposed to be on his side?' Anne said. 'You know, comrade this-and-that and all?'

'Theoretically, yes. Practically, I don't have a lot in common with a cleaner.'

Anne laughed. 'You're a *snob*.'

Tanya grinned back. 'Guilty as charged. Decadent as the West is, I do find some of its pleasures rather appealing.'

Anne found Tanya something of a puzzle – but, then, she probably felt the same way about Anne. 'Do you feel brave or decadent enough to tackle this processed food of theirs?'

'We shall have to be at some point. Why not now?' The two of them wandered off to look for the dining room.

Lethbridge-Stewart made his way back to the barrier.

He'd called Fiona, only to receive her daily report of *I'm fine; stop worrying and no, there's no sign of any problems with the baby.*

Standing outside the barrier, staring into the shrubbery

beyond, was incredibly frustrating. Since that one contact he'd had with the alien spokesbeing, there had been no further indications of life beyond the barrier at all. He'd almost have welcomed another whale attack to just hanging around impotently.

He imagined that Douglas felt pretty much the same in Siberia – only with the added strain of dealing with Bugayev. To have the possibility of nuclear annihilation hanging over his head must have made Douglas' position very stressful. Still, there was the good news that Anne was finding her aliens reasonably co-operative. He couldn't speak with her, of course, since she was on her faster-than-light trip to another planetary system, but he trusted her to do the right thing. She knew that the fate of the world rested upon her and her companions, and he had to simply trust her – as he so often did. She'd never failed him before.

This would be a bad time for her to let him down for once…

His guards were still on duty, and he saw there was a civilian with them, puttering around with some device or other. He started to get annoyed, and then he realised that it was Bryden's pet scientist… Fisher, that was his name.

'Any progress, Professor Fisher?' he asked.

Fisher glanced up from the device he was playing with. 'Ah… that's *doctor*,' he said, slightly nervously. He clearly didn't deal with the military every day.

'I'm sorry, *Dr* Fisher.'

'Ah – that's quite all right, Colonel.'

Was that a sly insult, or did the man not know military ranks? 'Brigadier.'

'Oh, ah… right. Um, what did you ask again?'

'If you're having any progress.'

'Oh, right.' He pushed his glasses back up his nose. 'Ah, as a matter of fact, yes. Yes, I – ah – think I've discovered something.'

'Well, that's a bit of good news for a change. Can you explain it in layman's terms?'

'Ah – I'll try.' Fisher concentrated for a moment. 'This – um – barrier of yours is quite intriguing. I'm not *entirely* certain how it works, but I've a rough idea. You do know that you can picture an atom as a sort of mostly hollow billiard ball, right? Nucleus – tiny – at the centre, surrounded by lots of empty space and then several shells of electrons? Yes?'

'I think I recall that much from basic science,' Lethbridge-Stewart admitted. 'Do go on.'

'Well, atoms can sort of – ah – bunch up, as it were, and some – like carbon – form a sort of orderly structure, bonding together.'

Lethbridge-Stewart searched his meagre supply of scientific knowledge. 'Like a diamond, you mean?'

'Yes,' Fisher said, happily. 'Just like a diamond. The atoms bond together, you see, and form a sort of tight net. Incredibly tough.'

'You mean that these aliens have somehow turned thin air into diamonds?'

'Ah – well, that would be an – um – crude way of expressing it, but, essentially, yes. They have somehow made the gaseous atoms of the air into an – ah – sort of chain-link business. It's really rather remarkable.' Fisher pushed his spectacles back up to the bridge of his nose. 'Most exciting.'

'Yes, I'm sure it is,' Lethbridge-Stewart said drily. 'Does this mean that you can whip up some sort of a gizmo to destroy it?'

'Oh, good heavens, no,' Fisher said, sounding shocked. 'It's far beyond anything we could ever manage. Ah, well, maybe in fifty years or so...'

'We don't *have* fifty years.'

'Ah, no, quite.'

'So, basically,' Lethbridge-Stewart continued rather relentlessly, 'you've discovered something that doesn't help us in the slightest?'

'Ah, well... I wouldn't go *quite* that far...' Fisher protested. 'There's a chance that I might be able to – ah – poke a hole in it, shall we say?'

'A hole? How *big* a hole?'

Fisher shrugged. 'Well, um, that would depend on the amount of power I have on hand. The more power, the bigger the hole.'

That sounded like it made some sort of sense, at least. 'How much power are we talking about?'

'Ah, well, I can't be – um – too certain about that until I've run some tests.'

'Then *run* them,' Lethbridge-Stewart growled. 'Do the four-minute-mile of testing.'

'Well, it would help if I wasn't constantly being – uh – interrupted,' Fisher said, quite crossly.

Just what he needed – a moody scientist. Lethbridge-Stewart was missing Anne quite badly. 'Oh, very well. Just tell one of my men if you need anything, and I'll see that you get it. And report any progress – to *me*,' he stressed.

'Ah – Mr Bryden is technically my boss,' Fisher pointed out. 'He pays my salary, and he told me to report directly to him.'

'And I represent Her Majesty's Government, Dr Fisher,' Lethbridge-Stewart said. 'And the government says that you report to *me*. Do we understand one another?'

'Um – yes. Yes, I believe we do.'

'Good. Then I shan't bother you anymore. Do carry on.' He tapped his palm with his swagger stick, and then strode away to speak to the guards.

'Well,' Colonel Hickenlooper said, 'they're on their way.' She'd just received the report from the guards stationed at the barrier.

Bishop nodded, trying to mask his concern for Anne. His air of pretended indifference didn't pass Hickenlooper's scowling scrutiny.

'Don't fret yourself, Captain, I'm sure she'll be okay.'

'Yes,' he said, struggling to believe this. 'You're probably right. These aliens don't seem like they'd do anything to *deliberately* harm her.' His fears were hard to suppress.

'Right.'

'Just like they're not *deliberately* aiming to harm our planet.' There – he'd said it. Might as well plunge on with his other fears. 'Just because they don't *mean* to cause trouble doesn't mean that this isn't going to happen. I'm sure they have the best of intentions – after all, this whole business is kind of humanitarian – if that's the right word – isn't it? They just want to help war refugees, and that's a noble sentiment. But their act of nobility might just lead to the end of the human race.'

'Well, you're a cock-eyed optimist.'

'I can't help it. That's my wife up there, trying to talk a group of crazy aliens into abandoning a plan to help other aliens because it will hurt us. But who do you think they'll have more concern about? Peoples they may have known for centuries, or the human race that they don't know at all? And, honestly, if they choose their friends, who are we to blame them?'

'Come on,' Hickenlooper said. 'They're clearly decent folks; their compassion demonstrates that. I'm sure they'll give us a fair hearing. And they'll look after that feisty gal of yours as best they can.'

Bishop sighed. 'Yes, I'm sure you're right, Colonel. But she's my *wife*, and I can't do anything to help her.'

'Now that's where you're wrong, fella. You can help *all* of us – that's why Al sent you here. He thinks you're a capable, resourceful *chap*. So *be* capable and resourceful. Speaking of which...' She picked up her phone. 'Put me through to the lab.' There was a momentary pause, and then she snapped, 'Who is this? Chun? Okay, tell me you've got good news for me...' Another pause. 'You sure you got that damned thing switched on? Check it out and get back to me, pronto.' She slammed down the receiver. 'I *knew* I shouldn'ta let Swift outta my sight...'

It was Bishop's turn to be consoling. 'I'm sure this Mr Chun is a capable man. He wouldn't be here otherwise, would he?'

'Oh, he's capable, right as rain – but he's no Swift. He's my second-best man, at a time when I really need my best man. Dammit, Bishop, we gotta find this phony king. I've got a really bad feeling about this.'

'What do you mean?'

'Well, lookee; whoever is pulling this scam is one smart honcho.' She started ticking off points on her fingers. 'He's got contacts here in this place – and, trust me, this ain't an easy place to infiltrate. He's been paying Bradley a whole passel of cash to steal him things. He suckered a whole blasted alien confederacy or whatever they call themselves into thinking he's humanity's monarch. And he's done all this without raising a single alert from the FBI, the CIA or the entire US government. That's one smart cookie. But. He's *bound* to have figgered out that we'd track him down eventually. A guy that smart has to have a plan. And he'd know that the arrival of these aliens was bound to set off five-star alarms around the entire planet, so whatever he's got in mind has to already be in motion… And we don't even know who he is, let alone what his damned scheme is.' She shook her head. 'Dammit, Captain, I don't like this. I don't like this one little bit.'

Bishop had to admit that she had a good point, and a real reason to be worried. 'What do you think our James Bond villain is after?'

'Beats me,' she admitted with a sigh. 'If he wanted to raid Fort Knox, I can't say I'd be too surprised. I—' She broke off as her office door was flung open, and a slightly dishevelled Chinese-looking man burst in. 'Dammit, Chun, what the hell are you doing here. Ain'tcha heard of the damned telephone? Or even knocking?'

Chun slammed a boxy structure down on her desk. It had begun life as a rather inelegant device, with wires, transistors and other electronic components that Bishop couldn't identify all hastily soldered together. It now looked as if somebody had fished it out of a volcano.

'*This* is your radio tracker,' Chun said.

'What in seven hells have you done to it?' Hickenlooper howled.

'Nothing. That's how I found it when I checked on it after your call.'

Bishop stared at the mess in silence. This… mess had been their only hope of tracking the spurious king. His spirits fell as Hickenlooper's voice rose.

'How in God's name could that happen? Didn't you have it *watched*?'

'Not watched, no,' Chun said, miserably. 'It wasn't doing anything. I had it on one of the lab shelves. That should have been safe enough.'

'Who had access to the lab?' Bishop asked.

'Dr Kleinman and myself. Nobody else has been in there since Dr Swift left. And it was fine when he left, because he showed me how to use it.'

'So you're saying that only you and Kleinman coulda done this?' Hickenlooper pointed to the device.

Chun suddenly seemed to realise that he was in potentially serious trouble. 'Uh, well… I guess if you put it like that…'

'I *do* put it like that. Nobody else has access to your lab. So, we got exactly two suspects.' She stared intently at him.

'I can assure you—'

'Assure me all ya like.' She picked up the phone. 'Get me security.' After a short pause, 'Go and get me Dr Kleinman – *now*. Escort him to me personally, y'hear?' She slammed down the phone and stared up at Chun. 'Now, I think that you and I have to have a little chat – don't you?'

The processed food on the ship didn't turn out quite as badly as Kwith had asserted.

There was no way to consider it a gourmet meal, Anne reflected, but it was edible and had reasonable taste. Tanya wolfed it down cheerfully. Anne imagined her impoverished youth had acclimatised her to eat almost anything. Anne took a little longer to finish hers.

As they were eating, one of the aliens approached their table. He looked almost entirely human and greeted them politely. He was dressed in a sort of shimmering white toga, with a large, dark collar. His blond hair was swept back. If he were entirely human, Anne would have judged him to be in his mid-twenties, but she realised that there was no way to judge the age of an alien. Still, he looked young and rather handsome.

'I'm Dellar,' he said, cheerfully. 'The ship's physician. Would you mind if I chatted with you for a while?'

'Not at all,' Anne replied, honestly. 'I'd appreciate the opportunity.' She waved him to a chair. 'You're not here to check us out for parasites or anything, are you?'

'Nothing like that,' he assured her. 'I can tell that you're both in extremely good health.'

'Without an examination? You're an unusual doctor. The ones I know are inordinately fond of testing.'

'Well, we do things a little different on Dulkis. I've had my senses enhanced, so I am effectively all the basic testing equipment that I require.'

'Really?' Tanya leaned forward slightly. 'What can you tell about me, then?'

He sniffed slightly, and then peered at her. 'Generally excellent health,' he said. 'Your cholesterol levels are slightly elevated, so I would judge that you enjoy the good life.' He frowned slightly. 'You are sexually active, but have been surgically sterilised. I can't imagine why, since you have very good genes that would be worth passing along. And you have a very mild fungal infection on one of your toes.'

He turned to Anne. 'Do you wish me to analyse you?'

'Thanks, no – I think you've demonstrated your skills already. But it's nice to meet a friendly person on this ship.'

'You're not feeling welcome?'

'Well… tolerated, perhaps,' Anne admitted. 'We are, after all, intruders on their way to file a complaint, so *welcome* might be a bit much to ask.'

'Oh, these sort of things happen all of the time. Nobody holds that against you. It's not possible to have a union of thirty-four worlds without a certain amount of… friction, shall we say?'

'Is it more that we're less technically evolved than the rest of you, then? Or merely that it takes a while for strangers to be accepted?'

'Perhaps a bit of both,' Dellar replied. 'Still, I'm happy enough to be friends with you.' Then he grinned. 'Mind you, I will confess that it's partly because I was hoping to be able to ask a favour of you.'

'Ah!' Tanya exclaimed. 'Enlightened self-interest. I heartily approve. What is it that you wish of us?'

'It's purely professional,' he assured them. 'As a medical man, I'd love the opportunity to check you out more thoroughly. I'd like to be able to include Earth humans in my database.' He added, hastily, 'A completely non-invasive examination, I assure you!'

'I think that might be an interesting idea,' Tanya said. 'I'd be very pleased to help your studies out.' She stood up, and pulled him to his feet, and then glanced at Anne. 'If you'll pardon me…?'

'He's all yours,' Anne replied.

Trust Tanya to take the lead. Still, she wasn't entirely sure how she'd feel about being a guinea pig for an alien doctor, no matter how non-invasive he meant to be.

Tanya went happily along, however. Anne heard her asking, 'So, have you heard of the practice of I'll show you mine if you show me yours?'

Honestly! The girl had almost no shame…

All things considered, Douglas decided, Siberia wasn't quite as bad as he'd expected.

The weather was cold, true, but no worse than the off-season in Blackpool. Of course, it wasn't yet winter when the temperatures would undoubtedly take a nose-dive. The landscape was quite pleasant – if you ignored the circle of crushed trees marking the extent of the alien barrier. And if the company was a bit taciturn, it was better than that to be found a few hundred miles north in the Gulags. In other words, things could be a lot worse.

And then it got a lot worse.

Bugayev had been on the radio, firing out instructions in Russian that Douglas couldn't follow. He knew a smattering of the language – these days it came in handy – but there was no way he could follow the rapid-fired orders. Bugayev didn't bother to enlighten him, naturally – the man was a Soviet operative, and was used to keeping his mouth shut, especially around potential foes. And, despite the fact that they were theoretically working together in this matter, Bugayev clearly found it impossible to break his secretive habits. When he wasn't giving instructions, he spent his time brooding and staring toward the alien base camp, far out of sight.

From time to time, aircraft flew over, as low as they dared. No doubt they were taking photos of what was happening off in the woods, but Bugayev shared neither pictures nor information. Finally, Douglas had had enough. He marched over to where the Russian was deep in thought.

'We're supposed to be co-operating,' he said. 'Would it be too much to ask you to share information with me?'

Bugayev blinked once and then glanced at him. 'What is it that you wish to know?'

'Well, we could start with what you're planning.'

'I have already told you that. Do you require me to

reiterate it every few hours?'

'You're still thinking about using a bomb on those aliens? The ones that – as far as we know – are pretty peaceful and relatively friendly?'

'I do not consider it either peaceful or friendly to invade Soviet territory,' Bugayev said quietly. 'I consider it an act of war. And that requires a response.'

Douglas couldn't help being angry. 'Dammit, man, you *know* we've made peaceful contact with them in Nevada. And Anne Travers, one of your own agents, and an American, are on their way to the alien base to talk with them. If you go ahead with your plan, you not only jeopardise their lives but any hope of a peaceful solution.'

'Tanya is a trained agent, loyal to the Motherland; she would be happy to sacrifice her life if it is necessary. Is your Travers agent not as steadfastly loyal to your state?'

'Anne *isn't* a spy,' Douglas growled. 'She's a scientist. And she's risked her life numerous times to save this planet. But that isn't the point. The point is that it's not the aliens endangering them but *you*. And your actions could undermine their mission.'

'I am willing to give them the opportunity to resolve this issue peacefully. I shall hold off any aggressive action until we hear from them. But if the negotiations fail, then I shall act, swiftly and decisively. And I shall be prepared to do so.' Bugayev gestured back down the mountainside. Douglas could see a heavy-duty transport carrier below them on the road. 'There is a transport from Kazakhstan. It carries a fifty-kiloton device that will be placed against the barrier. If the talks are fruitful, it will be simply taken away. If they are not…' He shrugged.

'Haven't you considered the consequences of that?' Douglas asked him. Just thinking about it made him sweat.

'Arrangements are being made to evacuate everyone possible within a twenty-five-mile radius,' Bugayev replied. 'I estimate a clearance success of about seventy percent.'

'And the rest?'

He shrugged. 'They will be vaporised. It should be painless.'

'Is that all you can say about thousands of deaths?'

'It is for the sake of Russia; they should be proud.'

Douglas shook his head in disgust. 'And what about the rest of the world? What about when the aliens decide that *they* have to retaliate for your bombing? Your actions could plunge us into war.'

'Whereas *your* inactions could thrust us into servitude to alien overlords,' Bugayev countered. He gestured at the barrier. 'They are here! They have taken our land. They are building on it, claiming it for themselves. If we do nothing, then they will expand their stolen territories. No, my friend, they must learn that they cannot force the Russian people to back down. Perhaps you British would be willing to roll over on your backs and accept the role of puppy dogs to these alien monstrosities, but the Soviets will never accept such a thing.'

'You are risking war – a war that could annihilate the human race, Bugayev! Just look at the technology that these aliens possess. We can't even understand it, let alone fight it!'

'We are all better off dead than slaves to some alien overlords. If you and the Americans don't have the stomach to fight, then you will all see that we do. We have fought for our existence before – against Napoleon and against Hitler. We will fight now, if it becomes necessary.'

'But Hitler and Napoleon were *human* foes, with weapons you understood. This… this is very different.'

Bugayev shook his head. 'No, it is precisely the same – fight or perish. And we choose to fight.' He glanced down the hillside again, and Douglas followed his gaze. The transport was a lot closer. 'Our vengeance weapon will soon be in place and readied. Once it is positioned, then we shall all retreat to a safe distance and await the results of the negotiations. But if your Travers and the others fail… then we shall not.'

Douglas stared in frustration and horror at the crawling transport. Firmly attached to the back of it was a box-like device. A device that could spell the end of the world…

CHAPTER ELEVEN
The Man Who Would Be King

LETHBRIDGE-STEWART FOUND Fisher happily hunched over some of his electronic gizmos close to the barrier.

He had four of the boxes set up, and was scurrying happily from one to another, taking readings and jotting them down in a small notepad he carried. Wright was watching him warily, but with a mostly hidden smile.

'He's as happy as a dog with a bone, sir,' he reported. 'Haven't the slightest idea what he's doing, but I imagine he does.'

'Let's hope so, Corporal. With Anne missing, we need all of the help we can get.'

Somehow, despite his absorption by whatever readings he was getting, the scientist caught at least a part of the last remark. 'I – ah – I've been meaning to mention that, Brigadier. With, um, Mrs Bishop off on a dangerous and, ah, potentially lethal mission, you should be thinking about an, ah, replacement for her.' He smiled. 'I'd like to, ah, offer my services as her replacement.'

Lethbridge-Stewart had to fight to avoid showing his anger at this callous, self-serving remark. He *did* need the man, after all, no matter how infuriating he was. 'Thank you, Fisher, but I have the utmost confidence in *Dr Travers*. I'm sure she'll be returning to us safely in the near future.'

And besides, if he wanted to find a permanent Head of Science & Research, he'd approach Arthur Grey, since Anne had recommended him before, and the man had served well in the role in a timeline now erased.

'Oh, ah, don't get me wrong, Brigadier,' Fisher said hastily. 'I, too, trust she'll, um, return in good health. But, just in case, you know…' His voice trailed off; perhaps he'd finally caught the flash of anger in Lethbridge-Stewart's eyes. 'Keep me in mind, eh?'

'If you could just get back to your work, that would be appreciated.'

'Ah, of course.' Fisher returned to muttering and scribbling.

That done with, Lethbridge-Stewart turned to Wright. 'Now, Corporal, where were we?'

Wright led Lethbridge-Stewart on a short inspection tour. Since nothing had apparently happened over the past couple of days, there wasn't much to see, save for the men on guard duty. By the time they returned to the jeep, Fisher was there, waiting eagerly for them.

'Do you have something to report, Doctor?' Lethbridge-Stewart asked.

'Ah, indeed, yes, yes.' He pushed his glasses back up his nose and consulted his little pad. 'I've got the frequency the carrier wave operates on, and, um, I'm sure I can build a nullifier that will be most effective – but, ah, as I warned, only over a small area.'

'When you say *small*, could you be a bit more specific?'

'Oh, um, a hole maybe ten feet across,' Fisher explained. 'Large enough to walk through, shall we – ah – say? Or drive a small jeep through?'

Lethbridge-Stewart felt a surge of excitement. 'We'll be able to go through this… nothing barrier, then?'

'Oh, yes, certainly.'

'Excellent.' Lethbridge-Stewart tapped his palm with his swagger stick. 'And how long do you estimate this device of yours will take?'

Fisher blinked. 'Oh, ah, a couple of hours should be, um, sufficient.'

'Then we can confront these blasted aliens in person,' Lethbridge-Stewart said with some satisfaction. No more waiting around… and no more being told *Keep Out!* He was looking forward to marching inside this force field and demanding an accounting… 'So, we could use this device of yours on all three barriers?' he asked, to be quite sure he was understanding Fisher correctly.

'*Three* barriers?' Fisher asked, puzzled.

'You weren't told about the other two?' Typical of Bryden not to keep his staff up to date…

'Oh, yes, but…' Fisher played with his glasses again. 'There are *four* barriers.'

Lethbridge-Stewart stared at him in surprise. 'Four?' he echoed.

'Yes, four.' Fisher had to stick his notepad in his pocket so he could use his fingers to count on. 'This one, Siberia, and the two in Nevada.'

'Two in Nevada?' Lethbridge-Stewart realised he was sounding rather dumb. 'We only detected one in Nevada – Groom Lake.'

'Ah, yes, well, that's probably because the second one in Nevada is, um, quite close to it. In a cursory survey, it might well *look* like there's only, um, one. Not that I'm faulting Dr Travers' work, mind you – just saying that a quick glimpse…' His voice trailed off as he saw the anger in Lethbridge-Stewart's eyes. 'Uh, yes. Four.'

Lethbridge-Stewart was finding the man increasingly irritating, but he was at least proving that he knew what he was doing. Anne had somehow missed the double signal from Nevada, but she'd been very rushed, after all.

'The second one in Nevada is, ah, quite weak,' Fisher said. 'Easy to miss, and all that. It's probably just a carrier wave, and the field isn't in actual, you know, operation.'

'Well, now that you've found it,' Lethbridge-Stewart growled, 'do you have the exact co-ordinates?'

'Oh, yes, well, I can calculate them quite swiftly…'

'Do so, then.' Lethbridge-Stewart crossed to the jeep and used the radio to contact Maddox back at Dolerite. 'Patch me through to Groom Lake,' he instructed. 'I'll wait.'

Wright joined him. 'What do you think this means, sir?' he asked, puzzled. 'Why would there be *two* force fields in Nevada, and only one elsewhere?'

'I think that it means that we've found what we're looking for,' Lethbridge-Stewart said grimly. Maddox interrupted to confirm the connection to Groom Lake, and a moment later he heard Maggie's growl. 'Ah, Colonel,' he said, crisply. 'It appears that we may have located the so-called King of all the

Earth – and he's right in your backyard…'

'What the hell are you talking about, Al?' Maggie demanded. Despite her tone, she felt excitement rising in her. 'Who's where?'

'One of my boffins has found a fourth force field generator, quite close to the one you know about at Groom Lake,' Lethbridge-Stewart's voice said, crackling somewhat over the transatlantic connection. 'He should have the exact co-ordinates for us in a few moments.'

'That's great news. Speaking of great news, how's your wife?'

'She insists she's doing fine.' His tone of voice informed her that he wasn't entirely certain that this was true.

'Try and relax,' she suggested, knowing that this was easy to say but hard to obey. 'Let nature take her course.'

'I am trying to do so. Meanwhile, there's another bit of news for you – Dr Fisher here thinks he can whip up some sort of device that will penetrate the barriers. A smallish hole, but it will allow us to pass through.'

'You *have* been busy! Is he with you?'

'He's the one doing his sums as we speak.'

'Great.' She yelled out, 'Corporal!' The guard outside her door appeared promptly and saluted. 'Go get me Dr Chun, fast as your little feet will carry ya.' He disappeared at a run, and she turned back to the phone. 'I've got my current top man on his way. When we're done, we'll let the pair of 'em have a chat, eh? I got to get me one of those devices.'

'Of course. Ah, here's Fisher now.' She heard him say as an aside, 'Do you have the figures? Good man.' Then, louder, 'Maggie, are you ready for these?'

'Hang on, Al.' Dragging the phone on its cord with her, she crossed to the wall, where she had a large scale map of Nevada hanging. 'Okay, read 'em off to me.' She pulled a pen from her pocket and used it to trace the co-ordinates he gave her. She made a dark cross at the intersection point and then her heart fell. 'Oh, crap.'

'Is something wrong?'

'Oh, yeah – I'll say there's something wrong.' She stared at the map in dismay.

'Are you going to tell me what it is?'

'I know who owns that land,' she admitted. 'This is bad news, Al. Real bad.'

'Are you going to explain?'

'It's Harrison Bailey.'

'And who is…' His voice trailed off. '*The* Harrison Bailey?'

'Yeah. The Harrison Bailey. Our President's favourite golfing buddy. Our funder of political parties, owner of industry and donator to all things donatable.' She felt like cursing. 'Al, this is gonna get sticky. Very sticky.'

There was a slight pause. 'Do you need backup? I can get a plane over and be with you—'

'Al, thanks, but no thanks.' She was glad he'd offered, though. 'One career flushed down the toilet today is enough. Besides, you got a wife and kid to support – if the brat ever shows up.'

Lethbridge-Stewart winced at the terrible choice of words, but said nothing. Maggie didn't know…

'I'll handle this end of things,' she continued, 'though God knows I wish I wasn't the one to tell the leader of the free world that his best buddy appears to be a traitor to the entire planet…' There was a rap on the door, and the corporal ushered Dr Chun in. 'Okay, my brains just arrived. Put your guy on, and they can converse in bigger words than either of us knows. Oh, and Al – thanks. I may curse you later – but thanks.' She handed the phone to Chun. 'Here – this guy has some super-duper science plans to tell you all about. Whatever it is, I want you to build me one – yesterday, preferably.'

She ignored the excited conversation that was going on behind her and simply stared at that cross on the map.

Harrison Bailey, of all people… Why did it have to be her in the crosshairs on this one? She was aware that she was simply trying to postpone the inevitable, and opened the door to glare at the unfortunate corporal outside.

'Go find me Captain Gazza,' she snapped. 'Tell him to report here, fastest. Go!' He took to his heels, and she reached for the wall phone. When the switchboard replied, she snapped, 'Put a call through to the White House, and tell 'em it's urgent. I want to speak to the President, and I don't care if he's in a meeting or in the crapper. This is *urgent.*'

She glared at the ceiling as she waited. 'Well, I suppose there are worse ways for a career to end. Off-hand, though, I can't think of many...'

*

Lethbridge-Stewart felt sorry for Maggie, but there was really no more that he could do to help her at the moment. Fisher was jabbering happily away with a sympathetic fellow scientist, so Lethbridge-Stewart turned away.

Wright was there, standing ready.

'I couldn't help catching some of that, sir,' he said. 'Is... is it really going to be a problem? I've never heard of this Harrison Bailey before.'

'No real reason you would, Wright. But he's a very large figure behind the scenes in politics in America. He's a multi-millionaire, and he's been friends with the last four presidents. He's particularly close with the current one. This is going to upset more than one applecart, and his influence could delay American response to the problem.'

It was a real mess. Lethbridge-Stewart couldn't imagine that the President would be too happy to get this news, and he might delay any response out of concern for his friend.

Wright looked puzzled. 'Why would a man like that get involved in something like this? Doesn't he have everything he could want already?' He snorted. 'If *I* had multi-millions, I'd be real happy, I would.'

'That's because you're easily satisfied, Corporal. The problem with having everything is that sometimes it's not enough to satisfy. There are always those who want more. And it would appear that Mr Bailey wants *everything*.'

Chun eventually hung up the phone. The expression on his face was a mixture of excitement and puzzlement.

Maggie stomped back into her office and glared at him. 'Didja understand all that?'

'Oh, yes... It's just... well, lovely.' Chun smiled at her. 'Some extremely interesting thoughts that hadn't crossed my mind before.'

'Well, go and cross the compound and get to work.' She hesitated, and then asked, 'Will it work?'

Chun blinked, surprised. 'Why, yes, I do believe so. You

see, it all depends on the molecular vibration rate and—'

'Spare me the science explanation. I won't understand any of it, and you'll just annoy the crap out of me. As long as you're sure it'll work, go build me one. No, on second thoughts, build me two. And tell me the minute they're finished!'

Chun nodded and hurried off.

Well, that was one problem solved – *if* this device of Lethbridge-Stewart's worked as advertised. She was anticipating using one of them to waltz into the closed-off zone and confronting this Captain Kwith herself… And she had a very good idea of where the other would come in very handy.

A few minutes later, Captain Gazza turned up and saluted smartly.

'At ease,' she ordered. 'Ya know where the Bailey spread is located?'

'Of course, ma'am.'

'Good. Get over there with a squad and stake it out – full surveillance. But – and I can't emphasise this strongly enough – don't set one foot onto his property, y'hear? This guy's pals with the President, and if you give him anything to complain about, you'll be lucky if you're left wearing any stripes.'

'Understood, ma'am. And what am I looking for?'

'If I knew that, I wouldn't need you playing superspy, would I? Just report whatever you can see. I'm ordering up an observation flight, so between you and it, I expect to know what I'm up against. You savvy?'

'Enough to do my job, ma'am.'

She cracked a smile. 'Attaboy, Captain. You'll go far. But, right now, go and spy on Bailey.' As he departed, she reflected that the easy part of her job was over.

She glanced at the phone, daring it to ring. The hard part was still to come…

She ordered the surveillance flight launched, and then sat scowling at her phone. She spent the time worrying – which, she reflected, seemed to be a major portion of her job these days. At least the upper brass weren't interfering much, or constantly asking for updates. They were probably all sighing with relief that they'd managed to dump this problem onto her shoulders. If they knew that Bailey was involved, they'd have been even happier they were out from in front of *that* target...

And then, *the* call arrived...

She wondered idly if she was expected to stand at attention when talking to the President, but that thought didn't last long.

'What in blue blazes is so all-fired important that they hauled me in off the golf course? Is it World War Three?'

'I sincerely hope not, Mr President. But it may be heading that way, I'm afraid.'

'What are those damned aliens up to now?'

'It's not the aliens – well, not directly, though they are involved. It's your friend Harrison Bailey. Uh – he wouldn't happen to be the one you're playing golf with, would he?'

'No such luck – it's the Vice-President, and he's absolutely hopeless. I wish it were Harry. Well, what's he done now?'

Damn. If it had been Bailey, they might have grabbed him immediately...

'Just a spot of treason, Mr President.'

There was a pause that was more pregnant than Al's wife, and then, 'You better not be joking.'

'I wish I were.'

She could almost hear him grinding his teeth. 'Spill the beans,' he ordered, and so she did, slowly and carefully.

'There's no chance of a mistake, Colonel?' he asked when she was done.

'Course there's a chance of a mistake. That's why I ordered out my men to check up. I don't want to set a foot wrong, especially given your friendship.'

'I 'preciate it,' the President answered, abstractly. 'But it sure does look like Harry's digging himself a deep pit. Damnation.' He sighed. 'You're doing the right thing, Colonel, much as I dislike it. But be *very* certain before you take any kind of real action, you hear? If this is somehow a mistake, I wouldn't want to piss Harry off.' He chuckled softly. 'He won't take it so easy on me in the next round of golf if we upset him.'

'Understood, Mr President.'

'I'll put this order in writing and get it to you asap. But you do what you think is necessary, and you have my full authority. But you be *real* careful, y'hear?'

'Trust me, sir – I will.'

'Good.' He hung up without another word.

Maggie replaced the receiver carefully. The call had gone better than she'd feared, but she was aware that she'd just placed her career on the sharp edge of a razor.

One slip... Well, she'd better not make one slip.

The day was hot – but, then, *all* days out here in the desert were hot.

Gazza had Mediterranean blood, so he liked the warmth, but some of his men didn't feel the same way. He couldn't blame them, but he couldn't take it easy on them, either. Colonel Hickenlooper hadn't been very specific about the number of troops he was to employ, so he'd decided on twenty squaddies and a camera crew from Intelligence. Bailey's spread was something like ten thousand acres of scrubland, and the captain had obtained a detailed map so that he could be very certain of not trespassing. The problem was that they were really too far away from the main house for anything to be visible to the naked eye at this distance. He hoped that the camera crew could come up with something, because all he could see was sand and a shimmering haze.

While they were setting up, he checked the map again, and then called base to find out the status of the overflight. Even as he did so, he could hear the far-off whine of an approaching jet. Base confirmed that this was the expected overflight.

'They'll be making two passes,' he was informed. 'Then heading back.'

'Understood.' As he watched, the jet flew almost directly overhead and then into Bailey's air space. He turned his attention back to the camera crew. 'You getting anything yet?'

'Almost ready, sir,' the sergeant in charge replied. 'Looks like there's some movement going on, but we can't tell what just yet.'

Gazza nodded. They'd not approached Bailey's property from the road – which was a few miles south-west of them – figuring they'd be less likely to be spotted here. There was no visible fence or boundary at this point, unlike the high walls at the main entrance. Even Bailey wasn't up to fencing off thousands of acres of this desert scrubland. It couldn't be used for ranching or farming, and it was clearly meant only to be a buffer for his privacy.

He tried scanning the wide open spaces with his binoculars, but couldn't resolve anything of consequence. The sergeant was right that there was movement in there, as there were dust clouds being kicked up, but no details were visible.

'Ready now, sir,' the cameraman called.

He'd stayed out from underfoot as they'd been setting up, but now he walked over to join them. 'Can you make anything out?'

'Hard to say, sir. Vehicles, definitely – a lot of them. Maybe twenty, thirty. They seem to be milling about a bit.'

Was that of any significance? He didn't know, but it really wasn't up to him to make the judgement calls. He was just there to gather information and report back. It wasn't much to report back, but orders were orders.

He returned to his jeep and called up Colonel Hickenlooper.

She seemed about as thrilled with the news as he was. 'Just moving around?'

'Yes, ma'am.' He glanced up as he heard the rising howl of an approaching jet. 'The fly-over is heading back now.'

'Well, he may be able to make out more of what's happening. Meanwhile—'

'Dear God!' Gazza dropped the microphone as the approaching aircraft was suddenly a ball of fire.

The sound from the explosion didn't reach him for another second or two. Bright rain fell down towards the desert below.

'What the hell was that?' Hickenlooper howled.

He didn't reply, watching the fire falling from the sky.

It didn't fall straight down. Instead, it dropped and then slid off to the east, as if...

He grabbed the microphone again. 'The plane's down,' he reported. 'In pieces. It seems to be hitting an invisible wall, and being deflected.'

'Bailey *does* have a barrier generator,' she growled. 'Did the crew get out?'

'No sign of parachutes, ma'am. I don't believe so.'

'Hell.' There was a short pause. 'Was the plane shot down?'

'I don't know. I didn't see anything. It might just have flown into the invisible wall. At that speed...'

'Yeah. Well, that's as neat a declaration of war as I've ever seen. You and your men had better get ready to get outta there. It's starting to hit the fan, and you're not a war party.'

'Captain!' the cameraman called. 'Vehicle heading this way – jeep, two men.'

'Sounds like a parley,' Hickenlooper commented when Gazza reported this. 'You'd better hang around and see what they got to say. But pack everyone up and be ready to head out.'

The camera crew started packing away the gear that they had just assembled, but there were no complaints. Everyone was clearly reflecting on what they had just seen, and they were not overly eager to hang around as the next potential target.

The approaching jeep came to a halt about a hundred feet away. One man clambered out and stood waiting. Gazza jerked his head for his sergeant to follow him, and he advanced to meet the newcomers.

'There's an invisible wall ahead of you,' the waiting man called. 'You'd better stop around there.' He grinned. 'Wouldn't want you to bump your dainty little heads.' He was dressed in military drabs, but with no recognisable insignia. The patches he wore probably meant something to him, but not to Gazza.

'Are you the people responsible for the downing of that jet?' he asked, coldly.

'They shouldn't poke their noses into other folks' business,' the man replied. 'Especially not King Harrison's.'

'Harrison is no king,' Gazza replied. 'We don't have royalty in the US.'

The man grinned again. 'We do now. You should think about coming over to our side, fella – we got the big guns.'

'And we have the United States Armed Forces,' Gazza pointed out.

The man shrugged. 'For the moment. Anyhow, I've been instructed to give you a message. King Harrison would really like for you to send some senior officer in here to have a chat with him. Whoever is chosen should come to the front gate, and will be allowed in – alone and unarmed.'

Gazza snorted. 'Sounds to me like he's asking for a hostage.'

'Safe conduct is guaranteed.' The man gave another twisted smile. 'Besides, I really don't think you got much choice, really. Do you?'

Gazza shrugged. 'That's not my decision to make. I'll report the request.' He scowled. 'And is there any word on what will be discussed?'

'Surrender.'

The captain was surprised. 'Bailey wants to surrender?'

The man shook his head. 'Not *his* surrender – *yours.*'

'You gotta be joking. He can't expect us to surrender.'

'Yeah, his Majesty figured that would be your response. So...' The man raised an arm and then brought it down, swiftly.

There was a flash of light, brighter than the sun – even out here in the desert. Gazza covered his eyes with a startled cry, but he was still blinded for a moment. When he could start making things out, the man beyond the barrier gestured, pointing behind Gazza. The captain turned to look and saw – nothing.

All of his men were gone. There were slight smudges in the dirt, and nothing more. All that was left of his patrol was himself and his jeep.

'Does that look like a joke to you?' the other man asked. His voice became harsher. 'Get back with your tail between your legs and tell them that they can expect this to happen over and over again – unless they send in a negotiator.' He climbed back into the jeep, which reversed, turned and roared away.

Alone, Gazza looked at the desert sands. Twenty men dead in an instant...

CHAPTER TWELVE
Battle Beyond the Stars

ANNE DRAGGED herself reluctantly away from watching the stars at the insistence of her stomach and headed back to the alien mess hall.

There actually hadn't been that much to see outside the ship – just the vast expanse of space – but she was simply revelling in just *being* there. She had dreamed of going into space, of course, but there had never really been an opportunity.

And now, here she was, flying faster than light, heading to a touchdown on an alien world. She still didn't understand how stars were visible even though the ship was travelling in some sort of mad trans-light manner, but she knew that her understanding was bound to be limited compared to that of the builders of this amazing vessel. Well, amazing in all but culinary matters – there was definitely room for improvement there. Still, the mush wasn't *that* bad; she could endure it a couple of days, but she'd definitely ask Bill to take her out for a good meal in Vegas after all this was done.

She was pleased to see that Tanya was already in the mess, and the woman waved her happily over. Even if she wasn't entirely to be trusted, Anne couldn't help but like the outgoing young woman. And she was munching away on something that looked vaguely familiar.

'What *is* that?' Anne asked.

'Dr Swift called it a *cookie*. He has not been wasting his time on this ship – he learned how to programme the food machine.' She nudged a second plate across to Anne. 'He even made you one, too. Believe me, it's *much* better than alien chow.'

'Thanks.' Anne sat down. 'So… how did the examination

by Dr Dellar go?'

'Ah, that.' Tanya giggled rather girlishly. And Anne wasn't sure she wanted to know anymore.

'Was he as intrigued with your anatomy?' she tried instead, trying to be delicate.

'Naturally. But, alas, purely in a hypothetical way.'

'Well, there's always Dr Swift…'

Tanya made a face. 'He expresses no interest in me at all, beyond wary friendship. It is possible that he holds my being a communist against me. Some American males are like that. Or it is possible that he is interested in men, I suppose.' Her eyes sparkled. 'I don't suppose you—?'

Anne held up her hand, ring finger prominent. 'Married, remember. And very happily so.'

Tanya laughed. 'Pity. But, to be honest, I am feeling rather tired – it's been an eventful day. I shall go and lie down.'

'Sleep well.' Anne watched the other woman head off and then chuckled to herself. Then she eyed the cookie with interest. Swift had done well to be able to make this using the food machine. It would make a nice desert after whatever sludge the machine would spew out for her.

She went and collected whatever the dish of the day was. As she returned to her seat, she caught sight of Dellar, and he headed across to join her.

'I understand you found examining Tanya… interesting,' she commented.

'I like to expand my knowledge. Our two species are alike in many ways, and so different in others. I have a lot of data to process. Though I should add that asking me for pharmaceuticals is better than self-medicating.'

Anne was confused by this. 'What are you talking about? I'm on no medications.'

'Well, it's understandable that you might have trouble sleeping, given the excitement of this day, but you're overdoing it.'

'Okay, I honestly have no idea what you're talking about.'

He gestured at the biscuit. 'You've put too much soporific in that food,' he explained. 'It will put you to sleep for several days.' He smiled brightly. 'I have a nose for that sort of thing, remember?'

Anne stared at the cookie as what he was saying started to finally make sense. 'Trust me, I've put nothing into that biscuit. But I have a strong suspicion that I know who did. That two-faced...'

Dellar stared at her. 'You did not intend to sleep?'

'Not for two days, no. But *somebody* wanted me out of the way...' She put down the food she was carrying. 'Dellar, maybe you'd better come with me. Tanya might well need a doctor by the time I'm finished with her.'

She hurried back to the cabin they shared, Dellar hurrying to keep up with her.

For once, she didn't observe or marvel at the technology all around her; she was too mad. She wasn't angry as much with Tanya – who, after all, was just doing what she perceived as her job – as with herself for allowing herself to be lulled by the Russian woman's likeability. How could she have been so naïve as to even think of trusting her? Obviously, she wanted Anne out of the way at the upcoming confrontation on Dulkis.

'Idiot, idiot, idiot!' she muttered to (and about) herself. Dellar said nothing, merely cast an occasional worried look in her direction.

Reaching their shared room, Anne tapped the door controls and almost ran inside.

'Tanya!' she yelled into the darkened room. 'You got some explaining...' Her voice trailed off. Tanya was in the bottom bunk, snoring very softly. 'Tanya!' she yelled again, but there was no response.

Dellar pushed her aside. 'You'll have to yell a lot louder than that,' he said. 'She has ingested a large amount of that same soporific.' He bent to examine her. 'Her body functions appear quite stable. She is in no danger, but she is unlikely to wake up for a few days.'

Idiot was the right description for her, Anne realised. It hadn't been Tanya who had drugged the biscuits... It could only have been their creator, Swift. And the only motivation he'd have for doing such a thing was if he were working for the so-called king...

Anne turned to Dellar. 'Can you give her some sort of an antidote?'

He frowned. 'Possibly,' he said, cautiously. 'I'd need to experiment a bit, as I'm not familiar with human physiology. Fortunately, my computers are currently processing the data I took of Tanya earlier. That should be finished in a couple of hours… Then I should be able to model the potential reactions to any such antidote.' He gave her a tentative smile. 'The *safest* course would just be to allow the drug she's taken to work its way through her system. She's not in the slightest danger from it.'

'No, but *you* could be,' Anne informed him. He gave her a blank stare, and she smiled. 'If she sleeps right through what is coming next, she's liable to take it out on you. And she's a trained assassin…'

'Oh. I'll get right on it.' He paused in the doorway. 'I'd tell you to let her sleep, but there's no need.'

'Hang on!' Anne said, sharply, halting him before he could flee. 'Maybe you could let it slip that *both* of us are sleeping like babies.'

He looked puzzled, and then his eyes widened. 'Making your attacker think he has succeeded in his plan?'

'Exactly. Give him false confidence. I'll stay in here and pretend to be asleep if anyone turns up.' Then she recalled the cookie. 'You'd better stop off in the food hall and dispose of that biscuit – if Swift sees it, he'll know I didn't eat it.'

'Right.' He grinned. 'We'll be landing on Dulkis in about eight hours, so it won't be too long to pretend.' He closed the door.

Anne stared down at Tanya. She looked almost frail and vulnerable, and Anne felt guilty that she'd jumped immediately to the wrong conclusion about the Russian. But at least Swift hadn't attempted anything lethal, as Bradley had done. Swift had only sought to keep them out of the talks, not to kill them.

Unless, of course, he had planned to drug them so he could kill them without a fuss…? Which meant that he might be along shortly to try and finish them off. Anne wished for a brief second that she'd thought to bring a weapon along, but that really wasn't her thing. Alistair and Bill took care of the action side of things; but neither was here right now.

Then she realised that Tanya *was* here, of course. And she had that wicked little knife of hers… Wherever she kept it.

Anne glanced down at the sleeping woman. She was wearing only her see-through nightie under the covers. Anne let the bedclothes fall back into place. No sign of a knife there. She glanced at the pile of clothing the Russian had neatly placed on a chair, and went through them without finding a thing. Well, no weapons, at least.

The small backpack she'd brought with her…? Again, nothing obvious – just a few personal items like a hairbrush and a change of underwear. Yet Anne was certain that the woman would not be unarmed; that would be against her nature.

Tanya rolled over in bed, murmuring something softly to herself in Russian. She appeared to be having a pleasant dream, at least. Anne looked at her a little more closely. The mass of dark hair had ridden up, and there was an odd shadow between her shoulder blades… Anne touched the shadow, and realised that it was actually a flesh-coloured sheath that normally lay hidden beneath the woman's long hair. The knife was within it, and Anne pulled it out with a smile of satisfaction. It was the perfect place to hide the weapon, really – invisible normally, and all Tanya needed to do was to reach over her shoulder to grip it swiftly.

Armed with the knife, Anne retreated to the upper bunk and prepared to wait in case Swift turned up to finish them off.

It was a long night, but absolutely eventless.

It looked like Swift was content with simply drugging the two of them. Not that this made him any more likeable or easy to forgive, and Anne had plenty of time on her hands to contemplate what she would do with the traitor.

Most of her thoughts she knew she would never go through with, but it did help her pass the time pleasantly. One thing that was obvious was that Swift must know who the would-be King of Earth was. If Maggie hadn't managed to uncover him, Anne might be able to get the information from Swift. With a wicked grin, she considered letting Tanya know and giving her back her knife…

But there was hardly any point to that, of course. Whoever their unknown foe was, he was clearly a very smart person.

He would have to know that his identity and plot would be uncovered once the aliens arrived on Earth to commence their building project. That meant that he had to have a plan in place to deal with it. The likelihood, therefore, was that he had probably already revealed himself and that Maggie and Alistair would be facing a very new problem already.

She wished that there was some way she could contact Earth and talk this out with Alistair. But she knew that these aliens, at least, couldn't transmit that far – they needed to send a ship. So, everyone back home was on their own, and they were relying on her to fix this end of the mess.

Ship's morning arrived eventually. Feeling totally dragged out, she managed to sit up when Dellar – looking absolutely fresh and infuriatingly cheerful – turned up.

'How is it going?' she asked him.

'Fine,' he replied. 'We'll be landing within the hour. I met Dr Swift, and he asked after the both of you. I informed him that you'd both apparently taken a sleeping draught to cope with all of the excitement, and I'd left you both to rest. He seemed to be happy to hear that.'

'I'll bet. He's undoubtedly gloating that his scheme is working.'

'Yes, he'll be heading off to the council chambers with Brond shortly after we land. I thought we'd give them a little head start and then follow.' He grinned. 'I hope you don't mind my tagging along…? I'm quite eager to see how this all turns out.'

'You'll be very welcome. Now, do you have a pick-me-up for Tanya?'

He reached into the pouch he had across one shoulder. 'And a little something for you, too. I'm sure you're probably rather exhausted, so a little boost…'

Anne accepted the bluish liquid he proffered gratefully. Her brain was a bit muzzy from lack of sleep, and the liquid made her feel better in a few moments. Dellar gave the Russia her dose as a sort of nasal spray. Within minutes, she groaned and jerked into a semblance of life. She blinked several times and then stared at them, puzzled by their looks of concern.

'Did I oversleep?' she asked, hazily, and then shook her head. 'Oh, I feel nauseous.'

'Only to be expected, my dear,' Dellar told her. 'You were drugged.'

'Drugged?'

'Doped cookies,' Anne informed her.

Tanya was becoming more alert. 'Swift…'

'Right the first guess,' Anne agreed. 'It's only thanks to Dellar that we're both not playing sleeping beauty right now. He has a very sensitive and useful nose.'

Tanya's hand moved to the back of her neck. Anne grinned and held up the knife. 'I stood guard all night, in case he had worse designs on us. Turns out he didn't.' Tanya held out her hand, but Anne shook her head. 'You don't get it back until you promise not to murder him. We need information he can give us right now.'

'I promise not to murder him,' Tanya murmured. 'At least, not while he can be used.' She gave a rather nasty smile. 'I'm very good at getting information…'

'Down, girl,' Anne said, handing over the knife. She was pretty certain she could trust Tanya – for the moment. She turned to Dellar. 'Thank you for all of your help. Can you come back once we've landed?' She sighed. 'I'd have loved to watch that, but we'd better stay hidden until Swift has left the ship.'

'Of course,' Dellar said. 'You'll want to freshen up. I understand.'

'I have to pee very badly,' Tanya announced, heading for the small bathroom.

'Side effect of the drugs,' Dellar called. 'It should wear off shortly.' He smiled again at Anne and left them.

Anne went to her bag and pulled out clean clothing. It seemed that there would be plenty of time for a shower. Whatever Dellar had given her was quite a tonic – she felt clear-headed and refreshed and ready for the upcoming confrontation. There was a squeal of pleasure from the bathroom, and then a naked Tanya peered around the doorframe.

'It's a bidet also,' she said. 'I am feeling rather spoiled. Is it okay if I take the first shower?'

'Be my guest.'

In some ways, the Russian spy was like a spoiled teenager…

*

They were both refreshed and ready when the signal sounded for landing.

Anne bitterly regretted not being able to watch the approach to Dulkis. Her first alien planet, and she was stuck hiding out in her room… Another thing to blame Swift for.

Tanya was pacing up and down, clearly overflowing with energy and just as bothered by being confined as Anne was. But they couldn't take the chance that Swift would see them before he revealed his hand in the promised meeting in the council chambers.

Dellar arrived, with hooded cloaks that he insisted the two humans wear.

'We can't take any chances of your being seen and identified until we're ready,' he explained. 'For all we know, Swift has allies aboard this ship. Don't forget that he – or, at least, his boss – has been in contact for almost a year.'

Anne thought he was overdoing the precautions, but it couldn't hurt to comply. She felt like Little Red Riding Hood heading for the wolf in Granny's bedroom. Tanya acted as if she were on a fashion runway, obviously enjoying herself.

'You know,' Anne said thoughtfully, 'this is the first time I've met somebody who is literally cloak and dagger…' That sent the Russian spy off into peals of laughter.

Dellar escorted them off the ship. Anne couldn't discern anyone obviously keeping an eye open for them – but, of course, anyone that obvious would be useless as a lookout, so it didn't mean that nobody was watching for them.

And then they were in the spaceport.

Anne couldn't help pausing to look about.

There was a clear resemblance to an airport terminal, though the docked vessels were far larger than any aircraft. There was a flurry of movement, with what appeared to be conveyor belts taking things from and moving them to the ship. There were technicians running diagnostics and passengers and crew disembarking. She couldn't see Swift, of course – Dellar had made certain he'd left the ship before coming for her and Tanya – but there were lots of other… well, *people* wasn't quite the word for it. Many of them looked human at first glance, but then showed subtle differences.

165

There were a group that had tendrils instead of hair that waved about like Medusa's snakes. There were a couple of octopoids in floating chairs that were clearly of Kwith's species. There was even something that looked like a cloak that fluttered through the air. So many alien species…

Anne wished she had the time to simply stand and study everything. Instead, Dellar hurried them to a waiting transport pod.

'The council chambers are only a short distance away,' he informed them. 'It's more convenient to have it close to the port. Swift is on his way there, so we'll be close behind him.' He saw the look on Anne's face and smiled sympathetically. 'I'm sure there will be time for you to look around after all of this is resolved. For the moment, though, urgency is the key.'

'I know,' she said. 'But I can wish…'

Their vehicle looked something like a large bubble, resting on a framework. There was a door in the side that opened gull-winged, and a circle of seats within. There was a small panel on a stalk in the centre of the craft, and Dellar used this to control everything. Once they were inside, he closed the door, and started the pod off. It rose from the frame and zipped off quite speedily.

Below them, the buildings were mainly architectural swirls and towers, very congested, with ground vehicles and what looked like hovercraft zipping along. It all seemed so very Dan Dare…

'It's not as busy if you get out of the city,' Dellar informed her. 'Dulkis is really quite nice when you go out to the islands. If you get to stay, I'd be happy to take you to my family retreat.'

'I wish I could take you up on it,' Anne admitted. 'But I suspect we'll be wanted back on Earth as soon as possible.' She couldn't keep the longing out of her voice, though. So much to see… and no time in which to do it.

In a very short while, they reached a rather imposing edifice. It was obviously a public building — it was of stonework, with elaborate stylings and carved artwork. It looked to be several centuries old, and Dellar confirmed this.

'Our off-world contact building,' he said, quite proudly. 'Coming up on five hundred years old, but freshly renovated to accommodate all of our visiting delegates. The chamber we want is in the heart of it.'

He brought the bubble to a gentle landing on another of the frameworks, and hurried them from the parking field into the building.

It was vaguely cathedral-like in style and size. The huge windows allowed light to stream onto marble floors and sprawling stairs. Passageways led off to the various rooms and chambers. Aliens of all shapes, sizes and speed scurried about. Some were diminutive, hairless slug-like creatures. Others were humanoid (mostly). There were even semi-robotic species, with various body parts replaced by slick metal and machinery. Anne's head was in a whirl as she tried to take all of the sights in and still follow on behind Dellar. He seemed to know where he was going, amazingly. Then she realised he was following guidance from a device he wore on one wrist. She could see the need for it in these vast halls, long passages and lofty ceilings.

Eventually, though, he slowed his pace down. 'Almost there,' he informed them.

'You could house all of Moscow in this one building,' Tanya muttered, clearly impressed. 'And still have room for London in the cellars...' She gave Anne a cheeky grin.

The council room proved to be almost as stately and ornate as Anne had imagined.

It was large, almost a hundred and fifty feet long and a hundred wide, with vaulted ceilings and rows of columns supporting the architecture. It was almost entirely made from some sort of semi-gloss pinkish stone that might have been marble. The furnishings were in some intensely dark material, an almost jarring contrast with the lighter stone. There were tall, alien plants that appeared to be growing out of the marble in dozens of places, giving an almost jungle look to various patches of the room. There was seating for hundreds of beings in all shapes and sizes.

But the place was almost completely empty. There were six beings in view in the room, all down at the front. Five of them were alien – two that looked human, one of the squid-beings that looked like a larger version of Kwith in a dark floating chair, a tall, blue creature and one of the dark, cloak-like beings.

Facing them, with his back to them, was Swift. He stood at a stone lectern, his attention on the alien committee. Anne, Tanya and Dellar moved quietly down to stand behind him and listen.

One of the humanoid aliens was asking most of the questions. 'You say, then, that the reports we have received from Earth are inaccurate?'

'Yes – deliberately so,' Swift answered. 'I can understand Captain Kwith's concerns, but he has been too accepting of the lies he has been fed by the rebels.'

The octopoid gave a loud belching sound. 'I've known Kwith for over a century,' it snorted. 'I have never considered him gullible.'

'Nevertheless, he accepted false tales given him by a rebel who doesn't have the courage to stand before you and make a case.'

'Oh, I don't know,' Anne said loudly, 'I think we're pretty brave, don't you, Tanya?'

Swift jerked around, startled and momentarily speechless.

'I think so,' Tanya agreed. She held something out in her right hand. For a second, Anne was afraid that the Russian was about to stab the traitor in the council room. Then she relaxed as she saw what it was. 'Have a cookie,' Tanya said, smiling. 'They're quite... restful.'

The squid made another unpleasant noise. 'You, I take it, are the rebels who are too afraid to face us?'

'So it would appear,' Anne agreed. 'Of course, since he's already been shown to be a liar, I think *rebel* is a bit strong.'

Swift was regaining his confidence. 'It is my word against theirs – and you know that I represent the man you've been dealing with all along, the King of Earth. They have no authority whatsoever.'

'We know no kings,' Tanya said. 'Where I am from, all men are equal; we do not have monarchs.'

'*Rebels,*' Swift accused.

'Patriots,' Tanya returned, proudly.

'This is all very well,' the leader of the council said, 'but trading accusations proves nothing either way.'

'Then shall we proceed with evidence?' Anne suggested.

'Swift claimed we were too afraid to stand before you.' She gestured at Dellar. 'In rebuttal of that, I offer you the testimony of one of your own, Dr Dellar.'

The squid snorted in his direction. 'You have knowledge pertinent?'

'Indeed,' Dellar said, 'I discovered that this man made an attempt to drug both of these humans to prevent them from testifying.'

'Something he would only do if he knew our testimony would harm his cause,' Anne pointed out.

'I have no idea what they are talking about,' Swift said, arrogantly.

'Then take this cookie,' Tanya said. 'Eat it in front of these beings.' She held it out again.

Swift paled slightly. 'This is outrageous! I don't know what you've put in that thing.'

'She has put *nothing* in it,' Dellar stated. 'I myself made it this morning – using the same codes that you fed into the food machine last night. The ones you used to make the cookies you gave them.'

'You can't have done,' Swift said. 'I erased the codes.'

Anne smiled. 'So, you admit to making them?'

'I...'

'And then deleted the codes out of... What? A guilty conscience?'

'I... was afraid that if some alien accidentally ate one, it could cause them problems.'

Dellar snorted in amusement. 'That's *my* concern,' he pointed out. 'But you're not as clever with our computers as you think you are. I used the backups to restore your settings.' He gestured at the cookie. 'I am willing to stake my professional career on what I say: that food item will not harm you in any way. *If* you are telling the truth.'

The second humanoid on the panel leaned forward. 'I've known Dellar for a good number of years,' he stated. 'I am quite convinced of his abilities and integrity.' He looked at Swift. 'If you tell the truth, then I am certain that this food item is harmless to you.'

Swift stared at the biscuit as if it were a bomb. 'I am taking nothing that they offer.'

Anne grinned. 'Draw your own conclusions,' she suggested to the panel.

'It's still their word against mine,' Swift said, stubbornly.

'Then I would suggest a simple solution,' Dellar said, innocently. 'The mind probe.'

Swift paled again. 'The *what?*'

The octopoid shifted uneasily in its chair. 'You are aware that what you suggest is... dangerous?'

'I will be present to monitor any side effects,' Dellar promised.

'The mind probe has not been tested on this species,' the leader said. 'We do not know if their minds will be able to tolerate it.'

'What *side effects?*' Swift demanded.

'They vary,' Dellar informed him. 'It can cause several kinds of problems. Agony is not unknown. Neither is permanent mental damage.'

'You expect me to undergo such a... disgusting prospect?'

'Expect? No. But these side-effects only occur if you attempt to lie.' Dellar spread his hands wide. 'If you are telling the truth, then you will experience at most a mild discomfort. If you *are* telling the truth, then you have little to fear. I estimate only a two percent chance of incapacitating permanent mental shock.' He looked at the panel. 'I ran a full medical scan yesterday of this co-operative young woman,' he explained, indicating Tanya. 'I am confident that what I stated is quite accurate. As long as the witness tells the truth, he has very little to fear.'

'Well...?' Anne asked, facing Swift. 'If it helps you to make up your mind, I am perfectly willing to testify myself under the mind probe...' That wasn't *strictly* true – the thought of even a small chance that her brain might be fried terrified her. But she was gambling on the fact that she knew she would be telling the truth – and Swift knew that he would be lying...

He hesitated and then shook his head. 'No,' he said. 'Not the mind probe.'

The council leader leaned forward. 'Then you admit that you have been lying to us?'

Again, Swift hesitated, but then he sighed. 'Yes.'

'And that what these two witnesses may say against you

is the truth?'

He glanced at Anne. 'Yes, I believe it will be.'

'Very well.' The council leader turned to Anne. 'State your information for the record.'

Anne took a deep breath, and marshalled her thoughts. 'The earth is not a united planet. We have over a hundred different segments, all independently ruled. We have attempted to come together in what we call the United Nations in order to resolve our differences. Its success rate is… not high. There are constant conflicts and even outright wars underway on our world at this moment. I am not proud of these facts, but they are true.

'The existence of life on other worlds is not a generally known fact on our planet. Most people believe that we are alone in this vast universe – or, at the very least, uncontacted. This is not strictly true, of course, as I for one have been fighting against a number of alien incursions on our world. These events we have kept secret for fear of causing hysteria and panic among our peoples.

'I am afraid that placing millions of refugees on our world will be massively disruptive to the human race. We have enough trouble accepting and tolerating peoples of different countries, races and creeds; there is no telling what might happen if we have to add *species* to that list. Violence, at the very least. Prejudice and panic, certainly. I am ashamed to admit that, as a species, humans generally do not react well to those they perceive as outsiders – either of our own people or of those like you, from other worlds.'

The octopoid's tentacles twitched. 'You firmly believe that our refuges will be disruptive?'

Anne glanced at Tanya, who took over. 'We do,' she said firmly. 'While we feel for those beings who have been displaced by wars – and we have had many such amongst our own races – we do not believe that settling them on our planet is a viable solution. Their location has not been approved by our peoples, and their arrival would be seen as an attempt to invade our planet. There would be war.' She sighed. 'My parents were killed in a war, and, believe me, I can understand and sympathise with how your refugees must feel. But moving them onto an unknowing and unwilling Earth is not the right answer.'

The leader looked at Swift. 'Now that you have elected to tell the truth, how do you feel about what they claim?'

'That this is the case *now*,' Swift said. 'But that it is about to change.'

'What do you mean?' Anne asked, sharply.

He turned to look at her. 'I know you must think I'm some sort of a traitor, a sell-out, bought and paid for with money – but that isn't the case. What I have done is because I *believe* firmly that it is the best thing for the human race.'

'How? You've taken money to betray your people and to lie and cheat these aliens. How can that be for the good of humanity?'

'Precisely because of the reasons you offered,' he answered. 'Because we are disunited, warring and preying on one another. Isn't it time to cry *enough*? To admit that what we are doing is *not* working? All of these nations, all of this hatred of others… It's time to just stop it.'

Anne could see the tears in his eyes. He was either an Oscar-level actor, or sincerely believed in what he was saying.

'A year ago,' Swift continued, 'I heard that one of my very best friends I've known since childhood had been killed in Vietnam. Caught in an ambush and shot down. And for *what*?' He gestured at Tanya. 'Because her government and mine can't get along? Because she believes one philosophy is right, and we believe in another? And look at you in Northern Ireland – one people, unable to tolerate each other over a religious difference? How can you want that to continue?'

'I don't,' Anne admitted. 'It is why I do what I do – to try and ensure a future for the human race.'

'And that is why I work with Harrison Bailey,' Swift said. 'Because it is time to put an end to all of that… Way, way past time to end it.'

Harrison Bailey. Anne stored that information to give to Alistair upon their return to Earth.

'And how is he any different?' she demanded.

'He has alien technology,' Swift said. 'It was what he traded with the council here for. It is far in advance of anything we humans can do, and with it he can impose strict control. He can take power, and put an end to all of the bickering and politics.'

'By *force?*'

'It is the only thing that people understand – and respect.'

Anne shook her head at how naïve he was. 'And how many people will die before he gets to power? You're not *ending* conflict this way; you're extending it.'

'No. Harry has such power at his command that nobody in their right minds would attempt to stand against him.'

'You idiot!' Anne yelled, and immediately shook her head, offering a silent apology to the council. 'Isn't that the entire point of what I've just been saying? That far too many human beings are *not* in their right minds?'

'She is correct,' Tanya said. 'There is no way that the Soviet Union would surrender to him. All you will achieve is war.'

'I don't believe that,' Swift said flatly. 'I cannot accept that there is no hope for the human race.'

'Neither can I,' Anne said. 'I firmly believe that humanity can improve. But *that* is not the way to go about it. A man who aims to rule the world is not a man who can be trusted.'

'And even if *he* can be trusted, can those who work with him?' Tanya asked. 'Are all of his co-conspirators to be trusted? Or are they simply going to allow him to take all of the risks and then attempt to seize power from him?'

'And how about the *next* generation?' Anne added. 'Too often, things begin with good intentions, but degenerate. Look at the Roman emperors – for every good one, there was a bad one… and a mad one.'

'Look at my country,' Tanya said. 'After Lenin comes a Stalin…'

Swift shook his head and crossed his arms. 'No. I *believe* in Harry.'

'Then you're a fool,' Tanya said. 'And a dupe.' She turned to Anne. 'We must return home with this information. I've met Harrison Bailey, and I know how dangerous he can be.'

'You *know* him?'

Tanya shrugged and grinned. 'I attended one of his parties. He found me… quite attractive. But he was not my mission, so I had to turn him down.'

'There's a novelty,' Anne muttered.

Tanya laughed. 'Indeed. But I spoke with him for a while, and found him… disturbing. He is a strong believer in imposing his will upon others, and he possesses a good deal of charisma. I am not surprised that Swift has been taken in by his promises; that is how the man operates. If he has futuristic technology and a fighting force, then he is most dangerous.'

'He's not like that,' Swift insisted. 'He wishes to unify the human race and make us able to withstand any alien incursions. And if there is one thing our knowledge has made clear, it is that there are plenty of hostile alien beings out there that might want our planet.'

'I've met some of them,' Anne snapped. 'And while I'd agree that a unified humanity would be a big advantage in combatting extra-terrestrial threats, *this* is not the way to go about it. The only way we can ever have unity, is for all concerned to *want* it – not to be forced into it.'

Swift glared at them both. 'We can never work in concert with the Russians, or the Chinese, or any of a hundred other nations. We need to abolish all such distinctions. And that means a centralised power structure, led by one capable man.'

Tanya winked at Anne. 'Oh, I think I am working well with the British here. And we are both in agreement that you are an idiot.'

'You're working together *now*,' Swift snapped. 'While it's convenient, and suits both of your purposes.'

'But that's the point,' Anne observed. 'We *can* work together when needed. We simply need to discover common goals.'

The octopoid cleared its throat rather obscenely. 'While I, for one, enjoy a good, healthy debate, I confess I'm growing bored with all of this… pontificating. Reminds me of the stories of the old days of Dulkis…' He glanced at the council leader. 'Before they reached and joined the larger community.'

The leader bowed his head in acknowledgement. 'Distant memories.'

'Frankly,' the octopoid said, 'I don't really care what you all decide in the end, this is a meeting of *our* council, so knock it off and listen for a while.' It turned to the other panel members. 'I think it is quite clear that the person we have been dealing with – Harrison Bailey – is a fraud.' There was a murmur of agreement from the other members. 'Then I propose that the agreement has been abrogated and should be abandoned. All in favour?'

There was a quick vote, and all of them were in agreement. Anne was surprised at the lack of debate – these beings *were* bureaucrats, after all! But who knew how many years (or decades, or centuries?) they had been working together.

The leader of the council now took up the reins again. 'It has been decided that the treaty that was concluded is invalid through fraud. Harrison Bailey claimed to have authority to speak for a unified planet, and it is more than clear that he does not have this authority. Therefore, the refuges must be relocated to a more honest world. We cannot allow refugees to be contaminated by human subterfuge. We will reconsider this matter in the event that Earth *does* become united. Until then, it is to be declared an interdicted world, and our members cautioned to stay clear of it.'

'You're going to order the withdrawal of your workers on Earth?' Anne asked, wanting to be absolutely clear on the matter.

'Indeed. Any construction in place will be dismantled.'

This was a huge relief.

'And what about Harrison Bailey?' she demanded.

'He is forbidden to deal with the council again, unless his claims become valid and he makes himself the king.'

'What do you mean?' Anne had a terrible sinking feeling in the pit of her stomach. 'Aren't you going to take away the weapons you gave him?'

'No. We just informed you that we are withdrawing from contact with your world. You must deal with your own problems now.'

Anne stared at the council members in shock. She could see that they were all in agreement with this insane decision.

'But... but... *you* gave him alien technology. He has... Well, I don't know how much power, but he believes he can conquer the earth with it! You *can't* allow him to keep it!'

The octopoid leaned forward in his chair. 'We cannot take it from him. The only way to do that would be to attempt force. And, believe me, that would create a far larger problem for your planet. We would have to land with overwhelming force, resulting in a far more devastating war than you face now. No, Harrison Bailey is one of *you*, and you must deal with him without our aid.'

Anne was furious at the injustice of all of this. 'You're willing to start a war on our planet – and then just wash your hands of it and walk away?'

'*We* start nothing,' the council leader said. 'It is this human, Harrison Bailey, who is responsible, not us. He is therefore a human responsibility. You must deal with him. We will order our workers to leave your world immediately. You will be returned to your planet on the ship bearing our orders.' He looked at Dr Dellar. 'You will accompany them, as you seem to have a favourable relationship with these humans. You will see that they are safely returned, and then report back to us.'

'I understand,' Dellar said.

'But… but…' Anne spluttered.

'That is all,' the council leader said firmly. 'We will hear no more from you.'

Dellar touched her elbow gently. 'Further argument will avail you nothing. Come along with me.'

Anne stared again at the implacable faces of the council, and then turned her back in disgust. She caught a look of triumph on Swift's face. She also saw Tanya's expression. In the interest of diplomatic relationships, she decided to allow the Russian woman the first shot at Swift.

'Not you,' the council leader said to Swift.

Anne had seen no signs, but somehow two beings that were clearly security guards had arrived in the hall, and they both moved to intercept Swift.

'What is this?' Swift scowled.

'*You* are not dismissed,' the council leader said, coldly. 'You have admitted to deceiving this council; that is a crime, and you are to be sentenced for it.' He turned to Anne. 'What is the life-span of your species?'

'Uh… well, not many of us make it past a hundred,' she admitted.

'My condolences.' He turned back to Swift. 'You are sentenced to a term equal to a quarter of your life-span.' He gestured to the guards. 'Take him away.'

'Wait!' Swift yelled. 'You can't do this!'

'Our worlds, our laws,' the octopoid said. 'You attempted to lie and gain advantage. You admitted this in open hearing. You are guilty and hereby sentenced.'

'But I have a wife and daughter back on Earth!' Swift yelled.

'Ah. We are not without mercy. We grant them leave to visit you during the term of your imprisonment here.'

'You'll bring them here?' Swift asked.

'Certainly not!' one of the other councillors snapped. 'The expense cannot be allowed. They must make their own way here.'

'But… but my race doesn't have space flight capabilities like that.'

'Then I am sorry for your species, but we must, above all, be frugal in our dealings. After all, your lies and deceits have led us to lose as great deal of money and time as it is. Now we have to budget for relocating the refuges. Be thankful that you have not been ordered to repay us!'

The guards dragged Swift off, howling and complaining.

CHAPTER THIRTEEN
Beginning of the End

LETHBRIDGE-STEWART WAS back at the barrier once more, staring through the nothingness to the woods beyond.

Though RAF photographs showed that the building project had expanded, there was still nothing visible from this spot. His mind was in a turmoil. He'd spoken to Fiona at breakfast, as always, and she'd admitted that she felt a little under the weather – nothing to be worried about, she assured him. Just a little tummy trouble. That bothered him, mostly because he wasn't sure whether he *should* be bothered. Fiona insisted that this was all completely natural, and he'd probably agree with her – if it were somebody else's baby. But, since it was *theirs*, he couldn't help being concerned.

And then there was Anne. They had heard nothing from her since she had blasted off for this alien world. She'd stressed that this was only to be expected before she'd left, as there was no way for her to get a message back to Earth. He could grasp that, but it did nothing to settle his mind. Having no idea what was happening inevitably led him to imagining the worst. And, until she returned – *if* she returned! – he was left only facing uncertainty.

On which score, he was now awaiting Fisher's arrival. The man had constructed his so-called barrier buster, but it needed to be tested in a practical setting. Another uncertainty – would the blasted device actually work? Or was it back to the drawing board time?

And – a minor point – where the blazes was that Russian liaison they were supposed to be getting? He could almost have walked there by now…

Wright huffed his way up the hill towards him, the radio

operator in tow. He saluted, a little out of breath. 'Call for you, sir,' he reported. 'From Nevada.'

Nevada? Had something gone wrong there now? He took the handset. 'Lethbridge-Stewart here.'

'Al?' It was Maggie. 'Glad I got through to you.'

He did a quick mental calculation. 'You're up before the sun.' The US was some seven hours behind them – it had to be about 2am there.

'Up late, ya mean,' she growled. 'No rest for the wicked, and all that. There's been a real development in the situation, and you won't like it. I sure as hell don't.' She brought him up-to-date about Bailey, and the slaughter of her patrol. 'It's a damned declaration of war,' she concluded. 'But he wants a face-to-face to discuss *our* surrender. Can ya imagine that?'

It was bad news indeed. Still, at least they now knew, finally, who their opponent was. 'What are you going to do?'

'Talk, a'course. If there's even the hope of defusing this situation with no further deaths, I have to try it.'

'Of course,' Lethbridge-Stewart agreed. 'Who are you going to send?'

'Myself, naturally. Who'd ya think?'

He felt a growing alarm. 'Maggie, Bailey's already demonstrated that he's prepared to kill to achieve his goal. There's a good chance you'll be walking into a trap.'

'Yeah, I already figured that part out. On the other hand, he might prefer to have a colonel as a hostage. And if he's serious about negotiating, then he's gonna have to let me at least communicate out.'

He didn't like the sound of that. 'You'll be taking an awful risk.'

'Ya think I don't know that? Whatya want me to do; order some poor sap in to take my rightful place? Ya know me better'n than, Al. I gotta go. It's why I get paid the big bucks.'

'Maggie…'

'If you say *be careful,* I promise I'll whop your limey ass.'

'You'd have to come back to be able to do that,' he pointed out. He changed tack slightly. 'There's no chance that your government will surrender to Bailey, though, is there?'

'Not a hope in hell,' she admitted, cheerfully. 'The good old US don't knuckle down to threats.'

'Then there will be no reason for him to let you leave.'

'None that I can think of.'

'Dammit, Maggie, you're talking suicide here.'

She laughed, but it was thin and brittle. 'Only maybe. Give me a reason to come back. Name your baby after me. I always wanted to be a godmother.'

'I'll be damned if I call any child of mine *Maggie*.'

That did make her laugh. 'Anyway,' she informed him, 'there's only a problem in this scenario if Bailey remains in command of the situation. I plan on cheating, a'course.'

That made him feel better. 'What do you have in mind?'

'I've got Chun hard at work on building me a couple of those force field zappers your guy invented,' she explained. 'I just need ya to tell me that it works. We won't have much time for a trial out here.'

'I'm awaiting just such a trial myself. Hang on.' He called out to Wright, 'Go and find me Fisher. Tell him he'd better be ready to test it right now.'

'Sir.' The corporal saluted and hurried back down the hill, muttering under his breath. It was probably just as well that Lethbridge-Stewart didn't hear what he said.

'We'll know very shortly,' he informed Maggie. 'When do you intend going in?'

'I'm assembling a small team right now. Bailey wants me unarmed, a'course, but I can take in a small radio; to get terms of surrender out, no doubt. My men won't be allowed in, naturally. But if the barrier puncher works, I'll have a second team sneaking in the back way.'

'Will that be enough?' Lethbridge-Stewart asked, worriedly. 'If Bailey has an army with alien weapons at their disposal…'

'We're aiming on playing sneaky, not taking on his entire army, Al. If we can take out Bailey, with the head gone, the body could just fall apart.'

'Could,' he stressed.

'Yeah, well, this entire plan is built on clouds of *could* and *maybes*. What else can we do?'

'I see your point.'

There was the sound of footsteps, and he saw Wright and Fisher approaching. The latter was carrying a flimsy-looking device in his hands the size of a typewriter. It looked like someone had just stuck electronic parts together in the night wearing a blindfold. He could only hope that this had not indeed been the case.

'Hold on, it looks like the test model is here.'

'He was just arriving, sir,' Wright reported. 'I just had to chivvy him along a bit.'

'Thank you, Corporal.' Lethbridge-Stewart turned to the bespectacled scientist. 'Is it ready to be tested?'

Fisher looked a little nervous. 'Um, yes, yes, I think so.'

'Right, let's go, then.' Lethbridge-Stewart gestured towards where the invisible barrier stood.

'Right.' Fisher adjusted the device, and there was a faint hum of power. Taking a deep breath, the scientist squared his shoulders and stepped up to where the line of broken bushes and trees showed the placement of the force field. He hesitated momentarily, and then stepped forwards.

There was a faint shower of sparks around his body, but he moved on unimpeded, and then turned back to give a shaky smile to Lethbridge-Stewart, who smiled widely in return.

'It works, Maggie, it works,' he informed her happily.

'Glad ta hear it. Right, no putting it off now. I'll be heading out shortly. I want to get there real early, make him get outta bed to meet me. It's a small psychological point, but I'll take every advantage I can get.'

'I'll talk to you once you're back out,' Lethbridge-Stewart promised her.

There was a short pause. 'I sure hope so, Al,' she said, his voice a little strained. 'But – just in case – it's been nice knowing ya.'

'You'd better come back,' he warned her, his own voice a little tight. He knew that her chances were not good, and he also knew that neither of them would admit it. 'You volunteered to be my child's godmother, and I aim to make sure you keep your promise.'

'Sure thing, Al. Be seeing ya.'

The line went dead.

He looked at the mic in his hand rather foolishly, wondering if he would ever hear from her again. The odds weren't good – but both of them had beaten pretty wretched odds in the past, so… He could, at least, hope. He handed the mic back to the radio operator, who saluted and left.

Lethbridge-Stewart turned to look at Fisher, who was now grinning and dancing in short, jerky motions. He'd obviously not been a hundred percent certain that his device would work, and was extremely pleased that it did.

'Right, Dr Fisher, it's a lovely day. What do you say to the pair of us taking a stroll to personally see what these aliens are up to?'

Maggie replaced her phone and looked up to Dr Chen's accusatory glare.

'What?' she demanded, scowling.

'You lied to him. He's your friend and you lied to him.'

'So? Are you trying to make a point of some sort?' She knew she sounded defensive, but she didn't care.

'Shouldn't you have told him the truth?'

'No, I shouldn't. He's got enough to worry about right now, and I sure as hell don't need him as well as you nagging me. And, trust me, he *would* nag.'

'Because he cares for you?'

'Yeah, because he cares for me. Now shut the hell up about this. You heard him; this gizmo actually works, so get busy installing it. Once you have, report back immediately, and I'll go and irritate Bailey instead of you.'

Chun hesitated. 'You don't have to do this.'

'You're wrong, I *do* have to do this. I wouldn't send one of my men to do it. And, as I outrank you, you don't get to offer unsolicited advice. I gave you an order, so go and do it. Now!'

He hesitated still, then saw the fire in her eyes and departed with due alacrity. Maggie grunted, and tried to focus on what she had to do.

She had to admit to herself that the idea of sending one of her men to confront Bailey was very tempting, but she knew it wasn't feasible. For one thing, Bailey wouldn't talk to anyone lower than a colonel. For another, she couldn't allow a task of this sensitivity and risk to be placed on the shoulders of somebody else. Much as the job scared her, she was simply the only person who could do it.

'Crap,' she muttered to herself. Her stomach was giving her pains – or she was giving it pains; one way or the other, pain was involved. She swallowed a couple of antacids, knowing they couldn't help with the underlying cause of her fears, but wanting to do *something*.

There were photos spread out on her desk. Some showed aerial views of Bailey's compound, others the same kind of views of the aliens' work area. It was a hell of a distance from Korea. She poured herself a generous shot of bourbon from the bottle in the bottom drawer, and silently toasted Lethbridge-Stewart. They had both been incredibly young back then. He'd had some crazy idea about becoming some kind of a teacher, but she had seen so much potential in him. It was a shame that the romance angle hadn't worked out, but she'd been more wedded to the Armed Forces than to her biological urges. And here she was now, at her desk, just waiting for the next few hours to crawl by. And there was Al, back in England, with a healthy career and a wife and a baby on the way. That might have been her place.

Ah, who was she kidding? She could never picture herself as a mother, with a baby upchucking on her, changing diapers six times a day. That was a future she'd never wanted, never envisioned for herself. More power to Florrie or whatever her name was, if that was what she had always dreamed of. Maggie had wanted – well, maybe not *more*, but *different*.

And here she was in the Nevada desert, dealing with aliens and a megalomaniacal multi-millionaire. Yeah, that certainly was different, all right. Had it all been worth it? 'Hell, yeah,' she decided. She contemplated another shot, but then replaced the bottle. It wouldn't do to show up to this very important meeting drunk, no matter how tempting it might be.

There was a rap on her door, and Captain Gazza entered. He saluted crisply. Even at 3am, he looked sharp and alert; she hoped he thought the same of her.

'Everything's in order, ma'am,' he reported. 'Transport will be ready at six precisely.'

'I'm sure it will be, Captain.'

He was an admirable officer, and would go far – maybe into this chair in a couple of years.

He hesitated. 'Permission to speak, ma'am?'

'Does *everybody* want to give me advice?' she snapped, and then regretted it. *Damn nerves...* 'Yeah, go ahead, don't pay my temper any mind.'

'I think I should accompany you into the compound,' Gazza said, slightly stiffly.

'Ya do, huh?'

'Yes, ma'am.'

'Well, forget it, Captain. For one thing, Bailey wouldn't let you in – he said just me, and he's a man who expects to get what he demands. Rich folks are like that. For another, I need somebody on the outside I can trust to do their job – unquestioningly. No matter how they feel. And I *can* rely on you, right?'

'Of course.' That was *very* stiff; he felt insulted that she questioned his integrity, obviously. Well, she couldn't blame him.

'And that's why I need it to be you,' she said, gently. 'So, off ya go. Come and fetch me when everything's ready, okay?'

'Ma'am.' He saluted and left.

A good officer; shame she had to keep pissing him off.

She remained lost in her thoughts until Gazza returned. She had no real idea how much later it was, but she realised that the sun had risen while she'd been worrying.

It was time to face the future.

There was a three-jeep convoy waiting. Gazza – stiff and formal – ushered her to the centre one. She had a driver, and two armed escorts. The captain entered the lead jeep, and then signalled for them to leave. They drove to the gates and then out.

Thankfully, none of the brass had shown up to see her off; they probably wanted to isolate themselves from the consequences of her actions. Blame it all on the woman. The hell with them.

The drive to Bailey's front gate seemed to take forever as well as, somehow, no time at all. She glanced around at the desert as they drove, and thought again how much she hated it here. She was a city gal, not some nature freak, and this just looked like so much wasted opportunity to her. Well, the odds were that she wouldn't have to see it ever again, so it looked somehow more appealing this time around.

Harrison Bailey had an armed guard at the gate, of course. In other circumstances, they'd probably have been dressed in black suits and packed discrete handguns, but now they wore quasi-military uniforms and had Parabellum MP5s slung across their shoulders. As the small convoy approached, the gate guards unslung their weapons and held them ready.

'At ease, boys,' she said, as her jeep drew to a halt. 'I got me an invite.'

One man stepped forward. 'Colonel Hickenlooper?'

'It ain't Beetle Bailey.' She grinned. 'You reckon he's related to your boss?'

Not a crack of a smile, of course. Well, she hadn't expected a sense of humour in a gate guard.

'Please get out of the vehicle,' he said, politely enough. He gestured toward the gate, where there was another jeep idling. This one had a driver and two guards also, but Bailey's men, not her own. 'You will be escorted, ma'am.' He glanced at the three jeeps. 'Your men may now leave.'

'We're here to guarantee her safe conduct,' Captain Gazza said, pointedly.

'Don't worry yourself, Captain,' she drawled. 'Bailey wants to talk ta me, not execute me. I'll be fine.'

'Ma'am—'

'*Go,*' she snapped. She held up the walkie talkie he had given her. 'I'll call ya when there's any news.'

He hesitated and then saluted. 'Yes, ma'am.' He made a circular motion with his hand, and the convoy reversed and sped away.

'Just like a puppy,' she remarked to the impassive guard. 'Wants to look after me.' She strode over to the waiting jeep. 'Going my way, boys?'

There was the barest flicker in the air, like a stray glint of sunshine. She realised it was the barrier being lowered to allow them inside. The jeep drove through, and the flicker returned, showing the barrier was back in place.

Interesting – they didn't have a hand unit, like the one Chun had built. They had to turn the barrier completely off and on again. That was good to know.

They drove through more scrub desert, with nothing more

than the odd shrub or lizard basking in the sun to break the monotony. After about fifteen minutes, though, she saw a line of greenery ahead, and the odd flash of sunlight on glass. As they drew closer, she saw that there was a line of evergreens on either side of the dusty road, incongruous in a desert. They invited one's gaze forward, and she saw that it opened up into a huge formal lawn ringed with plump trees. And beyond that was the house.

From there, she realised, you wouldn't be able to see any sign of the desert at all; it was a little wonderland of its own, shielded from reality.

The house itself was just as ostentatious and inappropriate. It was shaped like some immense W, flowing away from the approach road. The main entrance was in the dead centre, towards which they were heading. The building itself looked more like a university building or a hospital than a mansion, and it had to have a couple of hundred rooms. Most of the frontage was floor to ceiling windows, except for the central portion, which – as she'd rather expected – was like a majestic bank or Greek temple; stone-faced, with gigantic pillars, and a huge double oak door. It spoke of money, and a complete lack of originality and taste.

Not visible from this angle, of course, was the rest of the main compound. She knew from her briefing that behind the main house was a golf course (just as green and verdant as the front lawn), several swimming pools, tennis courts, a shooting range and more trees. And beyond those were the buildings that housed the workers and their equipment. And beyond those the military compound. It was the size of a village, and with as many people as a decent town. Money, of course, could get you almost anything.

The jeep pulled to a halt at the base of the steps leading up to the main doors. They would have put Fort Knox to shame. She grinned at her escort.

'Guess this is my stop.' She jumped out and marched up to the main door. Then she looked back at her escort. 'Where's the bell?'

The door opened without the need of one, of course. They knew she was coming; probably had it timed down to the second from the gate to the door. There was a footman holding it open for her. 'Thanks, Jeeves.'

She walked into the lion's den.

It was pretty much what she'd been expecting; long carpeted corridors, paintings on walls, sculptures on pedestals, and a bunch of flunkies.

She followed one to what she imagined was a formal greeting room; she'd been brought up in a poor family outside of Houston, so this was utterly alien to her. Her folks had moved a lot – one step ahead of sheriffs and creditors – and she'd joined the service in her teens mostly to get away from all of that. She was annoyed that she felt intimidated by this ostentatious display of wealth.

The room looked like it was influenced by early Vatican – wood panelling, ornate table and furniture, and even naked, fluttering cherubs painted on the ceiling. At the far end of the room was a chair that had pretentions of being a throne, and in it, sipping tea from a China cup, was Harrison Bailey himself.

He carefully placed the cup in a saucer on a small table beside his seat and rose to greet her.

'Harrison Bailey,' he said, completely unnecessarily, and extended his hand.

She didn't take it. She looked conspicuously at it and then up at him. 'I hardly think that shaking the hand of the man who's trying to threaten the U S of A is appropriate – do you?'

He didn't seem annoyed. He looked down at his own hand, used it to make a throwaway gesture, and then indicated the pot on the table. 'May I offer you tea? It's a blend I have made up especially.'

She glared at him. He was every inch the multi-millionaire; in an immaculate suit, neat tie, white shirt and shoes that probably came from Italy, hand-made by a blind paisano and costing a thousand dollars a pair. His hair he wore like a cap – neatly groomed, not a hair out of place – mostly white, but with flecks of black and grey. He had the appearance of everybody's favourite rich uncle.

'I'm a coffee drinker myself,' she informed him. 'But we're not here to drink coffee or tea, are we? We're hear so you can talk treason.'

He spread his hands. 'I imagine it must seem like treason to you; to me, however, it is simply common sense. Ah, I'm sure you'll understand if one of my men searches you before we get down to business?'

He gestured, and she saw that one of the guards had crept up silently behind her. The carpets were thicker than they looked; she'd not heard a thing.

'Fine. But I expect him to buy me a nice dinner if he gets too personal.' She laid her walkie talkie on the tea table, and held her hands up.

Bailey chuckled, and gave his man a slight nod. The search was brief and impersonal. He found nothing, of course, since she wasn't armed.

'I trust that wasn't too upsetting?' Bailey asked.

She shrugged. 'As searches go, I'd say he owes me a cup of coffee – definitely not dinner. You ready to talk now?' She looked around, and the man had vanished again. 'Damn, he's a quiet one.'

'I pay him for his efficiency.'

'Well, he'll be out of a job shortly.' She scowled at her host. 'The President is a mite upset with you; he had thought you were a personal friend.'

'I've been friends with four presidents. It seemed to be the appropriate thing to do at the time. But I have found them all weak and lacking in the moral fibre needed to rule this country properly. They concern themselves far too much with unimportant details, and they are allowing us to lose our rightful place in the world.'

Rule, of course, not *serve*. He didn't want to be a leader, but rather a dictator.

'And what would that place be?'

'In charge of it, of course. No more of this nonsense about negotiating with communists and terrorists; rule them with an iron grip. *My* iron grip.'

'Yeah, I figured we were leading up to that. Like all crazy folk, you think you're the only one fit to rule.'

There was a momentary flash of anger in his dark eyes before he managed to make his face neutral again. 'I am a realist, my dear. I know that the only way to get things done right is to take charge of them oneself. It works for me in business, and it will work for me in politics.'

She grimaced. 'With your kind of money, you could have bought yourself a senatorship somewhere with ease.'

'*One* seat of so-called power in that anthill of Washington? I think not, my dear. It is a waste of time trying to get anything done in all that tedious discussion of morality and ethics. We need a strong hand, a firm hand – a capable hand – at the reins, with no dissent. *My* hand.'

'The creed of every would-be dictator and petty tyrant. This country was founded on better.'

'What? The ridiculous notion that the common man – the man in the street – knows best? They know *nothing*. I have worked for decades to rise to the top of my field. I have proven that my methods and theories are correct, and it is now time for me to take my rightful place.'

'King of the world?' she scoffed. She knew that pushing him to anger could be a very dangerous thing – he might simply decide to execute her out of hand because she annoyed him – but she had to make him talk and reveal what she needed desperately to know.

'Naturally,' he said, shrugging slightly. 'There is no one better qualified – or in a position to achieve it.'

'You don't have the men on this ranch of yours to take on the US Government.'

'It's not the number of men that counts,' he informed her. 'It's the power that they wield. And my men wield power from the stars.' He smiled cheerfully. 'Come with me and see.'

He set off across the room, and she fell into step slightly behind him. He led her through a side door and into a brief corridor that led to double doors. There was a flunky there to open them for him, and he stepped outside onto a balcony that overlooked the back of the house.

The rear lawn and fields beyond it were filled with troops. They were in a feverish state of preparation, packing trucks and jeeps. She guessed that there were probably several thousand of them here. But she had to be certain.

'This is it?' she scoffed again. 'A handful of mercenaries who think they can take on a country…? A world…? You should think about turning this shack of yours into a mental hospital. There's a need for it, trust me.'

His calm superiority cracked a little before he managed to control his temper. 'You persist in insulting me – and in underestimating me. These men are all that I require; combined with my alien weaponry.'

'This is it?' she asked, scornfully. 'Is this all you have?'

'It is all I need.' He gestured to one of the fields. It was filled with strange-looking devices on the backs of flat-bed trucks. 'Those are weapons from the stars.' He gave her a smile. 'I'd be happy to demonstrate them on your ridiculous base at Groom Lake.'

'I don't think that will be needed,' she said, coldly. 'The last time you did that, you wiped out one of my patrols.'

'Indeed.' He smiled smugly. 'And I can do it, over and over again, with those star weapons. Unless the President comes to his senses and surrenders to me. That would save several million lives – *his* lives, not my men. Behind this force shield, we are untouchable.'

'They wouldn't be behind it if they left here.'

'We have portable generators. Once they leave my compound, these screens will be activated. My men can fire *out*, but nothing can get *in*.'

And that was all she needed to know.

'Let's go back inside,' she said, quietly. 'The President is waiting for my recommendation, and I left my radio in your tearoom.'

'By all means,' he agreed, cheerfully. 'Though I have to say that it shows poor judgment on his part to send a woman to assess the situation for him.' He led the way back to the greeting room.

'So, you're sexist, atop all of your other failings?'

He frowned. 'I am aware that the women's liberation movement seeks to assure everyone that women are the equals of men, but – seriously? Women are weaker, more emotional and, let's face it, more nervous than men. It is only right that we hold all of the power, and they know their place; for their own good.'

'Trust me, I know my place.' She picked up her walkie-talkie. 'But do you know yours? I'll give you one last chance. Give up this insane ambition of yours and surrender to me.'

He stared at her in genuine astonishment. '*Me* surrender

to *you*? I *knew* it was a mistake to talk to a stupid woman. You don't have a grip on reality, do you?'

'I'll take that as a *no,*' she said. She clicked on the radio. 'Captain Gazza?'

'Ma'am?' came the prompt reply.

'Mr Bailey has declared war on the U S of A. The word is given.'

There was the briefest of pauses. 'Understood, ma'am.'

She switched off the radio and tossed it aside. Then she turned to face Bailey.

'You stupid, arrogant son of a bitch,' she snapped. Now the moment had come, she discovered that she was no longer afraid. 'I don't give a damn how many presidents you've played golf with – *nobody threatens my country and gets away with it.*'

'You are just one woman,' he said, scornfully. 'What can you possibly do to harm me?' He stared at her in sudden suspicion. 'Unless you're a trained assassin?' He sounded worried, finally.

'I'm no assassin,' she spat. 'I'm a soldier in the service of my country. I am doing my duty to end a serious menace to not just this country but the world.' She gave him a thin smile. 'If you like, I'm the exterminator, putting an end to a plague.'

He stared at her, some of his cocky self-assurance gone. 'One woman? There is nothing you can do that could possibly stop me.'

'You said it yourself, Bailey. It's not the numbers, it's the power that is wielded. And my power outmatches yours.'

'You're crazy,' he said, but his voice lacked conviction. 'You don't have any power. You don't have any weapons, and you're trapped here, inside my force field. There's nothing you can do.'

'It's already done,' she said. 'You heard my command. You and I and all of those traitors outside your back door, camped out on your back lawn – we're already dead.'

He stared at her in dawning shock. 'What? What? Are you some sort of a plague-carrier?'

'No.' She shrugged. 'That was considered, but there was no way a plague could have spread fast enough to stop everyone. We opted for something considerably faster.'

He was clearly bewildered. 'You're not getting out of here.'

'I never expected to get out of here, you jackass. I'm going to die with the rest of you. But, one life against maybe millions? It wasn't really much of a choice.'

She was surprisingly calm. There was no way of knowing how long she had left, but it couldn't be more than minutes. And that was fine – she had stopped Bailey, and that was what mattered the most.

'There's no way to get at us!' Bailey insisted, frantically.

'You're wrong about that.' She was quite enjoying seeing him coming unhinged. She was calm, and he was terrified. 'You're so damned sure that you're deserving of power, to rule over others. Well, it's over now. You see, we built a device that will make a hole in your force field – not a big hole, but one large enough for a bomb to come through. An atomic bomb. And the hole will seal itself up right afterwards, so when the bomb explodes, it will *only* affect everyone and everything inside the barrier. The field will contain it; at least till its generator is destroyed.'

'You'll die too,' he said, weakly. 'You walked in here *knowing* you'd die?'

'I had to be certain that all of your alien weapons were still in here,' she said. 'We couldn't afford to let any get away, and now we're sure they won't be.' She smiled at him. 'And I'm willing to give my life to stop you, you crazed son of a bitch. It should happen any time…'

CHAPTER FOURTEEN
The Day After

LETHBRIDGE-STEWART WAS feeling rather pleased with himself.

He was no expert on aliens, but even he could see that the blue-skinned spokes-being he'd met earlier was startled when he'd looked up and observed Lethbridge-Stewart and Fisher walking onto their construction site. It had been very satisfying to see that. Oh, the alien had recovered quickly, and then played the gracious host rather well in fact. But that moment of sheer shock had been well worth it.

They'd been given a quick guided tour; Fisher had been most impressed, and asked intelligent questions that were far above Lethbridge-Stewart's head. The sheer size of the buildings was enough to impress him, and he let the scientist rabbit on with his technical questions. He simply noted that the installation being built had a sizeable portion that extended into the waters of the bay. The 'monster' that the Navy had spotted turned out to one of the underwater construction crew, and seemed amiable enough. Overall, Lethbridge-Stewart found the mixed bunch of beings was quite a collection of curiously gentle and pleasant creatures. As well as potentially the most dangerous menace he'd yet faced.

Lethbridge-Stewart had no problems ordering all-out attacks on ICUs or Egyptian gods, but he would hate to be ordered to deal with these – well, *people* in the same way. Yet there was no way that they could remain.

Their host dropped them off from a floating platform near the barrier and left them. Lethbridge-Stewart tapped his leg with his swagger stick, still enjoying the memory of that shocked expression.

'Well, Fisher, well done. That showed them we're not quite the backward barbarians they took us for, eh?'

Fisher snorted. 'To be quite frank, Brigadier, we are. What they can manage is almost unbelievable. What we could learn from them—'

'Is incredibly dangerous. Look at Bailey, he gained access to alien technology, and what he wanted were tools with which to conquer the world.' Lethbridge-Stewart shook his head. 'No, Doctor, the human race must earn its technical advances honestly, by their own efforts. And you can tell that to Mr Bryden when you report back to him. All of this...' He gestured behind them. '...simply convinces me that *not* allowing access to the alien technology we have locked away is the wisest course of action.'

'He won't like that.'

'Fortunately, I am not charged with making Mr Bryden happy, but with keeping this country – this planet – safe.' They had reached the barrier again, and he could see Izzy and Wright standing there, looking anxious. 'You can stop worrying. We're perfectly fine.'

'Hell, we ain't worried about you, Al,' Izzy said, but without his usual grin. 'But we've got what you'd call good news and bad news.'

Fisher triggered his device, and they stepped through the force field, which closed behind them. Lethbridge-Stewart frowned at Izzy.

'Is this the sort of news best met with an upraised glass?'

'Yeah – both parts of it.'

'Then let's head back to town,' Lethbridge-Stewart suggested. 'You can fill me in on the walk back.'

'It won't take long. The good news is that we have met the enemy and he is dead. Bailey's compound and all his crazy-ass followers have been nuked.'

Lethbridge-Stewart raised his eyebrows. 'Wasn't that a trifle extreme?'

'Couldn't chance any of 'em getting out. We had to get every last alien gun and whatever. Dropping a bomb in their laps was the most certain solution.' Izzy shrugged. 'The barrier held up long enough to contain the explosion from spreading, then collapsed. Fallout radiation seems to be low. The would-be king of the world just got deposed.'

'Well, that's certainly a very good outcome,' Fisher interjected. 'We can only hope that the aliens all hear about this and it causes them to rethink their decisions. Now they will know that they're no longer safe from us. We could take them all out as well, with minimal side effects.'

'They are not our enemies, Dr Fisher,' Lethbridge-Stewart said, rather sharply. 'With Bailey now gone, their agreements to be here are worthless. I'm sure we can persuade them to leave this planet – peacefully.'

'Let's hope so, Al,' Izzy agreed. He gave Lethbridge-Stewart a concerned look. 'You ready for the bad news now?'

'By all means. After that update, I can't imagine what could be considered bad.'

'There was one casualty on our side.'

'Only one? That's remarkable.'

'It was Colonel Hickenlooper.'

Lethbridge-Stewart stared at Izzy blankly. 'Maggie? Maggie?'

Izzy nodded.

All of Lethbridge-Stewart's good humour evaporated, as if the bomb had gone off inside his own skull. 'How?'

'She was the spotter for the bomb,' Izzy said slowly. 'She went in to talk to Bailey, and to make certain that we could get the whole works in one blow. She went in knowing that she wouldn't be coming back out again.'

So *that* was why she'd spoken to him as she had. That was what she was hiding from him! She'd known at the time that she was already dead… She had done her duty, and perished…

'She went out in a real blaze a' glory,' Izzy said. 'She'll probably get a whole chest full of medals for this.'

'But nowhere to pin them. Let's step up the pace a bit, Izzy – I really need that drink…'

She was home. Well, on Earth at least…

Anne felt a surge of relief, and a sense of urgency. She had to contact Lethbridge-Stewart and alert him to the results of her trip – the impending withdrawal of the aliens, and the news as to who their true foe was. Tanya, on the other hand, seemed to be as cheerfully casual as ever.

As their ship was docking and preparing for them to leave, Dellar came to them. He was smiling, a little wistfully. 'We will be returning home after this,' he said. 'It is highly improbable that we shall meet again, so I wished to express my regret at that. And to state that I hope the pair of you manage to resolve your situation here.'

'I'll miss you, too,' Anne said. 'Thank you for all of your help. We both appreciate everything that you've done for us.'

Tanya simply grabbed him and kissed him. 'It's a shame we're incompatible,' she murmured. 'It would have been… interesting.'

As they disembarked, Anne caught sight of a familiar face. Hovering, waiting, was Kwith. He waved a tentacle in greeting, and she and Tanya moved to greet him.

'So,' he wheezed – cheerfully, for him, 'it appears that you managed to get your way. I have orders to dismantle every damned thing we've built and haul it off-world. You've created more work for me.'

Anne grinned. 'Sorry about that.'

'Are you really?'

'No,' she admitted. 'And neither are you, you old fake. You'll be relieved to get off this desert and back somewhere more suitably slimy.'

The tentacles quivered. 'True enough. I don't mean to insult, but I shall be very glad to get off this dung heap of yours. You humans are more than welcome to it.' His huge eyes studied her carefully. 'You, on the other hand…' One tentacle reached out to gently touch her. She found it surprisingly warm and dry. 'You managed to make the council change their decision. Believe me, that's no mean feat. Will you reconsider my offer? I could *really* use someone that persuasive on my team.'

'Thank you,' she said, genuinely touched. 'And, believe me, it's *very* tempting. To see more of the stars…' She shook her head. 'But I'm needed here on Earth, Kwith. And my husband and friends are here.'

'I was afraid of that.' He looked at Tanya. 'How about you?'

The Russian laughed and shook her head. 'I must agree with my friend. I have a duty to my people here. I must make my report, and I am certain there are further tasks for me already being planned.'

Kwith gave a very human sigh. 'I expected as much, but am still disappointed. Well, I've laid on transport to get you back to those friends and family of yours…'

'Thank you.' Anne felt as though she was taking leave of a friend. 'Perhaps we shall meet again someday.'

'Not if I can help it,' Kwith grumbled. 'If I never even hear of this planet again, I shall be most happy.'

Anne was still laughing as a small transport disc controlled by a small snail-like being drew up beside her and Tanya. They jumped aboard, and it sped off in the direction of Groom Lake.

Tanya turned to Anne. 'I had better say my goodbyes now,' she said. 'Once we reach the barrier, I shall have to be Russian, first and foremost. But… I have enjoyed working with you greatly.'

Anne smiled, genuinely touched. 'And I with you. Once I got over my suspicions. Thank you, Tanya.' She hugged the other woman.

'Though I should still enjoy borrowing your husband for a night.'

'Not a chance.'

As they approached the barrier, Anne could see there was a small group awaiting their arrival. Her heart jumped as she spotted Bill immediately. It had only been a few days, but she missed him so much. As soon as she could, she jumped into his arms and kissed him. At least a small portion of that was to warn Tanya off her man.

'We did it,' she informed him. 'And we've found out who the king is.'

'So have we,' he said, holding her tightly. 'He's already been dealt with.'

She felt a huge surge of relief. 'So, everything's good?'

'*Almost* everything,' he agreed. 'The Americans have laid on transport back home for us. We'll be leaving within the hour to join the Brig.' Then his face fell. 'Colonel Hickenlooper is dead. I'll tell you all about it on the plane.' He turned to Tanya. 'I believe there's a message waiting for you back at the base.'

'My next mission, no doubt,' she said, grinning. 'Farewell – friends.'

Major Bugayev walked slowly, thoughtfully, back to where Douglas was waiting. Douglas stirred, apprehensively.

Bugayev stopped several feet away, and eyed the prepared bomb. Then he gave a sharp instruction to one of his men, who saluted and hurried off.

'It appears,' Bugayev said, thoughtfully, 'that the order has been rescinded. Moscow has just been informed that the aliens have agreed to leave. Peacefully.'

Douglas almost collapsed from relief. 'Thank God for that.'

Bugayev gave a very tight smile. 'If I were not an atheist, I might share your sentiment. It is an acceptable culmination. My bomb will be removed and returned to… storage.'

Douglas nodded, and turned to look beyond the barrier. The herd of mammoths was still there, shovelling the snow aside with their tusks to reach the grass below. 'What will happen to them?' he wondered. 'Will the aliens return them to their own time? Or simply leave them?'

'I do not know,' Bugayev admitted. 'But it may be interesting to find out…'

Back at the pub, Lethbridge-Stewart was still enjoying a well-deserved whisky when there was a call for him. He wasn't too surprised to discover that it was from Captain Kramer.

'I thought I'd better give you the straight story before you heard a garbled version from someone else,' she said.

'Izzy already told me about Maggie,' he informed her. His chest tightened as he said this. The loss was very real.

'Yeah, I figured he would; he never knows when to keep his mouth shut.' Her voice softened slightly. 'She's going to be getting a state funeral. Probably a posthumous promotion. She's a goddam hero.'

'She always was,' Lethbridge-Stewart said. 'And her coffin will be empty. A gesture, that's all.'

'Recognition,' Kramer said, disagreeing. 'She'd really have liked that, finally. But that's not the news I wanted you to hear.' She paused, and sounded both embarrassed and annoyed when she continued. 'The top guys have decided on the story they'll be giving out about Bailey.'

'Oh? And will I like it?'

'I can't see why. Personally, it rubs me the wrong way. The President has decided that his good golfing buddy can't be the villain because it might make him look stupid. Which he is, of course, but that's supposed to be a state secret. So the official line is gonna be that Bailey was the target of international terrorists, trying to make a statement of some sort against the West. From some Podunk Arabic country, 'cause they always make a good villain, and it will enable the President to ask for more money from Congress for anti-terrorist activities and more funds for the CIA.'

Lethbridge-Stewart felt a momentary surge of anger, but killed it quickly. He was far too used to the way things worked in the real world for this to surprise him. 'So, he died a hero also?'

'Yeah. I'm really sorry, Brigadier. But it could have been worse.'

'How so?'

'I am reliably informed that the President's first idea for a cover-up was to have had Bailey be a lover of puppies and kittens who was taken out by crazed animal rights activists. They did finally manage to convince the President that the ASPCA doesn't employ hit squads.'

Lethbridge-Stewart sighed. 'You have my sincere sympathies.'

'Yeah.' She sighed in her turn. 'Things like this would drive me to drink – if I wasn't there already. Speaking of which, you're in a pub, aren't you? Go and raise a glass to Maggie.'

'My very plan.'

Two days later, Lethbridge-Stewart walked up the hill to the barrier for the final time.

The aliens had promised him that they would be gone today. He'd already sent most of his men back to Scotland, and only Wright and six men remained. And Izzy, of course, who seemed to be in no hurry to return to the States.

Anne and Bill were due on the Isle of Man shortly, and as soon as the aliens went home, he'd shut down the site. Albert and Elsie Rudley seemed to be a little unhappy to lose their guests – and the additional bar tabs. Queenie, as dogs tended to, seemed to sense that there was something going on, and had been hanging about the soldiers all morning.

Lethbridge-Stewart had dispatched Dr Fisher back to Bryden, though not without the scientist making another pitch for Anne's job. The man simply didn't know how to take no for an answer.

'I'll be heading home shortly,' Izzy informed him. 'Got my marching orders. I'll be stopping off on the way to see Stu.'

'He won't be going with you?'

'He's in hospital in New York,' Izzy answered. 'Nothing serious!' he added, reassuringly. 'He just pigged out on mammoth meat. Who'd have guessed he's allergic?' He grinned. 'Got lots of spots and what they call *intestinal distress.* Serves him right.'

'Is it too much to expect that you'll be going to comfort him?'

'Yep. I'm gonna have fun getting plenty of cracks in.' Izzy gestured down the hill. 'Somebody's coming.'

Lethbridge-Stewart looked down and frowned. He didn't recognize the figure. The man was puffing away as he hurried up the hill. When he reached them, he caught his breath and then said, in a thick accent, 'I must apologise for my arrival. Am I late?'

'And who might you be?' Lethbridge-Stewart asked.

'Chernov,' the man said, standing straight. 'You have been expecting me?'

'About a week ago.'

'There have been… delays,' Chernov explained. 'Not at all due to Soviet inefficiencies, of course.'

'Of course.' Lethbridge-Stewart's moustache twitched very slightly. 'Well, I'm afraid you've missed absolutely everything.' He gestured at the barrier with his swagger stick. 'The aliens will be off any time now.'

'Oh.' The Russian's face fell. He thought for a moment. 'I had better report back to the major.' He nodded formally. 'Good day.' Then he turned and trotted back down the hill.

Lethbridge-Stewart felt rather sorry for the man.

'Think he'll get sent to Siberia?' Izzy asked, grinning.

'He's *from* Siberia.'

'Even better.' Izzy held out his hand. 'I'd better get going, Al. It's been a pleasure. Next time you're based in a pub, give me a call. I'll join our friend down there and needle him all the way back to town.' And he hurried off.

Lethbridge-Stewart turned to Wright. 'Well, Corporal, you'd better see about getting the men together. As soon as the aliens leave, we'll be pulling out.'

'Yes, sir.' Wright hurried off, leaving Lethbridge-Stewart alone for the moment.

They'd come through again. There had been a cost, of course; he still felt pain when he thought about Maggie. The funeral was to be the following week, and he'd already applied for permission to attend. Meanwhile, the Russians had cloaked their own incident in their usual veil of secrecy. That left only this Isle of Man incident to explain away to the public somehow. He'd think of something to explain that sea monster sighting – deep-sea squid, perhaps? Didn't whales sometimes attack those? Or vice versa…?

Still, he felt a sense of relief. Now he could go back to worrying about Fiona and the growing baby once more…

There was a faint sighing, and Lethbridge-Stewart realised that the barrier had been deactivated. That meant that the aliens must be about ready to depart.

Wright came back. 'The men are all packed and ready once you give the word, sir.'

'Thank you, Corporal. We'll—'

He broke off as there was a sudden blast of warm air that washed over them. They both stared straight ahead of them.

There was an immense flash of bright light, and then a rumbling. As they watched, a large spacecraft lifted slowly above the trees, shaking the ground. It paused momentarily, hanging perfectly visibly in the rushing air. Then, with a howl, it accelerated abruptly upwards, flying out over the Irish Sea… right over the town of Peel below. Lethbridge-Stewart watched as it vanished into nothingness.

'Dear Lord,' he muttered. 'There is absolutely no way we're going to be able to cover *that* up… Half of the island must have seen and heard.'

*

Halfway down the hill, and now out of sight of Lethbridge-Stewart and any of his men, Izzy paused and took out his radio again.

He hated doing this behind Al's back, but he had his orders. He switched on, and pushed back the feelings of guilt. There was no other option. He waited nervously for IntOps to reply, and then he sighed internally.

'It's about Lethbridge-Stewart… Yeah, I'll wait…' He stared at the transmitter in his hand, wishing he could just toss it into the woods and walk away and not look back. But he couldn't.

He had to follow his orders – no matter what the consequences were for Alistair Lethbridge-Stewart.

Coming Soon from Candy Jar Books

THE GRANDFATHER INFESTATION BY JOHN PEEL
THE ILLUSTRATED EDITION

The late 1960s and pirate radio is at its height.

Something stirs in the depths of the North Sea, and for Radio Crossbones that means bad news.

Lethbridge-Stewart and his newly assembled Fifth Operational Corps are called in to investigate after the pirate radio station is mysteriously taken off the air, and a nuclear submarine is lost with all hands.

This book will be accompanied by *The Grandfather Club* by John Peel, a new Lucy Wilson story, and a postcard of the new cover art by Martin Baines.